PRAISE FOR REED FARREL COLEMAN AND EMPTY EVER AFTER WINNER OF THE SHAMUS AWARD

"Reed Farrel Coleman is a terrific writer.... a hard-boiled poet ... If life were fair, Coleman would be as celebrated as [George] Pelecanos and [Michael] Connelly."
  —Maureen Corrigan, NPR's *Fresh Air*

"Among the undying conventions of detective fiction is the one that requires every retired cop to have a case that still haunts him. Reed Farrel Coleman blows the dust off that cliché in *Walking the Perfect Square* ... with a mystery that would get under anyone's skin."
  —Marilyn Stasio, *The New York Times*

"In the dark, compelling fifth Moe Prager mystery from Anthony-winner Coleman (after 2007's *Soul Patch*), the PI and former New York City cop pays a heavy price for a choice he made in the late 1970s after locating the missing Patrick Maloney. While this appears to be the end of the series, fans of well-written PI novels will hope to see more of Prager."
  —*Publishers Weekly*

"Moe Prager is the thinking person's PI. And what he thinks about—love, loyalty, faith, betrayal—are complex and vital issues, and beautifully handled."
  —S. J. Rozan, Edgar Award-winning author of *On the Line*

"Whenever our customers are looking for a new series to read, they often leave with a copy of *Walking the Perfect Square*. It has easily been our best-selling backlist title. Thank you, Busted Flush, for bringing this classic 'Moe' back into print!"
  —Gary Shulze, Once Upon a Crime (Minneapolis, Minnesota)

"The biggest mysteries in our genre are why Reed Coleman isn't already huge, and why Moe Prager isn't already an icon. Both are to me. Read this book and you'll find you agree."
  —Lee Child, best-selling author of *Worth Dying For*

"Reed Farrel Coleman is one of the more original voices to emerge from the crime fiction field in the last ten years."
—George Pelecanos, best-selling author of *The Way Home*

"Originally published in 2001 … *Walking the Perfect Square* has been reissued by Busted Flush Press, good news for mystery lovers, since Reed Farrel Coleman is quite a writer, and this is only the first of five books about Moe Prager. The story and the characters will hook you, and Coleman's lightly warped take on the world will make you laugh, dark as the tale is."
—Marilyn Dahl, *Shelf Awareness*

One of crime fiction's finest voices, Edgar Award-finalist Reed Coleman combines the hard-fisted detective story with a modern novel's pounding heart and produces pure gold. Moe Prager belongs with Travis McGee and Lew Archer in the private eye pantheon. Coleman's series is a buried treasure—dig in and hit the jackpot!"
—Julia Spencer-Fleming, best-selling author of *Once Was a Soldier*

"In a field crowded with blowhards and phony tough guys, Reed Farrel Coleman's hero stands out for his plainspoken honesty, his straight-no-chaser humor and his essential humanity. Without a doubt, he has a right to occupy the barstool Matt Scudder left behind years ago. In fact, in his quiet unassuming way, Moe is one of the most engaging private eyes around."
—Peter Blauner, Edgar Award-winning author of *Casino Moon* and *Slow Motion Riot*

"Reed Farrel Coleman makes claim to a unique corner of the private detective genre with *Redemption Street*. With great poignancy and passion he constructs a tale that fittingly underlines how we are all captives of the past."
—Michael Connelly, best-selling author of *The Reversal*

"Moe Prager is a family man who can find the humanity in almost everyone he meets; he is a far from perfect hero, but an utterly appealing one. Let's hope that his soft heart and lively mind continue to lure him out of his wine shop for many, many more cases."
—Laura Lippman, best-selling author of *Life Sentences*

BY REED FARREL COLEMAN

Moe Prager novels
Walking the Perfect Square (2001)
Redemption Street (2004)
The James Deans (2005)
   Winner of the Anthony, Barry, and Shamus Awards
   Nominated for the Edgar®, Gumshoe, and Macavity Awards
Soul Patch (2007)
   Winner of the Shamus Award
   Nominated for the Edgar®, Barry, and Macavity Awards
Empty Ever After (2008)
   Winner of the Shamus Award
Innocent Monster (2010)

Writing with Ken Bruen
Tower (2009)
   Nominated for the Anthony, Macavity, Spinetingler, and Crimespree
   Awards

Writing as Tony Spinosa
Hose Monkey (2006)
The Fourth Victim (2008)

Dylan Klein novels
Life Goes Sleeping (1991)
Little Easter (1993)
They Don't Play Stickball in Milwaukee (1997)

Edited by Reed Farrel Coleman
Hardboiled Brooklyn (2006)

EMPTY EVER AFTER

A MOE PRAGER MYSTERY

REED FARREL COLEMAN

BUSTED FLUSH
♥♣♥♥♥ PRESS
2010

Empty Ever After
Originally published in 2008 by Bleak House Books

This edition, Busted Flush Press, 2010

ISBN: 978-1-935415-19-0
First Busted Flush Press paperback printing, October 2010

BUSTED FLUSH
♥♣♥♥♥ PRESS
www.bustedflushpress.com

FOREWORD
BY S.J. ROZAN

HERE'S THE THING I learned right away about Reed Farrel Coleman: there's no BS to the guy. This isn't to say he's nothing more than the shaved-headed, Brooklyn-accented oil-truck-driving tough guy novelist he appears to be. He is that. He's also a poet, an editor, a work-at-home devoted dad, the cook of the house, and a hell of a loyal friend. Hell of a basketball player, too. He can also discourse at length—and will, if you give him a chance—on movies and rock music. And books, and how much weight a coat of paint adds to an airplane.

The guy works hard. This is important. He writes fast, turning out short books with short words and short sentences, and if you don't look closely you might think he's just tossing it off. This idea could be reinforced when you learn he has rewriting in the needles-under-the-fingernails category. But if you're thinking he's just a wild man, slamming down on paper whatever comes into his head, you're wrong. He puts in long hours and he sweats over every word. He revises as he goes, word by word and phrase by phrase. For Coleman writing is a conscious, full-throttle effort. Like playing basketball. No airy cogitating, no waiting for inspiration to strike, for the muse to waft into the room and lay a soft hand on his shoulder. The hell with that. It's all about the heavy lifting.

So where does the poetry come in, and where does it come from? No less an authority than NPR's Maureen Corrigan called Coleman "a hardboiled poet." She's right, because in poetry every word, the sound of every word, its shape and meaning and the flow of every phrase, is critical. No slack, no fat. That's how Coleman writes. Any word, any phrase that's not doing two or three jobs at once: out. That's why it's short and that's why it looks simple.

Just try it.

That's where the poetry comes in, and that's hard enough. But where does it come from? That's even harder. That's not technique. That's the part you've heard about, the part where you open a vein. Coleman's books can make you cry but they're not tearjerkers. With him you don't get cheap cathartic tears, have a good cry and you'll feel better. You get the real thing and you sometimes feel like an oil truck hit you. People whose powerful love for someone isn't enough to make them overcome their own bad ideas. People who're lost, for whom finding each other doesn't mean finding themselves. In Coleman's world, love does not redeem. Good intentions buy you nothing. Small mistakes have huge effects, and good deeds backfire. History, your personal history and history written before you were born, horns in on your life throws you around and leaves you bleeding. It's not comforting. But it's true.

Coleman writes about the shape of the world as it is. As it really is, and we know it. He puts it into high relief, makes it starker than it is in our everyday lives, but it's the same stuff we're living with and living through and we recognize it. That's what art does, isn't it? Not show us something new. "New" is just surprise. Fun, but not art. Art shows us what we're deeply, intimately familiar with, blasting away everything nearby so we can really *see* what we've been looking at all along.

That's what you get with Reed Farrel Coleman. You get the truth. No BS.

S. J. Rozan is the multiple award-winning author of *On the Line*. She lives in Manhattan.

To the survivors

ACKNOWLEDGMENTS

I would like to thank the late David Thompson for this new edition. His belief in me helped Moe to live on. It's a debt I can never repay.

I would also like to thank Peter, Megan, Ken, and Ellen for being my first readers and listeners. And for their help with Chinese, a nod to Alice Wang and Dr. Fuh-Lin Wang. And a nod to Sara J. Henry.

None of this would have been possible or worth it without Rosanne, Kaitlin, and Dylan.

"I'm trying to escape. Escape to anywhere, but I'm not. I'm not going anywhere. There isn't any anywhere, is there?"
—Daniel Woodrell from *Tomato Red*

PROLOGUE
1984

THE MOURNER'S PRAYER

WE WALKED THROUGH the cemetery, Mr. Roth's arm looped through mine. The cane in his left hand tapped out a mournful meter on the ice-slicked gravel paths that wound their way through endless rows of gravestones. The crunch and scrape of our footfalls were swallowed up and forgotten as easily as the heartbeats and breaths of all the dead, ever. The swirling wind demanded we move along, biting hard at our skin, blowing yesterday's fallen snow in our faces.

"Bernstein!" Mr. Roth defied the wind, pointing with his cane at a nearby hunk of polished granite. "You know what it means in English, Bernstein?"

"No. I know stein means stone."

"Amber."

"Amber, like the resin with the insects in it?"

"Amber, yes. Bernstein, like burned stone. German, such an ugly language," he said, shrugging his shoulders. "But at least the words sound like what they mean."

We walked on.

"A lotta dead Jews in this place, Mr. Moe."

"I think that's the point."

"When I die, I don't want this … this nonsense."

"Why tell me, Mr. Roth?"

"And who else should I tell, my dead wife? Wait, we're almost at Hannah's grave. I'll say Kaddish for her and then I'll tell her, but I don't think she'll listen. I wasn't a very good husband, so it's only right she shouldn't pay attention."

"What about your son?"

1

He stopped in his tracks, turning to face me, taking a firm hold on my arm. There were very few moments like this between Israel Roth and me. He'd suffered through the unimaginable, but he very rarely let the pain show through.

"I'm serious here, Moses." He almost never called me that. "This is not for me, to be cold in the ground. Kaddish and ashes, that's for me."

"Okay, Izzy, Kaddish and ashes."

"Good, good," he said. "Come already, we're almost there."

I stood away from the grave as Mr. Roth mumbled the prayer. *"Yis-ga-dal v'yis-ka-dash sh'may ra-bo, B'ol-mo dee-v'ro ..."*

"Amen," I said when he finished.

As was tradition, we both placed little stones atop Hannah Roth's tombstone.

I never said Kaddish for my parents. Israel Roth had tried to rekindle whatever small embers of my Jewish soul still burned. Even so, they didn't burn brightly. I wondered if they'd burn at all when he was no longer there to stoke them.

"Would she forgive me, do you think?" he asked, again twining his arm back through mine.

"Would you forgive her?"

His face brightened. "See, there's the Jew in you, Mr. Moe. You answer my question with a question."

"*I* would forgive you, Izzy."

The brightness vanished as suddenly as it appeared. "You do not know my sins."

That wasn't quite true, but I didn't press.

As we got close to my car, I slipped on the ice and landed square on my ass. Mr. Roth took great joy in my fall. His joy seemed to dissipate as we rode out of the cemetery and back to Brooklyn.

"Poland had miserable winters," he said, staring out at the filthy slush and snow-covered reeds along the Belt Parkway. "The camps were muddy always, then frozen. Rain and snow all the time. The ground was very slippery."

"I'd think that would be the last thing people in Auschwitz would worry about. Slippery ground, I mean."

"Really? Part of self-preservation was to busy myself with the little things. Did you ever wonder what became of the ashes?"

"What ashes?"

"The ashes of the dead, of the ones the Nazis gassed, then burned. They didn't all turn to smoke."

"I never thought about it."

He cupped his hands and spread them a few inches apart. "One body is only a little pile of ashes, but burn a few hundred thousand, a million, and you got piles and piles. Mountains. In the winter, the Germans made some of us spread the ashes on the paths so they shouldn't slip. Everyday I spread the ashes. At first, I thought, 'Whose ashes are these I am throwing like sawdust on the butcher shop floor? Is this a handful of my mother, of the pale boy who stood beside me in the cattle car?' Then I stopped thinking about it. Thinking about the big things was a dangerous activity in such a place. Guilt too."

"But you survived."

"I survived, yes, by not thinking, by not feeling. But I've never stopped spreading the ashes."

We fell silent. Then, as I pulled off the exit for my house, Mr. Roth turned to me.

"Remember what I said in the cemetery, no burial for me."

"I know, Izzy, Kaddish and ashes. But where should they be spread?"

"You already know the answer to that," he said. "And we will never speak of these things again, Mr. Moe."

We never did, but never is a funny word. Time makes everyone's never a little different.

EMPTY EVER AFTER
2000

CHAPTER ONE

SOME THOUGHTS ARE traceable, but I don't know why I was thinking of Israel Roth and that winter's day in the cemetery. He was long dead now and I was all cried out. I was all cried out for the both of us. In death he was beyond the reach of my love and scorn. Even now, I am amazed at how he feared losing my affection. "You don't know my sins," he'd said. Hell, he didn't know mine. It's funny how that works. We were men of sins and secrets, Israel Roth and me. We could share love, but not sins. Too bad he died before mine were out in the open, before he could witness the bill come due.

You would think I'd be good at grief by now, having mourned a mother, a father, a marriage, and a miscarriage before him. Miscarriage, what an asinine term. *Oh, dear, I seem to have miscarried that baby. How clumsy of me!* That child had been a part of Katy and me, not a tray of dirty dishes. As I recall, no one shouted, "Oops!" But experience had taught me that God doesn't say oops. You have to have faith in God's big plan, so I'm told, and that misery is all just part of it. For Mr. Roth, misery had been a big part of the big plan. No more misery for him. He had gotten his wish. Kaddish and ashes, ashes and Kaddish. *Yis-ga-dal v'yis-ka-dash sh'may ra-bo, B'ol-mo dee-v'ro ...* I hadn't been quite so lucky.

Sure, there was some sense of relief in the secret being out, with Patrick dead and buried and buried again. Just lately, I find relief is overrated and secrets, no matter how potentially corrosive, can often sustain a man much the better than truth. I would know. Patrick's vanishing act had changed the course of my life. Without his dis-appearance in December '77, I would never have met his sister, Katy Maloney, my future and now ex-wife. With Katy and me, as with all things, the seeds of destruction were sown at birth. Even if we hadn't made Sarah, the most glorious child ever, I would not regret my time with Katy. She had taught me love and comfort and how not to be only an observer to my own life. So no matter what Patrick had or had not done, I could never hate him.

The same could not be said of my late father-in-law, Francis Maloney. I knew exactly how I felt about that cruel and callous fuck. My father-in-law chilled the earth when they laid him in it, not the other way around. He too had known the secret of his son's disappearance, that I had found Patrick all those years ago and let him slip away. For twenty years, neither of us had managed the courage to confess our sin to Katy. We held the secret between us like a jug of acid, both of us scared to let it drop for fear of being maimed by the backsplash. We were right to fear it. For when, in death, Francis let go of the jug, the splash scarred us all.

Foolishly, he had assumed it would burn me worst. But the anticipation of the burn, the years of his taunting about ghosts and payback had hardened me. Secrets do that. If the secret's big enough, you build a wall around it until there's only wall and very little left of yourself. And Patrick's secret was only one of many. As a PI, I had become a collector of secrets, a gatekeeper of orphaned truths. I kept the secrets of the murdered and murderers alike.

Since the divorce, secrets and loss were my only companions. I suppose, then, that it wasn't such a mystery, my thinking about Israel Roth on a rainy Sunday in July. Katy and I had tried briefly to reconcile, but there are some wounds from which recovery is neither possible nor truly desirable. We had sold the house even before the divorce was finalized. Katy moved back upstate to Janus and I bought a condo in one of the new buildings across from the water in Sheepshead Bay. Sarah stayed in Ann Arbor over the summer instead of coming home to work at one of the stores. The wine business wasn't for her. Like father like daughter. *Christ, I hoped not.*

The phone rang and there was someone at the door. Amazing! I had sat alone for hours staring out at the rain making shiny little ripples out of the petroleum film floating atop the bay. Now I was pulled in two directions at once.

"One second!" I shouted at the door.

I picked up the phone, "Hello."

"Dad!"

"Sarah! What's wrong? Where are you?"

"At school still. It's Mom."

"What's Mom?"

"Call her."

"Sarah, what's going on?"

"Somebody disturbed Uncle Patrick's grave."

I would never get used to her calling him Uncle Patrick. It was weird, like me thinking of him as my brother-in-law. As it happened, Patrick had been murdered before Sarah was born. She was now older than he ever was.

"What do you mean, someone disturbed his grave?"

"I don't know, Dad. Mommy was hysterical crying when she called me. You better call her."

"Okay, I'll take care of it." There was that banging again. "One second!"

"Dad, did you say something?"

"No, kiddo, there's somebody at the door."

"So you'll call Mom?"

"As soon as I get the door, yeah. I promise."

"Call me later and let me know what's going on."

"I will. Thanks for calling me about this."

"I love you, Dad."

"You too, kiddo."

The banging at the door was more insistent, but I wasn't in the mood for anyone else's crap. Divorce, no matter how amicable, isn't easy, and Katy, Sarah, and I were still in the midst of realigning our hearts to deal with the new tilt of our worlds. That's why Katy had moved back upstate, why Sarah had made work for herself in Michigan, and why I was watching raindrops in Sheepshead Bay. The last thing I wanted was to be dragged back into the thing that had blown us all apart. I must've looked pretty fucking fierce to Mrs. Dejesus, the maintenance man's wife.

"For chrissakes!" She didn't quite jump back at the sight of me. "I'm sorry, Mrs. Dejesus. I was on the phone with my daughter and ..."

"Look!" she said, pointing down at my threshold and along the blue flecked terrazzo floor of the hallway. "Mud everywhere, Mr. Prager, to your door. And this!"

I knelt down to try and compose myself. There, on my welcome mat, was a withered red rose and, beneath it, drawn in the mud, was the Chinese character for eternity.

CHAPTER TWO

BONEYARDS WERE ABOUT the only places yellow crime scene tape seemed not to attract a crowd. The bold black CRIME SCENE DO NOT CROSS was rather beside the point. There wasn't much of a crowd inside the tape either. Even that number was shrinking. With the one deputy sheriff gone to pick up his boss and Katy headed back to her car to dry off, only the younger deputy and myself remained inside the perimeter. The longer I stood out there, the easier it was to see why Katy was distraught. Her father's headstone was toppled and smashed to bits, while eleven rain-soaked red roses had been neatly arranged in a circle on her mother's grave.

Then there was Patrick's resting place. Although Patrick Michael Maloney's grave wasn't quite empty, *he*, or what was left of him, was gone. The lidless coffin box was still at the bottom of the hole, buried now not by dirt but under several feet of rainwater and murky runoff. Splinters, jagged shards, and larger chunks of the muddy coffin lid were strewn about the family plot. Even in death, the most damage was done to Patrick.

"Fooking kids, vandalous little gobshites," the caretaker said.

"Watch your mouth, Mr. Fallon," said Father Blaney.

"Sorry, father, but it had to be them kids."

I didn't agree. "Kids? I wouldn't bet on it. This was a lot of work, not just random vandalism."

"And kids don't leave roses," added the priest.

"A sin writ large, no matter," said Fallon. "In Ireland tis not how you treat the living by which yer judged, but by yer care for the dead."

"Amen to that, Mr. Fallon." The priest crossed himself.

Both men stood under the priest's umbrella just beyond the yellow tape, neither seeming much bothered by the rain. The same could not be said for either the young deputy sheriff or myself. Father Blaney took notice.

"Come lads, get out of the wet."

The deputy, feeling he had to prove himself, politely refused. I was too old to worry about proving anything to anyone, even if it meant sharing an umbrella with Father Blaney.

I'd known the man for more than two decades. He was an old world priest, as avuncular as a meat hook and as politically correct as a minstrel show. He didn't exactly get touchy-feely with his parishioners. So it was no wonder that he and Francis Maloney had been thick as thieves and equally disdainful of me.

"How have you been getting on, Moses? I mean, since Katy's seen the light and ridded herself of you."

"I'm good," I lied.

"A pity." He showed me a crooked grin of gray teeth and chapped lips.

I almost laughed. One thing about Blaney, you always knew where you stood with the man.

"Do you suppose Katy will return to the church now that she's returned to her senses?"

"I was born a Jew, Father. Katy chose to be one. What do you think the implications of that are for you?"

Fallon smiled. I'd never met the caretaker before that day, but I liked him for his smile. Blaney saw it too and scowled. When Blaney scowled, clouds darkened.

"Such a lovely place, even in the rain," said the priest, changing subjects.

"'Tis that," Fallon agreed.

The Maloney family plot was in a secluded corner of an old Catholic cemetery up in Dutchess County. This section of the graveyard, a grouping of low hills overlooking a stream and woods beyond, was reserved for the families of the local movers and shakers. My late father-in-law had certainly been one of those. Back when our paths first crossed in the winter of '78, Francis Maloney Sr. was a big time politico, a major fundraiser for the state Democratic party. Francis was an old school power broker in that he kept a low profile but wielded influence from the Bronx to Buffalo. A valedictorian at the Jimmy Hoffa Charm School, Francis Maloney Sr. traded in nepotism, patronage, kickbacks, and threats as easily as most men breathed. He'd have rather paid for your vote than make his candidate earn it. "Cleaner that way, less risk involved," he would have said.

Blaney, who'd baptized all the Maloney children and had performed Katy's first wedding ceremony, took inventory. "A shame," he said.

Fallon took the bait. "A shame?"

"Such a big plot of land and it will never hold the family but for Francis Sr. and Angela. With Francis Jr. in Arlington and Katy ... Well, never mind about Katy." He crossed himself again.

"What about Patrick?" I asked.

"The boy, please God, will never rest for his sins. His spirit is destined to roam."

"Resurrection, Father?"

"Don't be an ass, Fallon. Pushed out like a splinter more likely. His kind are a blight on holy ground."

I was far away from laughing now and stepped out from under his umbrella to stand in the rain with the young deputy. At that point the rain was preferable to inhaling the fumes that malicious old bastard breathed out. It was more a matter of principle than kinship with Patrick. The truth was that Patrick and I spoke only once, very briefly. That was on February 15, 1978. I stood on one side of his boyfriend's bedroom door and Patrick on the other.

"Do I have your word?" I asked.

"Yes."

That was it, the entire conversation, and for twenty years I thought his one word was a lie. The irony is that his lie became my lie and my lie became my secret. He had promised to turn himself in that coming Saturday, to stop hiding, and to finally face his family. God, I was so full of myself that day. I found Patrick. *I* found him! Not the NYPD, not the daily busloads of volunteers, not the newspapers, not the fortune hunters, not the passels of PIs his family had hired before me, but me. That day I proved I was worthy of the gold detective's shield I was never to get. Whether I deserved it or not was moot. I'd already been off the job for months by then.

But that Saturday came and went. Nearly twenty years of Saturdays came and went without word of Patrick. Oh, there were a thousand false leads and sightings that amounted to nothing. Offer a reward for anything and the roaches will crawl out from under the floorboards, the hyenas will come out of the bush. Only once, in 1989, when I was looking into the suicide of my old pal and NYPD Chief of Detectives Larry "Mac" McDonald, did I ever truly believe I was close to getting a handle on what had become of Patrick. But that lead was crushed beneath the wheels of a city bus when the Queens District Attorney Robert Fishbein was run down on a Forest Hills street. None of it mattered now, not any of it.

The rain was letting up some. Katy had just gotten out of her car. She seemed composed, but it was hard to disguise the distress deepening the lines around her eyes. There was a time when I believed it could never hurt me to look at her. Even after the miscarriage, when she took her guilt, fury, and indignation out on me, it was grace to look upon her. And when we hit that inevitable dead spot in our marriage, when the sameness of our days made me feel light years away from her, the sight of her face was always reassuring. Now it stung. What we had was gone. I broke it. Francis broke it. There was far more breakage out here than a headstone and a coffin.

I looked away.

Over Katy's right shoulder, I could see a Janus Village sheriff's car pulling into the cemetery followed by a dark blue and yellow State Police SUV. My cell phone buzzed in my pocket.

"Excuse me," I said to no one in particular, pulling the phone out of my soaked jacket. I ducked under the tape and hurried along the path toward the stream below the Maloney family plot. "Hello."

"Mr. Prager?" It was an older woman's voice, but a familiar one somehow.

"Yes, this is Moe Prager."

"I don't know if you'll remember me, it's been a few years. I'm Mary White, Jack's—"

"—sister. Of course. How are you, Mary?"

There was silence at the other end of the phone, an unsettling silence.

Jack White had been an actor, a painter, and a bartender at Pooty's in Tribeca. Pooty's was the bar Patrick Maloney disappeared from in December of '77. Beside Jack's other interests, he was Patrick's lover. It was behind Jack's bedroom door that Patrick stood and uttered the only word he ever spoke to me. Jack was the man who sat across from me, hand clamped around my wrist, promising me Patrick would return to his family. When Patrick broke that promise and vanished again, Jack went back home to Ohio. He taught drama to troubled teens until he died of AIDS in 1986. After we discovered the truth about Patrick, I'd flown Mary in for Patrick's funeral.

"Mary, what is it? What's the matter?"

"It's Jack's grave."

My heart stopped.

"What about Jack's grave?"

"I've visited him there every Sunday since the week I buried him. No one but me and a few of his old students has ever left flowers at the grave. Then last Sunday …" She trailed off. I could hear her fighting back tears.

"What about last Sunday?"

"Roses."

"Roses?"

"Almost six dozen red roses were laid on Jack's grave."

"Maybe one of his students hit the lottery," I said without an ounce of conviction.

"No, I checked. We keep in touch. They are very loyal to Jack even after all these years."

"Wait, Mary, let's back up a second. What did you mean there were *almost* six dozen roses?"

"There were seventy-one roses. Five bouquets of twelve were propped up against his headstone," she said. "But on his grave itself, there were eleven individual roses—"

"—arranged in a circle, the tips of the stems meeting in the middle."

There was that ominous silence again.

"There's more, isn't there?" I asked.

"My God, Mr. Prager, how did you know?"

"In a minute, Mary. First tell me the rest."

"This afternoon, when I went to his grave ..." Now she could no longer fight back the tears. I waited. "I'm sorry."

"No, that's fine. I know this is hard for you."

"On the back of Jack's headstone someone had painted that Chinese symbol with the rose, the one Jack had tattooed on his forearm. Do you remember it?"

"I do." I'd seen something just like it on my welcome mat a few hours ago.

"And at the corner of the painting were the block letters PMM. Why would somebody be so cruel, Mr. Prager? Jack never hurt anyone in his life."

Now the silence belonged to me.

"Mr. Prager ..."

"Sorry. I'm here. It's just that someone's disturbed Patrick's grave as well."

"Oh, my God!"

"Mary, would it be all right if I called you later? It's too complicated to talk about now."

"That's fine. You have my number. Please know that my prayers are with you and your family."

"Thank you, Mary."

When I wheeled around, Katy was coming down the path toward me. The sight of her stung a little less this time. Maybe it was repeated exposure. Or maybe it was that the thickest clouds moved east and what was left of the sun shone like an orange halo behind her head.

CHAPTER THREE

MR. FALLON'S QUARTERS were small and tidy, not unlike the man himself. His house—a bungalow, really—was way on the other side of the cemetery, close to the tool shed and equipment barn. All three—shed, house, and barn—were of similar rustic construction and painted a thoroughly depressing shade of brown, but everything looked neat and well-maintained. Fallon himself was less than thrilled at the prospect of our company, but the sheriff thought the bungalow was the best available option given that the station house was on the opposite side of the hamlet. So we formed an odd cortege, my car behind Katy's behind the priest's behind the sheriff's behind the caretaker's backhoe, and snailed across the fields of stone in the dying light. The youngest, wettest deputy and the crime scene investigator from the state troopers stayed behind.

Sheriff Vandervoort was a gruff, cinder block of a man who, in the space of a very few minutes, had twice boasted that his ancestors had lived in these parts since New York was New Amsterdam. He wore his insecurities like a rainbow. He was well aware of who the Maloneys were—everyone around here was. They knew about the hero son shot down over 'Nam and his big wheel father. Although nearly three years dead, the mention of Francis Sr.'s name still turned heads in Janus. Vandervoort knew, all right, and if he'd forgotten, there was little doubt Father Blaney would take the time to refresh his memory.

Vandervoort was just the sort to do things his way, like interviewing us as a group. It was a dumb move, but I wasn't going to moan about it. In the end, it would probably save me some leg work. Small town policing, even in the new millennium, was different than any policing I understood. I'd gotten my first taste of that when I saw how the deputies mishandled the crime scene. As far as I could tell, they'd done nothing to preserve the scene beyond stringing the yellow tape. For a while there, I thought they might invite any passersby to add their footprints to the increasingly muddy mess that was the Maloney family plot.

The deputy who'd accompanied Vandervoort sat at Fallon's small kitchen table taking notes as the sheriff asked his questions. Katy sat at the table too, as did the priest. Fallon had dried off a spot on the counter near the sink where the two of us sat. Most of the early questions were for Fallon and they were pro forma, the kinds of things you'd expect to be asked.

Did you hear anything? "Not me own self, no."

Did you notice anything suspicious last night or this morning? "No."

When did you first notice the damage? "Near noon. Was a slow day with the wet. Not one visitor I can recall. A disgrace to be sure. It took me that long to work me way over to that part of the cemetery."

Has anything like this happened before? "Like this? Jesus and his blessed mother, no! In thirty years as caretaker, I've had but two incidents and then only a few stones were toppled."

When? "Years ago."

Who did you call first? "The father there."

Other than revealing that he had been the one to alert Katy to the desecrations, Blaney's answers shed less light on the matter than Fallon's. I could tell by the tone of the old priest's answers that he held the sheriff in even lower esteem than me. That was really saying something. I didn't know whether to feel sorry for Vandervoort or relieved for myself. The first part of Katy's interview was about the same. She had asked Blaney to meet her at the family plot. Afterwards she called the sheriff and Sarah. And no, she couldn't think of anyone who might want to do this sort of thing. I was glad he hadn't asked me that question in front of Katy. Then things turned ugly.

"Your brother Patrick was murdered. Is that correct?" Vandervoort asked.

"Yes, but what does that have to—"

"Can you describe the circumstances surrounding his death?"

Katy went white. She bowed her head and stared at the linoleum floor.

"I can answer that," I said, jumping off the counter.

"I'll get to you in a minute, Mr. Prager. Right now I'm asking your wife—"

"Ex-wife," Blaney corrected.

"I'm asking your ex-wife what happened to—"

"Okay, that's it! Interview's over." I grabbed Katy by the elbow and we started for the door. "You want to ask her anything else, you go through her lawyer. My *wife*," I said, glaring at Blaney, "is going home. She's had a terrible day. I'll be back in a few minutes to answer any questions you have for me."

I could see Sheriff Vandervoort doing the calculations. He might've been a bit of a bully, but he wasn't a total schmuck. There was little for him to gain by jumping ugly with the sole surviving Maloney. Town sheriff was an elective office and although the late Francis Sr. wasn't exactly a beloved figure, a lot of people around this town owed their livelihoods to him. Ill will has lost a lot of elections over the years and my guess was Vandervoort understood as much.

"All right." The sheriff stood aside. "I'm very sorry, Miss Maloney."

"Prager!" she snapped.

"I was just trying to do my job. If I need anything from you, I'll call. Rest up. I'm sure we'll get to the bottom of this."

Outside, I saw Katy to her car and told her to go back to her house and get some rest, that I'd call on my way home to Brooklyn to let her know how things turned out. She asked me to stop back at the house. I told her no. We had twice suffered the fallout from horizontal despair. Divorce creates new history, but it doesn't blot out the past. It was just too easy for people who'd once loved each other as much as we had to succumb. Yet, the thing that drove us apart was never far away and fresh regret makes the next time that much harder. Neither of us needed to compound the hurt, especially not after the grief of the day. I had skillfully avoided mentioning the rose on my doormat and my talk with Mary White. But I could see in her face what she must've seen in mine: it was happening all over again. I didn't watch her leave. I'd already seen that once too often.

"Sheriff," I said, stepping back into the kitchen, "I believe there's some things you want to know about Patrick's death."

"That's right."

"Short or long version?"

"Short," he said. "If I need any details, I'll ask."

"Patrick was a student at Hofstra University on Long Island in December of '77. He'd gone into Manhattan for a college fundraiser at a bar in Tribeca called Pooty's. Sometime during the night, he vanished. Eventually his parents got worried and contacted the cops. After the investigation turned up nothing, his folks started organizing twice-daily bus trips of volunteers to go down into the city to put up posters and look for the kid."

"I remember that. My folks went a couple of times. I think they just wanted the free ride to Chinatown." The sheriff amused himself.

Father Blaney gave Vandervoort a category five scowl. Christ, with this guy around I might rise to sainthood in the old priest's eyes. The sheriff got the message.

"Sorry, that was a bad joke. Continue."

"When that didn't work, the Maloneys hired PIs."

"That's where you came in," he said to me.

"I was just retired from the cops and I wasn't licensed then, but yeah. I tracked the kid down to an apartment in the West Village where he was staying with his lover."

"So the kid was a fag, huh?"

I ignored that. "When I tracked him down, he asked me to give him a few more days and that he'd come back to his family on his own and on his own terms. I agreed.

"But he never turned back up. For twenty years, I assumed he'd run again."

"Such hubris, Moses," said the priest, "to play God like that. You should have grabbed the boy by the scruff of his neck and dragged him back home."

So much for my beatification. Blaney was right, of course. Not bringing Patrick home was the single biggest mistake of my life. Not confessing the truth to Katy was a close second.

"So what did happen?" Vandervoort was curious.

"I'm surprised you don't know, sheriff."

"There were rumors," he said. "There was something about it in the local paper, but no details. Sometimes I think the people up here are still scared of the old man even though he's dead."

I was right, the sheriff was shrewder than he looked.

"A pissed-off dealer who worked the Village wanted to whack somebody as an example to his crew. It was Patrick Maloney's unlucky day. They took him back to Brooklyn, tortured him, killed him, and wrapped him in a plastic shower curtain. They buried the body in an empty lot out by a Cypress Hills cemetery. A couple of years ago, I got a call from a hospice in Connecticut. One of the members of that old drug crew was dying and he wanted to confess about witnessing Patrick's murder. How he located me is irrelevant. He died the next day. The cops found Patrick's body right where the guy said it would be and Katy re-interred his remains here."

"A Cypress Hills cemetery, did you say?" Fallon asked.

"I did."

"Is that not near where Houdini is buried, Mr. Prager?"

"That's right, Fallon."

A somber smile washed over the caretaker's face. "That being the case, it would seem the Maloney lad has perfected an escape Houdini never mastered."

All of us understood and let the line hang there for a moment.

"What about the dealer?" Vandervoort broke the silence.

"Dead."

"The lover?"

"Dead."

I withheld the information about Jack's grave and the muddy visit to my front door. Whatever was going on was beyond the capacity of a small town cop to manage and, more importantly, it was personal.

"Anybody else you can think of who'd want to do this?"

"Like you implied, sheriff, my father-in-law was more feared than loved. So if it was only his headstone that had been fucked—destroyed, I could understand it. But what was done to Patrick's grave was pretty extreme. I don't know who would do something like that."

That was no lie. This just seemed to come out of the blue. There was no significance to the date or season that I could tell, no precipitating event. There hadn't been any mention in the media of the Maloneys or me or my cases in years. My brother Aaron and I hadn't even opened a new wine shop in quite some time. With the exception of the phone call from Mary White, neither Katy nor I had had contact with anyone connected to Patrick or the events surrounding his disappearance since 1998. Even Rico Tripoli, the man who got me involved with the Maloneys in the first place, was dead.

"I'll be taking my leave then," the old priest said. He wasn't asking permission. "I've nothing to add. Fallon … Sheriff … Deputy … Moses …"

But as Blaney stepped to the door, there was a knock. The other deputy and state crime scene investigator came in without waiting for an invitation.

"Well …" Vandervoort prompted.

"The scene's a mess," said the crime scene guy, frowning at the sheriff, "but you knew that already. Took lots of pictures, foot impressions, dusted the coffin lid, the headstones, bagged the roses. I've got some samples to take back to the lab. I'll need elimination prints and shoe impressions from anyone who stepped on or near the site. Frankly, I'm not hopeful."

That made two of us.

I called Sarah on my way back to Brooklyn and minimized the situation. There was no need to worry her about this stuff and I didn't want her flying home. Although my secret about her Uncle Patrick had caused her parents to split, she really wasn't a party to it. I couldn't see a reason for making her one now. As promised, I rang Katy, but only after I got home. If we had chatted while I was close to Janus, it would have been too easy for her to talk me into coming over. Katy didn't pick up, so I left a message. I preferred thinking she was asleep.

CHAPTER FOUR

CARMELLA MELENDEZ WAS in a foul mood, not like that was headline news or anything. The first time we met, she was cursing at her partner in the lobby of my old precinct house, the Six-O in Coney Island. The first words she ever said to me were, "Yo! You got a problem?" *Nice, huh?* The thing was, I *had* been staring at her. Her looks, in spite of the tough-bitch demeanor and foul mouth, invited staring. Carmella had coffee-and-cream skin, plush and pouty lips, and straight, jet black hair. She had a pleasantly curved and athletic body, but it was her paradoxical brown eyes from which I could not look away. They were fiery and cold all at once. It was easy for a man to lose his way in those eyes.

That was more than ten years ago, when she was maybe twenty-four and one of the youngest detectives on the NYPD. She took a lot of shit for getting the bump to detective at that age. Women take a lot of shit on the job no matter what. You can set your watch by it. If a guy had gotten the bump at that age, he would have taken a lot of crap too. But not all crap's the same. For Carmella, no matter how it was couched, it always came down to her looks. Every day was a struggle for her to prove to the world she was more than just pussy on the hoof and that struggle put quite a sizeable chip on her shoulder. After I got to know her a little bit, I realized that chip had been there for quite a long time and for a very different reason. In any case, that chip got shot off her shoulder in '89 during a gun battle at Crispo's Bar in Red Hook.

Things had changed between us in the last eleven years. She was by no means less pleasing to look at. If anything, Carmella had blossomed from simply stunning to beautiful. The years had softened her harder edges and she had learned to dress and makeup to her strengths. If it sounds like I'm a little in love with her, maybe I am. We even shared a kiss once that resonates to this day, but there are reasons we can never be together, reasons as solid as the wall of secrets I built over the years between Katy and me. We were also partners now: Prager & Melendez Investigations, Inc., established 1998. As Ferguson May, the late great philosopher of the 60th Precinct, was wont to say: "Don't shit where you eat. Don't fuck where you work." Too bad Bill Shakespeare and Fergie May were born centuries apart.

"What the fuck's eating you?" I asked Carmella, who had just slammed down the phone.

"Brian."

"Brian what?"

"I told him the lawyer wanted both digital and Polaroids of the accident scene and that brain-dead asshole only took digitals. Now he's gotta go all the way back to the Bronx again today. Remind me why we hired him again."

"The knucklehead's trying," I said, regretting the words even as they left my mouth.

"Trying! What the fuck do you get for trying in this fucking world?"

She had a point, but there was something else going on. I knew better than to make a frontal assault. Carmella would just clam up completely if I kept questioning her.

"I got us a new client."

But instead of leaning forward as she normally would, she found something quite a bit more fascinating about her Starbucks cup.

"Hey, Carmella, did you hear me? Earth to Melendez, please come in."

She forced herself to look my way. "A new client, yeah. Who is it?"

"Me."

That got her attention and I explained about what had happened the day before. She did what a good detective does: she listened. When she was young, she'd been too much of a shark, too aggressive. Listening was a skill that had come to her over the years.

"Describe the tattoo again," she said. As I spoke, she pulled something out of a brown shipping envelope on her desk. "Did it look something like this?"

"Holy shit!"

Wrapped in clear plastic, it was a perfect likeness of a small illustration Patrick Maloney had done of the Chinese character and rose. He had given it to Jack when they were together. Jack left it to Mary. Mary had sent it to me in 1986 after her brother's death. I'd given it to Katy during our first try at reconciliation. As far as I knew, she still had it.

"When did you get this?" I asked.

"Friday, in the mail."

"Fuck."

"Hey, Moe, if you spent more time here instead of at those stupid wine stores …" She didn't finish the sentence.

"Yeah, yeah, yeah, I know. Let me have a look at that envelope."

She handed it over. "No return address."

"Mailed from … Dayton, Ohio." I got that sick feeling in my belly.

I flipped it over a few times, not sure what else I expected to find. There are few things in the world more generic than brown shipping envelopes.

"Bag it just in case," I said, handing it back.

"In case of what?"

"I don't know yet. Someone's fucking with me and I don't like it. Here, take this too." I handed Carmella a list of names. Next to the names were addresses, phone numbers, descriptions. "Some of them are probably dead and a lot of the other info is old. Put Devo on it now. I want as much info as I can get on these folks by the time I get back."

"Back from where?"

"Dayton."

"What's in Dayton?"

"Not what, who. Mary White, for one. And the person who mailed that package."

"Whatever."

Normally, I would have expected to get shit from Carmella for acting like the boss and telling her who to assign to what. And she would have been justified in giving it to me. Although I had put up seventy-five percent of the money to start the business, she was the one who did the heavy lifting. Carmella hired the staff and managed the office. She also worked the tough cases. For the most part, I worked cases here and there and collected my share of the profits. While I split my time between the wine stores and the office, Carmella was fully committed to Prager & Melendez Investigations, Inc.

"Are you sure you're okay?" I asked.

"So long, Moe. Bring me back some cheese."

"That's Wisconsin."

"What's Ohio got?"

"Buckeyes."

"I'm not even goin' there."

CHAPTER FIVE

MARY WHITE SMELLED of sweet perfume and mixed feelings when she greeted me at the door of her house. I think she was glad to see me as I was one of the few living connections to the best months of her brother's life, but unhappy about why I'd come. I wasn't too thrilled about that part myself.

"Come on in the kitchen. I'll make us some tea."

Jews are comfortable in the kitchen. As a people, we find vast comfort in food. We aren't great cooks, but we are great eaters. I sat at the Formica table and watched Mary fuss with her pot and cups. She seemed out of sorts. But what did I know about her, really? We'd only met once before—at Patrick's funeral—and spoken a couple of times on the phone. I did think having me there made her a little nervous. As heavy as Jack had been skinny, Mary wasn't the type of woman to have had droves of gentlemen callers. She kind of reminded me of my Great Aunt Florence. Nice, but a bit socially awkward. A spinster, my mother called her. What an odd word, spinster.

The little brick house on the outskirts of Dayton was a 1950s museum piece: neat and clean and with all the original equipment. Mary caught me staring.

"This was our folks' house and I inherited it. I suppose if Jack had lived longer, we might have sold it eventually. When you're done with your tea, I'll show you Jack's old room."

Walking around Jack's perfectly preserved boyhood room was more than a bit spooky and only reinforced that museum feel. It was also reminiscent of my first visit to the Maloneys' house. It was the second time Katy and I were together. The first time, we'd stood over a floater that had surfaced in the Gowanus Canal in Brooklyn. The cops thought it might've been Patrick. I couldn't help thinking things might've been easier if the body *had* been Patrick's. Anyway, Katy showed me Patrick's room that day much as Mary was showing me Jack's.

But in the Maloneys' living room, there'd been a shrine to the family's real pride and joy, Francis Jr. There were glass display cases that held all of the dead pilot's high school trophies, his game balls, ribbons, loving cups, and assorted memorabilia. The cases also held photos of him in his dress Navy blues, his wings, and posthumously awarded medals. Katy had since given the game balls and other sports memorabilia to the high school and packed most of the other stuff away. There were no such displays here. Jack told me once that when he came out to his parents, they thought the solution was for him to go to more Reds games with his dad. They weren't the kind of people to build shrines to their gay son.

I offered to take us over to the cemetery, but Mary insisted on driving. We made small talk on the way, Mary chatting about the nearby Air Force base, indicating local points of interest. Given the circumstances surrounding my visit, I wasn't terribly interested. As we neared the cemetery, her conversation took a more serious turn.

"I don't know what you hope to find, Mr. Prager. Like I said on the phone this morning when you called, I got rid of all the roses and I scrubbed the painting off the stone myself."

"Why'd you do that, scrub the paint off, I mean?"

"I don't know. I was angry, I guess. I want Jack to rest in peace, not to be part of …" She collected herself. "I just want peace is all, for Jack and myself."

That was easy enough to understand. I had been pretty vague with her that morning about what had been done to Patrick's grave, but I thought the time had come to tell her all the details.

"My lord!" Mary slammed on the brakes. And to her credit, it wasn't lip service. She seemed utterly horrified by what I described. "I'm so sorry, so very sorry." She repeated it several times as we made our way slowly to the gravesite.

"It's okay, Mary, it wasn't your doing."

"This is it."

We'd stopped along the way to buy some flowers—not roses—to lay on Jack's headstone. When Mary turned off the car, we both reached into the backseat to collect our bouquets. I asked Mary for a minute by the grave alone. She hesitated, her earlier discomfort once again showing through.

"Go on," she said, if not happily.

I wasn't a grave talker. I took no solace in speaking to bones, grass, and granite. Besides, it's not like Jack and I were old buddies. I liked what little I knew of him and he had seemed really in love with Patrick. No small accomplishment. Although I didn't know Patrick, I'd learned a lot about him during the course of my search for him. Much of what I learned, I didn't like. I didn't care that he was gay: not then, not now. I even felt sorry that he suffered from paralyzing OCD, but he could be a bully like his father. He'd even gotten physical with a girl he dated while working through his sexual identity. No, I hadn't requested the time alone to chew the fat with Jack about his old boyfriend.

Like Mary said, the roses were gone, but I could see where she'd scrubbed the paint off the back of the small headstone. It wasn't a grand thing, Jack's tombstone. It was a low chunk of beveled granite: tasteful, modest, Midwestern. I liked that. I liked that a lot. I laid my flowers down and extended my hand to Mary.

While not exactly Father Blaney, Mary wasn't much for touchy-feely either. She sort of winced when I held out my hand. I remembered her being warmer when we had her to New York, but this was her home turf and this was her brother's grave. Patrick had been an abstraction to her, someone who only existed in her brother's phone calls and letters. So his burial, twenty years after the fact, was almost surreal. Jack, on the other hand, had been very real to her.

"Hi, Jack," she said, laying down her flowers, "Mr. Prager, Patrick's brother-in-law, has come all the way out from New York to see you …"

I sort of tuned out to the rest of her chat. Mary was right, there wasn't much to see. But sometimes you have to see for yourself that there's nothing to see. It was like when I looked at the envelope in the office. I didn't figure there'd be anything on it, but I had to look for myself. Suddenly, I was feeling pretty beat. There'd be time to rest that night. I was going to stay over in Cincinnati and fly out early in the morning.

When Mary was done, I picked up a pebble and placed it on Jack's headstone. I did it without thinking. I noticed Mary staring at me and not with a glad expression.

"Why did you do that?"

"Habit. It's a Jewish tradition."

"But what is it for?"

"You know, Mary, I think it serves a lot of purposes. It shows other mourners that the person buried by that headstone isn't forgotten. I guess it also lets the spirit of the person buried there know too, though I don't think that's in the Talmud. But a wise man I loved very much once told me it was symbolic of adding to the mound, to show that a memorial was an ongoing thing and would never truly be finished."

"Oh."

"I meant no disrespect. Would you like me to remove it?"

Her mouth said no, but her body language said yes. I chose to take her at her word. That's what Israel Roth would have done. For the second time in two days I remembered our visit to the cemetery all those years ago. I was smiling as we pulled away, remembering Mr. Roth. I also saw that Mary could not take her eyes off that pebble.

I asked Mary if she'd like to go to dinner, on me, of course. She said no. I tried to contain my disappointment. It meant I'd have time to get a lot of rest and maybe call one or two of Jack's old students. Not that I thought talking to them would get me anywhere, but again, I just wanted to hear it for myself. At first, Mary was reluctant to share any of the names or numbers with me, though she eventually relented. Again, I understood. Mary just wanted this over with so she could get back to the way things were. She liked her routines. The older you get, the less you like change. And the disturbance of her brother's grave was a little more serious a change of routine than her dry cleaners moving to a new location.

I thanked her for her putting up with my visit. And when she said she was sorry for what had been done at the Maloney family plot, Mary got that sick face again. If I didn't know better, I'd swear that bothered her more than having Jack's resting place messed with. She was tired and we kept our goodbyes brief. Tired as she might have been, I was willing to bet that the second I turned the corner, Mary would be heading back to the cemetery. That pebble I left on Jack's headstone would have to go.

I RETURNED THE rental and caught a shuttle bus to my hotel. I got back early enough to have ventured into Kentucky or Cincinnati, if I was so inclined. I was not. I felt the allure of a quick meal and a long stretch in bed more than the need to feel blue grass between my toes or ... What was Cincinnati famous for, anyway? Chili, right? I could get some of that from room service. But first I ordered a double Dewar's on the rocks at the hotel bar and found a quiet table away from the TV. I took out the list of names and numbers Mary White had given me and punched the first number into my cell.

I left three messages before I got a live human being on the phone. Too bad, in a way. I was just perfecting my message.

Hi, my name is Moe Prager. I knew Jack White a long time ago in New York, and his sister Mary tells me you and Jack were close. I was just wondering if you wouldn't mind spending a few minutes of your time talking to me about Jack. It would mean a lot to me if you could. My numbers are …

But like I said, someone picked up on my fourth call.

"Yo."

"Hello, is this Marlon Rhodes?"

"Who da fuck wanna know?"

"My name's Moe Prager."

"Dat name s'posed ta mean sumptin ta me?"

"How about the name Jack White?"

That got Mr. Rhodes' attention. "Say whatchu gotta say."

"I knew Jack White a long time ago in New York. He was close with my brother-in-law Patrick. I was thinking about Jack this week and I asked his sister Mary if she could put me onto any of Jack's old students because I knew he meant a lot to you guys."

"Don't be lyin' to me, man. Dis about dat graveyard shit, right?"

"Right."

"You Five-O?"

"A cop? I used to be."

"Fuck y'all."

So ended our conversation. I waited a few minutes and called back. He didn't answer, so I left my finely honed message on his machine. I got two more of Jack's former students on the phone and though the conversations were longer and more polite than the one I had with Marlon Rhodes, they were equally unproductive. Both liked and admired Jack and both had, on occasion visited his grave, but neither had made a habit of it and neither had been there for months.

I drank another scotch, ate a bowl of awful chili, and went to bed. I had a long dreamless sleep without insight, vision or revelation. It was just exactly the kind of sleep I needed.

CHAPTER SIX

DURING THE PLANE ride home I realized I was doing it again. I was keeping secrets under the guise of protecting someone else. That's crap. Secrets protect their keepers. I hadn't told Katy about what had happened to Jack's grave or that I was going to Dayton. When I spoke to Sarah, I severely minimized the extent to which the Maloney gravesite had been desecrated. If it hadn't suited my purposes, I probably wouldn't have shared all the details with Mary White. Had I shared them all? It gets hard to know. But if there is any justice, it's that the protection of the secret keepers doesn't last forever. For when any two people share knowledge, their secret is a shared illusion.

Looking back twenty-two years, it seems like madness to have not confessed to Katy what I knew about her father and brother. I was afraid to tell her I had found her brother and that I had let him go. Afraid to tell her that her father had been thrown off the NYPD in the early '60s for a brutal assault and that it had been covered up. Afraid to tell her that her father and brother had been locked in a perverse game of chicken. Afraid to tell her that her father had ordered two of his underlings to beat the piss out of me on a SoHo street. The truth would have hurt her, sure, but it might've hurt me much worse. There's a reason people say, "Don't shoot the messenger." I wasn't willing to risk losing the only woman I had ever loved by being the bearer of bad news. And my original mistake was compounded by the day, by the week, by the year, by the decade. Even now there were things I hadn't told her, things she had a right to know.

It's strange how they say you can't teach instinct. Learned behavior is learned behavior. Instinct is inborn. Yet it's become nearly impossible for me to distinguish between the two. Once you replace reason with self-preservation, secret keeping becomes reflexive. For me there was little difference between a secret and the blink of my eye. Only in retrospect can I distinguish between the two. So there on the plane home, in seat 24C, I decided for the second time since 1978 to come clean.

My resolve lasted the time it took to get to New York and have the wheels of the 737 hit the LaGuardia tarmac. When we touched down, I turned on my cell phone and found a long queue of messages. The first was a hang-up from Katy. The other four were from my brother Aaron, Sarah, Carmella Melendez, and Sheriff Vandervoort. All of them were looking for me on behalf of Katy and their tone ranged from desperate to angry. Something was wrong, but no one would say what exactly. When I tried Katy's house and cell numbers, I got recordings. Now I was getting panicky. As a keeper of secrets, I was uncomfortable on the opposite side of the fence.

Although the Boeing was half empty, it took an eternity to deplane. When I finally managed to free myself, I did something I hadn't done for quite some time: I flashed tin.

"Listen," I said to a woman at the desk of the adjoining gate. "I need a quiet place to make some important calls."

"Follow me."

I was glad she took a closer look at my badge than at me. I was getting a little long in the tooth to be flashing a regular cop's badge at anyone. Like an aging comedian taking stock of his act, I realized the time had come to retire that joke. The gag was on its last legs.

"You can use this lounge, officer," she said, fiddling with a keypad lock. "No one will bother you in here and if you want to use the phone, just hit nine for an outside line."

I thanked her and waited for her to close the door behind her before getting back to my cell phone.

My first thought was to call Aaron, but it wasn't my second. Just the judgmental tone of his voice was enough to set my teeth on edge and I'd heard hints of it in his message. I was an enigma and a bit of a disappointment to my big brother. He didn't understand my being a cop in the first place and when I was forced to retire, he couldn't comprehend my missing the job so much. There was a lot he didn't understand about me. We were wired differently, Aaron and me. But the flash point between us for the last two decades was my stubborn refusal to leave my PI license in the sock drawer with the dust bunnies and the rest of my unrealized ambitions and accept my life as a wine merchant. That was always enough for him. It never was and would never be enough for me.

I tried Katy's numbers again to the same frustrating end. Again, I left messages. I hesitated to call Sarah before I knew anything. Trouble sucks, but it sucks worse when you're seven hundred miles away from it and you feel helpless. I didn't want to add to her frustration. Carmella was out of the office and not answering her cell, so that left Sheriff Vandervoort. At least he'd left me his cell number.

"Vandervoort."

"Sheriff, it's Moe Prager. What's going on?"

"Where've you been, Mr. Prager?"

"What the fuck does that matter? What's going on with Katy?"

"You better get up here."

"One more time, Sheriff, what's going—"

"Your ex-wife's had a little trouble. She's over at Mary Immaculate."

"Trouble! Is she hurt? What happened?"

"No, she's not hurt, not physically, anyway. We just had a little excitement and the doctors wanted to take a look at her."

"Sheriff, I'm an ex-cop and I respect other cops, but if you don't start speaking English to me, I'm gonna—"

"Mrs. Prager called us to her house and when we got there she was ... unhinged and talking a little crazy. Maybe it was all the heartache from yesterday or—"

"Crazy how?"

"She said she got a call."

"A call. A call from who?"

There was silence on the other end of the phone.

"Sheriff!"

"She said she got a call from her brother Patrick."

I'D BEEN TO the Mary Immaculate Medical Center only once, back in 1981. I was up in the Catskills looking into an old fire in which some of my high school classmates had perished. One of the dead was my fiercest teenage crush, Andrea Cotter. That's when I first met Mr. Roth. During the investigation, Francis Maloney suffered a stroke and I rushed to be with Katy. Now as I drove, I remembered that last time, how I prayed for the cold-hearted prick to die. He knew it too. Even with a partially paralyzed face and mild aphasia, he warned me to be careful what I wished for. He was right. Eventually all death wishes come to pass, and the fallout with them.

Vandervoort met me in the lobby. I wouldn't say he looked worried. Concerned was more like it. Oddly, I found his concern reassuring. As cynical a bastard as I could be, I had never been completely cured of hope. We shook hands.

"What happened, exactly?"

"I got a call at home from dispatch around seven this morning . . . Hey, you want to grab a cup of coffee? My treat." He was avoiding the subject.

"Sure. We'll talk as we go. You were saying ..."

"They said your wife—ex-wife, sorry, called in hysterical, begging for us to get a car to her house. The dispatcher couldn't get anything out of her about what was wrong, if there's been a break-in or what. So they sent a car out, but thought maybe I should know too. Like we were talking about yesterday, people up here still know the Maloneys."

"I'm glad they called you."

"I got there a little after Robby, that's the younger deputy who was out at the cemetery with you yesterday. He's green, but he's good with people and he'd gotten your wife—ex-wife—"

"Just call her Katy, Sheriff. It'll make our lives easier."

"Okay. Well, he'd gotten Katy calmed down, but he couldn't get anything out of her except that she'd gotten a call. She wouldn't put the phone down no matter what Robby did. How do you take yours?" he asked as we stepped into the hospital cafeteria.

"Milk, no sugar."

"Wait here."

He was back in a minute with our coffees. "Let's sit before we go up to the Psych Ward."

"We?"

"Sorry, Mr. Prager. You're not family anymore. They won't let you up there without me."

I didn't like it, but it wasn't his doing. It was mine. Divorce impacts couples in different ways. It's an equation of losses and gains. The gains, however large or small, are usually apparent early on. The losses, as I was discovering, reveal themselves slowly, in painful, unexpected ways. We sat at the closest table.

"When you got there, what happened?"

"I told Robby to wait outside and your—Katy broke down. She said she knew what she was going to say would sound crazy, but it was true. Her brother Patrick had called. She recognized his voice."

"Christ!"

"Exactly. What was I going to say to that?"

"What *did* you say?"

"I'm no shrink, Mr. Prager. I said maybe she was just stressed out by what had happened yesterday and how it can get rough sometimes with people you love when they're gone. But that set her off again. 'I'm not crazy. It was my little brother,' she started screaming. Then she started talking about little star or something."

"Little Star is a pet name she had for Patrick," I said. I hadn't heard those two words uttered in two decades.

"Oh, okay. Well, I told her I believed her, but that I needed her to come with me to the hospital. I gotta tell you, I expected that to flip her out, but she came along pretty calmly."

"Thanks for taking care of her, Sheriff Vandervoort."

He held his hand out to me. "Pete. Call me Pete."

"Moe."

We shook hands again and started for the elevator.

"So what do you make of it, Moe? You know Katy. I don't, so I'm just asking."

"Pete, my wife is the least crazy person I ever met. If she says she got a call, I believe her."

"From her dead brother?"

"I didn't say that. Someone's going to a lot of trouble to fuck with my family."

We stepped onto the elevator and had the car to ourselves. He pressed 6.

"Look, Moe, I gotta say this, so hear me out. This is a police matter and this is my jurisdiction. I'd hate for us to be at odds after making nice. You have to stay out of it."

I didn't say anything to that. He seemed relieved by my silence. I think he was even less anxious to hear me tell him lies than I was to tell them.

THE DAYS OF involuntary institutionalization have long since gone. It wasn't even that easy to keep people for observation anymore unless a crime had been committed, so it was no shock to me that the shrink at Mary Immaculate was sending Katy home. A big man with soulful eyes and a calm manner, the doctor's name was Rauch. He possessed the ability to make you feel you were the most important person in the room and what you had to say was absolutely crucial.

"I've given her a Xanax to calm her down and a prescription for more if need be," he said. "From what I understand, she's had a lot to deal with in the last thirty-six hours, gentlemen. I am not familiar enough with her to make a formal assessment, but I can say that there are always unresolved feelings when it comes to the death of a loved one. It is no great leap to see how the desecration of her father's and brother's graves might stir up those feelings and set her off."

"So you think she was hallucinating, Doc?" I was glad Vandervoort asked and not me.

"Well, Sheriff, how many confirmed cases of resurrection can you point to? If I had to guess, and this is off the record, I'd say someone called and Katy heard what she wanted or needed to hear. Guilt and wish fulfillment make a powerful and, oft-times, toxic elixir."

"Thanks, Dr. Rauch." I shook his hand.

"Mr. Prager, I don't think Katy is a threat to herself or others, but there is something troubling going on. I would strongly advise you try to get her to seek treatment. When that point comes, I can recommend some good people in the area. Now if you'll excuse me, I'll go sign the necessary papers."

Vandervoort and I had already agreed that I would take Katy home.

"You know, Moe, I am gonna get the LUDs for Katy's phone, just to make sure. Like the shrink, I believe in guilt, but I'm not keen on coincidences."

"Me either. Thanks. Can you excuse me a second, I've got to call my daughter."

OUR RIDE BACK to the Maloney house on Hanover Street consisted of silence bookended around a burst of anger. Early on, Katy wasn't talking and kept her head turned away from me.

"I'm not crazy, Moe," she said calmly, head still turned.

"No one says you are."

"It was him."

"Patrick? Katy, come on." I didn't want to argue with her, but I wasn't going to placate her either. "Patrick's dead. You know it. We saw him buried."

"Did we?" There, she said it. Someone was bound to. "We saw bones and rags and sneakers buried, not my brother."

"Yeah, Katy, *his* bones, *his* rags, *his* sneakers. The cops confirmed it with dental records. That was Patrick."

"Then how do you explain the call?"

"Someone's fucking with you, with us. That's what all this stuff with the graves was about. That's why someone screwed around with Jack White's grave and—"

Now she turned to face me. "What happened to Jack's grave?"

I told her about the package at the office, about the Sunday call from Mary, and my trip to Dayton.

"Fuck you, Moe. You're doing it all over again," she said, a tear in the corner of her eye. "You and your goddamned secrets. Just take me home."

When we got there, I expected her to run out of the car and flip me the bird, but she was full of surprises.

"Come in."

It was an order not an option. When I stepped through the front door, she called me into the bedroom. *Shit!* I hesitated to go in. There was already enough going on. But when I entered, Katy was standing by her night table, her face serene.

"When I called you, when I called the police, I used my cell."

"I know," I said. "That's the hang-up number I got."

"Do you know why?"

"Umm … look, Vandervoort told me. When the deputy got here, you wouldn't let go of the phone."

"That's right. I wouldn't."

"So."

"It was early when the phone rang and I was still asleep."

"And …"

"You call here sometimes, right?"

"You know I do, Katy. Just look at the red light on the phone machine. At least two of those flashes are my messages, but what's that—"

"Ssshhhh! How many rings before my machine picks up?"

"Four."

"Very good," she said. "You always were observant."

"Thanks, but—"

Before I could get the question out, she pressed the PLAY button on the machine.

You have seven new messages. You have one saved message. Playing new messages.

First message. Without hesitating, Katy hit ERASE.

Message erased.

Second message. Again.

Message erased.

Third message. And again.

Message erased.

Fourth message. And again and again and again until all the new messages were gone.

To play saved messages, press three. She flicked her right index finger.

First saved message. Six forty-three a.m. From outside caller:

"Hi."

"Hello … Hello, who's there?" Katy's voice was full of sleep.

"I miss you, sis."

"Patrick! Patrick!"

"Gotta go now. I love you."

"Oh, my God! Patrick don't hang—"

Click.

End of saved messages.

We both stood there across the bedroom from each other, as far apart as we had ever been. Even at the few low points of our marriage, even in the depths of her anger when the truth of Patrick's disappearance first surfaced, she had never looked at me so coldly. We were strangers.

"Now," she said, "I'm tired, please get out of my parents' house."

I turned and left without a word.

How, I wondered, had Katy and I grown this far apart? We had once loved each other beyond all reason. From the first, our bodies had fit together as if carved to do just so. Did we fight? Of course we fought, all couples fight, but we could always see the love behind the anger. Now, and over the course of the last few years, there was only anger. Even during the inevitable dead spots in our marriage, when every day was like a long drive through Nebraska, we had rediscovered the passion. We had come through everything. I think for the very first time, when I walked out of her bedroom, I accepted that we would not come through this. That cold look on her face, not a judge's signature on a piece of paper, was our divorce decree.

STILL A LITTLE stunned, I drove around aimlessly for a while. It was pretty country up here, though not as pretty as it once had been. Farms that I used to pass on my way up had been sold and turned into gated communities of McMansions with nine-hole golf courses and artificial lakes. Some of the farms had been cut up into bigger lots. Those parcels were for super-sized homes, ones with garages the size of aircraft hangars. Sarah had a friend who called them Garage Mahals. To me, no matter how lavish the homes might be, no matter how tasteful, they were ugly. They just didn't belong.

I loved New York City, but it could be cruel to its neighbors. I once heard it said that being in close proximity to New York was like sleeping in bed next to an elephant. Everything was great until the elephant rolled over. It was what ruined Long Island and what was slowly happening here. To its neighbors, the city was a contrary beast. As its influence spread to surrounding areas, it sucked the local flavor out of the landscape. It's funny how people try to get away from the city, but never quite escape its gravity.

As the light faded, I rode back into Janus. The sheriff's office was at the end of Main Street. Robby, the young deputy, was at the desk. I hoped he got paid a lot of money given the hours Vandervoort was working him. He recognized me and flashed a smile that still had a lot of little kid in it. It was nice to see. I wasn't sure there was a lot of that left in me.

"Robby, right?"

"That's right, Mr. Prager."

I thanked him for helping with Katy.

"Sheriff Vandervoort's not around. I'm sorry. You want to leave him a note or something."

"No, thanks, that's okay. Any results from the crime scene?" I asked just to make small talk.

He hesitated. "No."

He smiled like a kid and lied like a kid. The job would beat that out of him soon enough.

"Look, deputy, you saw my ex-wife this morning. You saw for yourself what this is doing to her. Just let me know so I can be prepared when the shit hits the fan. And it's our secret. Sheriff Vandervoort will never know we even spoke about it."

"I shouldn't. I'm on probation and this is the only job I've ever—"

I put my hand on his shoulder. "Listen, kid, it's up to you."

That did the trick.

"There were some shoe impressions that didn't match any of the elimination impressions," he whispered as if Vandervoort was lurking. "They were men's size nine running shoes that led away from the Maloney plot, across three adjoining plots, down into the stream."

"No big deal in that, right? Shit, in Janus alone, how many guys are out there with size nine running shoes?"

"You don't understand, Mr. Prager. These weren't just any men's size nine running shoes."

"What's that supposed to mean?"

"These were Shinjo Olympians."

"Shinjos? I've never heard of—"

"—Shinjos. That's right." He cut me off. "No one has. Not no one, very few people have. That's because they stopped making the Olympians model in 1976 and the company went out of business is 1987."

"Thank you, deputy."

I about-faced. Robby said something to me, but the blood pounding in my ears was too loud for me to hear him. I sat in my front seat for what seemed like hours. The next thing I was fully conscious of was unlocking the door to my condo.

CHAPTER SEVEN

THE SUN FILLED my rearview as I drove along the Belt Parkway to the Gowanus. This part of the Belt could be beautiful, especially in early morning. From Bay Parkway west, the roadway swooped along the shoreline and you could race with container or cruise ships sailing beneath the Verrazano and into the hungry mouth of New York Harbor. The deep blue of the water could seem almost structural and not a trick of light. In the orange of the sun the patches of rust on the skin of the gray bridge came alive. Not today. Today I was blind to beauty, to nearly everything, but I had made this drive so often I could do it in a coma.

Aaron and I owned four stores. City On The Vine near the American Museum of Natural History was our first. Two years ago we ventured into the wilds of New Jersey and opened Que Shiraz in Marlboro. Red, White and You was our big volume location on Long Island. But our second store, Bordeaux In Brooklyn on Montague Street in the Heights, was closest to my house and to my heart. I'd run the store for years and even after I turned it over to a new manager, it was my base of operations. It was also less than three blocks away from the offices of Prager & Melendez Investigations, Inc. That was no accident. I had to go into the store, but I had other business first.

When I got off the elevator at 40 Court, I found Devo doing yoga in the hallway outside our office door. Carmella and I picked 40 Court Street for practical reasons. Besides its proximity to the State Supreme Court Building and the Brooklyn Tombs, it was filled to the brim with law firms. Funny how cops have no use for lawyers until they're off the job and looking for work. Then it's no longer about them having use for lawyers, but lawyers having use for them. And if you are going to feed off their scraps, you better have a good seat at the trough. 40 Court was front row, ringside, orchestra. Well over half the jobs we worked were farmed to us by lawyers or other investigative firms that shared our address.

Devereaux Okum—Devo—was a thin black blade of grass with a shaved head, soft voice, vaguely feminine features, and a shaman's eyes. He was in his early thirties and claimed he came from down South somewhere, but would never say exactly where. Frankly, he was more off-worldly than out-of-state. He had that '70s David Bowie mojo working. It was probably foolish, but Carmella and I never pressed him too hard on his background.

What we knew about him was that he was a vegan with a sweet disposition and formal manners who was great at what he did and worked harder at it than anyone else in the firm. Devo did gadgets. Gadgets, that's what modern investigations were all about. From tracking devices to cameras to computers, he had it covered. We paid him a big salary and had several times offered to get him licensed, even to give him a piece of the business. He had so far resisted our offers. He seemed content. I had known what that was like once, being content.

"Hey, Devo."

He didn't say anything, slowly letting out a deep breath, prayerfully pressing his palms together in front of him, a few inches from his chest. He turned to me, removing a sleek, white metallic box from his shirt pocket.

"Good morning, Moe."

"What's that?"

"This," he said, removing the earphones, "is the coming revolution."

"Looks like a cigarette case, not a revolution."

"It's an Apple product that won't be out for another few months yet."

I didn't bother asking where or how he'd gotten hold of it. He was always getting things logic and the law dictated he shouldn't have.

"What does it do, tune your circadian rhythms and access the internet?"

"It stores and plays music."

"It plays music, that's it?"

"That's it."

"How much did it cost?"

That elicited a sheepish smile.

"Okay, I'll bite. How much will it cost regular schmos like me?"

"Around four hundred bucks," he said.

"Just to play music."

"Just to play music," he repeated.

"Some revolution. They won't be able to give those things away."

"We'll see."

I had called Devo before hitting the Dewar's the night before. I wanted him to come in early specifically to discuss my dead brother-in-law's voice mail message from the great beyond. Until I could get a copy of it—and I meant to get a copy—I wanted to have some idea of what I was dealing with. When we sat down in my office, I described as closely as I could what I had heard on Katy's machine. I tried to mimic the intonation of the voice, the timing involved in the dialogue, etc. Devo didn't hesitate to ask the million dollar question.

"Was it Patrick's voice?"

"He's dead."

"Moe, I did not ask if it was actually him calling. I asked if it was his voice. Those are two very different things."

"I don't know," I said. "We spoke only once, very briefly, but Katy seemed pretty convinced. Katy would know her brother's voice."

Devo was unpersuaded. "She has not heard his voice in twenty years."

"Twenty-two plus, but who's counting? I don't think that matters. I haven't heard my mom's voice in longer than that and I'd recognize it."

"Possibly. I think it is situationally dependent, Moe, but let us come back to that in a moment. First, tell me if there was anything obviously mechanical about the voice. Was it robotic? Did it sound spliced? Were there inappropriate pauses? Was it scratchy like an old vinyl recording? Was there any background noise?"

"No, there was nothing like that. It sounded pretty much like I did it for you before. Why? Does that mean it wasn't doctored?"

"No, not at all. With a reasonable laptop and software you can download from the internet, you can make sound sit up and beg or fetch the newspaper. There would be no limit to what a person or persons with more formidable resources could do. I simply wanted to make certain that we are not dealing with pranksters or rank amateurs."

"Okay, rank amateurs and pranksters eliminated."

"Did the voice sound conversational?"

"See, Devo, that's harder to answer. There were so few words exchanged and Katy was so emotional … and not for nothing, but what were you talking about before when you said recognition was situationally dependent?"

"Simply that the events of Sunday sensitized Katy for the call on Monday. The caller might just as easily have phoned late Saturday night before the desecrations were spotted, but he didn't. Why do you suppose that is?"

"Because Katy had to be primed to recognize the voice. The stuff at the gravesite played with her head. It got to those last shreds of hope and denial we hide deep inside."

Devo smiled a smile at me that made me feel like an apt pupil. Maybe he'd put a gold star next to my name.

"Do you have enough to make an educated guess about whether it was someone imitating Patrick's voice or some digital wizardry?" I asked.

"We are certain he is dead, are we not?"

"Everybody but Katy."

"Well, until I have a copy of the message, I cannot say. Even then, I may not be able to render a definitive opinion, but it is almost beside the point."

"How's that?"

"For someone to imitate a voice they have to hear it. And if Patrick is dead …"

"… they either had to have known him or have a recording of him. Even if the mimic knew Patrick, it would be hard to do his voice flawlessly simply from memory."

"Imitation is a matter of trial and error, of feedback and fine tuning," he said. "Hard to get accurate feedback from old memories."

"So," I said, "either way, if it's some digitally enhanced trick or a clever mimic, there's a recording of Patrick's voice out there somewhere."

"Find that recording and—"

"—I'll find my ghost."

I shook Devo's hand. "How are you coming with that list of names I gave Carmella?"

"I should be finished this afternoon," he said.

Had he been any other employee, I would have slipped him a few C-notes in an envelope or sent over a bottle of Opus One. But gestures like that were just wasted on Devo. He was old school in that he found the job itself reward enough. He wasn't interested in the perks. I guess I liked him for that.

I CAN'T SAY that I hate the wine business, although I have, at times, hated it. I've often thought that if I really despised the life, I'd be out of it. I've always had strength enough to walk away. The thing was, the business bored me. Like I once said, there's only so many times you can parse the difference between champagne and *methode champenoise* without completely losing your mind. For over twenty years the wine business had kept my bank account full and left my soul empty. It afforded me a few luxuries. I'd owned a house. I had a condo. I got to drive new cars every few years. My kid could go to whatever college she was smart enough to get into.

The wine business was never my dream. I wasn't a dreamer by nature. Even the profession I loved was the result of a drunken dare. I mean, how many college students in the late '60s were signing up to take the NYPD entrance exam? One year I'm tossing bottles at the cops, the next year I'm a cop getting bottles tossed at me. The wine business was Aaron's thing. The initial plan was for me to be an investor and then to come on board after I retired from the job with my twenty years in and a detective first's pension. Didn't work out that way and all because I fell prey to a conspiracy of fate. In a way, I was actually Son of Sam's last victim.

In August of '77, when Sam was finally captured, New York City was as close to defeat as it ever was or is ever likely to be. Beaten down by years of near bankruptcy, brutal winters, blackouts, and Mr. Berkowitz, the city was a madhouse. Any street cop would know. I knew. Rage was boiling just beneath everybody's skin, beneath the city's streets. We were always a pinprick away from explosion. And none of us was immune to the Vietnam hangover: our national headlong rush into pot, punk, polyester, and Plato's Retreat. I think sometimes if Gerald Ford had wanted to be a more effective president, he should have moved from the White House to Studio 54.

Anyway, when Son of Sam was arraigned, the brass wanted to make sure there were plenty of cops around for crowd control. So they bussed in uniforms from precincts all over the city. I was one of those uniforms. If you catch any of the old video from that day, you can see me standing just behind Detective Ed Zigo and to Son of Sam's left. Although I couldn't have known it then, it was my first appearance on television and my final shift in uniform. While I was gone, the precinct's linoleum had been waxed for the first time in months and some careless schmuck had thrown a piece of carbon paper onto the floor. When I returned, my foot found that piece of carbon paper. Cops who were there say the sound my knee made when all the ligaments snapped was enough to make you puke. Apparently, a few people did. I don't remember, because my head smacked the floor pretty hard. I woke up in Coney Island Hospital having taken my first misstep into the wine business.

Five months and two surgeries later, I was put out to pasture with pain pills and a patrolman's pension. Aaron had found the perfect store, but we were still a little short on funds and worried about getting our liquor license. That's when Rico Tripoli, my closest buddy from the Six-O, told me about some missing kid and how maybe, just maybe, if I found the kid, his influential father could get us our financing and license and how we'd be set for life. *Yeah, sure!* What Rico neglected to mention was that he didn't give a rat's ass about the missing kid or my future. I was to be his shortcut to a gold shield and the means to the end of Francis Maloney's political career.

Rico was right in a way. We all got what we wanted. Rico got his gold shield. His handlers got Francis Maloney to retire from politics. Aaron and I got our financing and our license and we were set for life. I got a wife and love and a family as well. Yes, we all got what we wanted, everyone but Francis Maloney. I hated my father-in-law, but I never blamed him for his hating me for my part in his demise. We all got what we wanted and the only happy one of us was Aaron.

My big brother was tinkering with the register as I walked through the creaky wooden doors of Bordeaux In Brooklyn. Aaron had aged well. His hair was thinner and all gray, but his shoulders were still broad and unbowed. Other than my chronic disinterest in the business, he had everything he ever wanted. Our success had washed away the sting of our dad's small-time thinking and big-time failures. He had a wife he probably loved more now than the day they married, great kids, a big house on Long Island, and good health. Aaron didn't think so, but I envied him. It was a blessing to be born knowing what you want and how to get it. With few exceptions, my wants shifted with my cases.

"Hey, big brother."

"Christ, will you help me with this thing," he barked.

"Here, shithead." I banged the side of my fist into the till and it slid open. "You should come to this store more often. The drawer's been sticking like that for years."

"You should come to any store more often."

"Touché."

"So what's this *mishegas* with your wife?"

"Ex-wife, as everyone keeps reminding me."

"All right, your ex-wife."

"What *mishegas*? What's wrong with thinking your dead brother dug his way out of his grave, smashed his dad's headstone to bits, and is making phone calls?"

"*Oy gevalt!*"

"Yeah, big brother, *oy gevalt* indeed."

"What are you doing about it?"

"I was just about to call Ghostbusters."

"Very funny, Moses."

"I'm doing the only thing I can do. I'm gonna look into it. First, I have to pick your niece up at the airport."

He grinned. My brother and Sarah had a special affinity for one another. "When does she get in?"

"I'm leaving for LaGuardia in about an hour."

"Does she know what's going on?"

"Some of it. Look, Aaron, I just want you to know, I'm going to take as long as it takes to find out what's going on."

"We've prospered for two decades without your full attention. We should be able to survive another few weeks."

"Fuck you!"

"Fuck you, he says to me," he stage-whispered to an invisible audience. "Let's face it, the best thing you ever did for us was getting us started. That shit with Katy's dad, look, you never wanted to tell me much about it, okay. It was your business, but enough already."

I wanted to explode. He was right, but he was wrong too. I put in my time. I got us some of our biggest accounts, hired our best people. Even Aaron would have to admit that much. Klaus and Kosta were integral parts of our success and had been with us from year one. Both now owned small percentages of the business. Kosta was our head buyer and Klaus, besides running the day-to-day operations of the New Jersey store was, along with our lawyers and accountants, looking into the possibility of our franchising.

"Without me, there'd be no business," I said.

"Yeah, I heard that refrain before. It used to mean something, too, when you said it last century. That was then. Four stores and twenty years later, it's enough already."

"Did Abraham Lincoln write that for you?"

"What?"

"Never mind."

"Go play cops and robbers with your Spanish hottie." Aaron was very much of my parent's generation. I'm surprised he didn't call our African-American employees colored. He wasn't a bigot. Far from it. He was just old. He was born old.

"Puerto Rican."

"What?"

"Carmella is Puerto Rican and she's not my hottie. Where do you come up with these terms anyway, *Reader's Digest*?"

"What's wrong with *Reader's Digest*?"

No matter what our arguments started over, they always ended in the same place.

"You want coffee?" I asked.

"Sounds good."

"The usual?"

"Always. Hey, little brother ..."

"Yeah."

"I love ya."

"I know. Me too."

THE NORTHWEST TERMINAL was bustling. The area airports were always busy, but there was just something about LaGuardia that brought out the closet claustrophobic in even the most hardened New Yorker. I found myself wishing *I'd* made the travel arrangements instead of leaving them up to Sarah. All this foot traffic was going to make things that much more difficult. No doubt a late afternoon or evening flight would have been a better option, but there was no use giving myself *shpilkes* over it now. For the moment, I only wanted to think about the best thing in my life, Sarah.

I loved the kid so much it hurt. Maybe it was her only-child status or that we were baseball buddies, but I had never gotten used to her being away from home. The sting was particularly sharp today with LaGuardia being just a stone's throw away from Shea Stadium. Sarah had a double-major as a kid, learning about baseball and aircraft as we sat and watched the big jets roar over Shea on their final approaches to the airport. I remembered the first game I took her to, a weekday matinee against the Padres. She lasted only a couple of innings in the baking sun and passed out on my shoulder. When she woke up, she said she was *firsty.* I remembered that day for other reasons too.

It was the summer of 1983 and I had been hired to look into the disappearance of a political intern named Moira Heaton. Moira was a plain looking girl, a cop's daughter, who had gone missing from State Senator Steven Brightman's neighborhood office on Thanksgiving Eve 1981. For two years Brightman had proclaimed his innocence. He'd done everything he could, cooperated completely with the police, posted a big reward, jumped through fiery hoops, but it was all to no avail. He had been tried and convicted in the press and in the court of public opinion. Trouble was, Brightman was the fair-haired boy, the next Jack Kennedy and he was too ambitious to just live out his days as a has-been that never was.

That's where I came in. Thomas Geary, one of Brightman's wealthy backers and the father of one of our former wine store employees, got the idea that I could magically clear the state senator's name. My reputation was for luck, not skill. As my early clients had too often said, "We tried good, now we're going to give luck a chance." I guess, if I want to be honest, they were right. I was lucky. My luck extended as far back as 1972. On Easter Sunday of that year, a little girl named Marina Conseco was kidnapped off a Coney Island street. And once seventy-two hours passed, the search for Marina silently morphed into a search for her remains. I found Marina severely injured but alive at the bottom of an old wooden water tank. She had been molested, then tossed in the tank and left to die. To this day, I'm not sure what made me look up and notice the tanks and think to search them. I was lucky then. I was lucky with Brightman too.

We were on the 7 train heading back home from Shea. Sarah was sleeping with her head of damp red curls resting on my leg. I was hot and tired too, but my eyes kept drifting to the front page of the *Post* that the man across the car from me was reading. On it was a picture of evil personified, a serial rapist the papers had dubbed Ivan the Terrible. He had scraggly hair, a cruel condescending smile, and black eyes. They were the blackest eyes I'd ever seen: opaque as the ocean on a moonless night. With a little bit of digging, I found a connection between Moira and Ivan. He eventually confessed to her murder. I was a little *too* lucky with that one. It all came just a bit too easily. In spite of it, I found the real facts behind the fabricated truths that had been sprinkled on the ground before me like so many bread crumbs.

I could never go to a game or drive past Shea Stadium without thinking of Sarah's first Mets game. Every year I renewed my Mets season tickets, but it wasn't the same without her and it was never going to be the same. These days I usually gave my tickets away to Aaron's kids or Carmella's little cousins or clients. I checked the Arrivals screen for the hundredth time in the last ten minutes and noticed Sarah's flight number was flashing. So far, I had been able to filter Ivan the Terrible's kind of evil out of my kid's life and I meant to keep it that way. I dialed Carmella's cell number.

"What?" she barked. "It's so fucking noisy in here."

"Her flight's landed."

"No shit! There's like a screen two feet from my face."

"You remember what Sarah looks—"

"For chrissakes, Moe! I know your daughter for ten years. I know what the fuck she looks like. I could spot that red hair from halfway across the state."

"What the fuck's eating you lately?"

"My stomach's been bothering me for weeks. I'm sorry, Moe, I know I been cranky."

"Okay, she should be getting down here in a few minutes."

"Don't worry. Anybody comes near her, I got it covered."

"Anything suspicious?"

"I got my eye on a few mutts, but you know these town car drivers try to scam rides. We'll see soon."

Not everything I got right was about luck. I was a good cop before my accident. I still possessed the ability to anticipate, to see what might be coming around the next corner, and what I saw coming was trouble for Sarah. Whoever had done this stuff with Patrick had gone through a lot of trouble. So far the only direct targets had been Katy and me, but if you really want to hurt, frighten, or generally fuck with people, you go after their kids. That's why I had arranged for Carmella to come to the airport before me and stake out the baggage claim area. She was less certain about the setup than me.

"What about that lady in Ohio? They fucked with her brother's grave, no?"

"Collateral damage," I said. "It enhanced the effect of what was going on here, a bit of sleight of hand to distract me. It worked, too. I was out in Dayton looking at a grave when I should have been home keeping my eye on the ball. I'm not gonna let them catch me off guard again."

She was right about one thing. We'd see soon enough.

My least favorite part of the airport was baggage claim. Baggage claim was like the final insult after the long ordeal, just another opportunity to hurry up and wait. Folks looked defeated waiting for their bags. And no matter how they spruced up the area, the machinery always seemed positively medieval.

My phone buzzed, then stopped. That was Carmella's signal that people were spilling into the baggage claim area. Sarah appeared. I couldn't help hoping that I was being foolish and over protective, that Carmella was right. She wasn't. Everything seemed to happen at once. Even before I was fully conscious of Sarah's presence, the pocket of space closed around her. Carmella came out of nowhere and tackled someone, Sarah screamed, a crowd surged in their directions. I put my head down and charged through the sea of bodies.

"Get the fuck off me, bitch! You breakin' my finger."

A chubby black kid of maybe seventeen was face down on the floor, Carmella twisting his thumb and wrist behind his back. Sarah's expression was more surprised than anything else. Then I noticed a brown shipping envelope in her hands that I hadn't seen her holding when she first came into view.

"Give that to me, kiddo." I held my hand out to Sarah and she placed the envelope in my palm. "Let him up, Carm, so we can talk privately."

Carmella pulled the kid to his feet as I assured everyone that it was all right.

"Just a misunderstanding," I lied, sounding authoritative as hell. I didn't flash my badge. When the cops showed up—which they would—I didn't need to try and explain away a potential felony charge. "Show's over, folks. Go get your bags and have a safe trip back home."

By nature, New Yorkers are disobedient bastards. On the other hand they take an inordinate amount of pride in their unshockability. This time unshockability won out and they went back to reclaiming their luggage while we hustled the kid into a corner. As we walked, I tore open the envelope. It was another wilted rose and a "self-portrait" of Patrick done on an eight by eleven piece of Masonite. The familiar initials PMM were in the lower right hand corner. This wasn't funny anymore.

"Okay, asshole, what's this about?" I said, pressing my face into the kid's. His wide, frightened eyes told me he knew I wasn't fucking around.

"Guy gimme a twenty ta give dat package to da red-headed girl come out dat door."

"What guy?" I asked, pressing my face even closer to his.

"Dat one," he said, pointing.

"Which one?" I stepped back to see where he was pointing.

"Him."

He was pointing at the portrait.

"Bullshit!" Carmella hissed in the kid's ear, tightening the thumb lock. He winced. "I ain't fuckin wich y'all."

Carmella yanked and twisted. The breath went out of the kid and I thought he might pass out from the pain.

"Carmella, stop it!" Sarah said. "Dad, tell her to stop it."

"Look! Der he at." The kid's voice was barely a whisper, but he pointed toward the exit doors with his free hand.

I turned and my heart jumped into my throat. There he was, tattoo and all. The world around me crawled. There was a muted roar in my ears. I could hear individual noises—the squeaky wheel of a baggage cart, the smack of a suitcase as it hit the metal railing, a limo driver screaming "Mr. Child. Mr. Child. Mr. Child," the whoosh of the doors—but none of it made any sense. I told my legs to run, but they wouldn't move. I tried to shout, but I could form no words. Something was tugging my arm.

"Dad! Dad!" Sarah was shouting, pulling my sleeve.

"Moe, what's up?" It was Carmella.

"Let the kid go," I heard myself say. "Let him go."

"What?"

"Let him go."

My legs finally started moving, but not fast enough. Strong arms grabbed me.

"Where the fuck you think you're going, buddy?"

"Huh?"

"C'mon, pal," the Port Authority cop said. "And the three of youse too, let's go. Now!"

I didn't argue, but kept watching the door as I moved.

I didn't know ghosts used doors.

IT DIDN'T TAKE long to straighten things out with the Port Authority cops, especially once we showed them our old badges and shields. You should never underestimate the power of the *us against them* mentality. Once cops, always cops. Raheem—that was the kid's name—was no fool either. He understood that he wasn't going to get a whole lot of sympathy once the policemen's love fest began. So for a hundred bucks and a sincere apology, he was willing to forget all about Carmella's tackle and death grip. For an extra fifty, he agreed to have coffee with Carmella so she could debrief him about how he'd been approached to deliver the package to Sarah.

I had to get Sarah back to my condo so we could talk about the full extent of what was going on with Katy and so she could decide if she wanted to stay with me or her mom. Having Sarah in the car to talk to was helping me not to obsess over who I thought I saw at the airport. The distraction of driving had also let me regain some measure of equilibrium. It wasn't Patrick—that's what I kept telling myself—but I was meant to think so. My new mantra was, "Don't fall for it. Don't fall for it. Don't fall …" But Christ, that guy in the airport terminal looked an awful lot like him.

"So talk to me, kiddo." I wasn't quite pleading.

"I didn't like that back there."

I didn't like it either, at least not the part where I saw a ghost. I didn't think Sarah had seen him, so I played dumb. "You wanna give me a hint here?"

"How you guys treated Raheem."

"We were only being cautious. Don't hold it against Carmella. She was trying to protect you. Blame me. More has been going on at home than I've let on."

"Not that part," she said, staring out the window as we passed Shea and smiling wistfully.

"Then I'm a little confused."

"How the cops blew him off because he was a black kid and you guys were cops. If the roles were reversed and he had tackled you or Carmella, the cops would have beat the shit out of him. They wouldn't have been slapping him on the back and inviting him out for drinks like they did with you and Carmella."

"You're right. I'd like to tell you it's not true, but it is. That's a cop's world sometimes."

"Well, it sucks."

"There's a lot of injustice in the world, Sarah. Some of it's big. Some of it's small. In the scheme of things, today's events were a small injustice."

"You don't have to talk to me like I'm a little kid, Dad. Besides, there's no such thing as a small injustice."

"I didn't say it was right. I just said it's the way it is."

"Is that how you rationalized yourself to sleep when you were a cop?"

"When I was a cop, I slept like a baby. Being a cop isn't about the big questions. It's about doing the job."

"Did doing the job include mistreating innocent people?"

"Sometimes, yeah, I guess it did."

"Then that sucks too."

"I'm glad I'm sending you to the University of Michigan so you can learn to use the word 'sucks' in every other sentence. You gonna try for the debate team next term?"

"Don't change the subject."

"Okay. Look, Carmella and me, we were just looking out for you. Raheem got the shit end of the stick today, but he also got a hundred and fifty bucks for getting his thumb twisted a little bit. You seem a lot more worried about his dignity than he did."

"That's not the point."

"Then I'm lost," I said.

"It wasn't necessarily what happened back there, but what it represented that bothers me. You guys got a free pass because you were once cops, not because of what you did or didn't do."

"Oh, kinda like how you got out of those speeding tickets last year because you were a cop's kid and had the PBA and Detectives Endowment Association cards in your bag that Carmella and I gave you."

Sarah had no snappy reply for that one, but sank into her seat and sulked for a few minutes.

"So what is it with you and Carmella anyway?" she said as we got off the Van Wyck and onto the Belt Parkway.

"We're partners."

"That all? Just business partners like you and Uncle Aaron?"

"Not exactly. I get along better with Carmella. I'm not a disappointment to her like I am to your uncle."

"Come on, Dad, Carmella is beautiful and you have that cop thing between you and—"

"Look, kiddo, if this is about me and your mother, forget it. What went wrong with us has nothing to do with Carmella."

"Not even a little bit, not even about you and Mom not getting back together?"

"I love your mom, but it just doesn't work between us anymore."

"But—"

"No buts. I hurt your mom and she can't get past it. Until this stuff with Patrick, we were both okay with that."

Patrick. *Shit!* I got a little queasy just saying his name. What had happened at the air terminal came rushing back to me. I worried Sarah might notice. Then, of all people, I thought of Francis Maloney and smiled. A reaction I had never before had nor was ever likely to have again. The strange thing about my late father-in-law and me was that in spite of our mutual loathing, we never fought, not really. We were engaged in a long cold war. And just like in the real Cold War, both of us kept a finger close to the button that would bring our worlds crashing down around our heads.

We barely spoke, but there was one question Francis Maloney Sr. never missed the opportunity to ask me, "Do you believe in ghosts?" He never explained the question, never once discussed it. He didn't want or expect an answer. After a few years, he didn't even have to say the words. The question would come in the guise of a sideways glance or a churlish smile. His favorite form of silent sparring was to raise his glass of Irish to me, a toast to his sworn enemy.

Only in death did he explain. The mechanics of his revenge from the grave were particularly cruel. Included in Katy's inheritance was a cold storage receipt. She thought it might be for her mom's wedding dress. When we retrieved the item from cold storage, it wasn't a wedding dress at all, but a man's blue winter parka, the blue parka her brother Patrick had been wearing the night he disappeared. Katy recognized it immediately. So did I. In the pocket of the coat was a twenty-year-old handwritten note from Francis:

"Your boyfriend gave this to me on February 17, 1978. Ask him where he got it and why he swore me to secrecy. Did he never tell you he found Patrick?"

And so I came to understand the question he had asked me hundreds of times in a hundred different ways over the years. The coat proved I had found Patrick, that I had let him go, and that I had conspired to keep the secret from Katy forever. Patrick's ghost had essentially ended our marriage. Francis, thinking that his death would protect him from the fallout, had miscalculated. For as angry as Katy was with me, the extent of it was nothing compared to the animus with which she regarded her late father. Katy and I might never reconcile and she would likely not forgive me, but we would always share Sarah.

Sarah was the best of both of us. On the other hand, Katy would hate her father for eternity.

So I sat there in the driver's seat, smiling, thinking of the late Francis Maloney Sr. and wondering whether he would have appreciated today's delicious irony. I closed my eyes just for a second and saw him raise his glass of Irish. In my head I heard him ask, "Do you believe in ghosts?" And this time I answered, "Maybe."

"Dad, what are you smiling at?"

"I was just thinking about your grandfather."

"Your dad?"

"No, Grandpa Francis."

"But you hated him, didn't you?"

"Yeah. That's why I'm smiling."

"You're so weird, Dad."

"I suppose I am, sometimes. At least you didn't say I suck."

CHAPTER EIGHT

FOR THE SECOND time that day I drove into Brooklyn Heights, but the road ahead hadn't gotten any clearer. Now I was facing down the sun sliding slowly behind the curve of the Earth and the blue of the water was less assertive. The green spaces and bike paths that ran along the Belt Parkway were crowded with couples, joggers pushing strollers, tanned skater girls, dogs on long leashes, dogs on no leashes at all. Kites bathed in dying orange light flirted with the Verrazano Bridge and dreamed of untethered flight. These were not the cheap, diamond-shaped kites I flew as a kid, kites made of splintered balsa wood and paper, trailing tails of my mother's old house frocks or whatever other *schmattes* were laying around. No, these were proper kites, fierce and sturdy things that loved the wind and did not fear it. I wondered if I were a kite, would I love the wind or fear it? It's odd what you think about sometimes.

By the time I turned off the BQE at the base of the Brooklyn Bridge and into Cadman Plaza, the sun and the kites were gone. There may be no silence in Brooklyn, ever, but there are lulls when its symphony quiets down just enough to hear individual instruments: a tugboat horn, the squeal and rumble of a lone subway, the *thwack, thwack, thwack* of a low-flying helicopter. I used to love this time of night. I would sit on the steps outside Bordeaux In Brooklyn and listen to the reassuring buzz of tires along the metal grate deck of the Brooklyn Bridge. The buzz was gone now that they had paved over the deck. I knew it was silly to miss it and that the bridge was far safer this way, especially in the rain. Still, I listened for the buzz as I walked from my car to the lobby of 40 Court Street.

Working nights never bothered me much nor did staying late at any of the wine stores. I did hate coming to 40 Court at night. Office buildings are depressing places, lonely and desperate places after dark. Bored square badges read the papers, slept in the shadows, spoke broken Spanish to the cleaning girls. As I walked from the elevator, I checked for light leaking through the bottoms of other office doors. I thought about the men and women behind those doors. *Was it always about the work? Was it about avoiding a loveless marriage? An empty apartment? Or worse, an emptier bed?*

Carmella didn't greet me when I came through the front door, so I went into my office and collected my bottle of Dewar's and two glasses before heading in to see her. Just lately, it seemed like she needed more than a few drinks and I'd been scotch jonesing since the airport. I hadn't wanted to drink in front of Sarah. Crazy, right? It's not like she'd never seen me drink before. I mean, she was twenty and I owned four fucking wine stores, for chrissakes. But she'd never seen me drink at home and never alone. She had never seen me drunk and I wanted to keep it that way.

I knocked on Carmella's office door and walked in. Her chair was turned toward the window, but not completely so that I couldn't see her profile. She was crying. I had seen her cry only once before, when the NYPD finally did to her what they had done to me. They had wanted to show her the door almost immediately after she was wounded at Crispo's Bar in Red Hook in '89, but the only thing Carmella Melendez ever wanted to be was a cop and she wasn't going to give up as easily as I had. Amazingly, she hung on for seven more years and made it to detective first before getting the boot. She'd taken a lot of shit to make it that far, but that last year had been particularly hard on her. And after her last shift, she broke down.

"Here," I said, as I poured. "You look like you could use this."

Carmella still did not face me. "I'm not drinking these days."

"No wonder you've been such a bitch." I was laughing. She wasn't. "Come on, you know I hate to drink alone."

"No!"

"What the fuck is the matter with—"

"I'm pregnant."

I drank my scotch, quickly, then drank the glass I poured for Carmella. After that, I said nothing. Sometimes, the two of us would talk about my divorce and what had gone wrong between Katy and me. We almost never talked about Carmella's social life. That was mostly my doing, I suppose. Her taste in men sucked and I wasn't shy about voicing that opinion. I also tended to pile on when the latest asshole would inevitably disappoint her. It didn't take her long to tire of hearing me say, "I told you so." She thought she could read my mind.

"Go ahead, say it. I know you're thinking it."

"No, I'm not. What I'm thinking is are you gonna be okay?"

"I'm always okay. You know what I been through. I can take anything."

She was right. She had been through a lot. Her whole life seemed to be one long drawn-out test of her will to survive. Outside her family, only I knew just how cruel that test had been. I walked over and knelt down in front of her chair.

"Just because you always survive doesn't mean you're always okay," I said, stroking her hair. I wiped her tears away with my thumb.

"What am I gonna do, Moe?"

"I don't know. What do you want?"

"I want not to have gotten knocked up is what I want." The anger shut off her tears. She looked up at the ceiling. "I pray to God, always. Since I was a little girl, I pray to God, but he don't answer my prayers."

She crossed herself, then flipped up the middle finger of her right hand. I went back around the desk and poured myself another scotch.

"You remember Israel Roth?"

"The *viejo*, your friend? Sure, I remember. Nice man."

"You know he survived two years in Auschwitz, right?"

"Yeah."

"What Mr. Roth used to say was that the problem with God wasn't that he didn't answer prayers. The problem was his answer was usually no."

"Smart man, but that don't help me."

"Have you told the father?"

"Fuck him!"

I didn't touch that line. "Who is he?"

"Doesn't matter, just another jerk in a long line of jerks." She stood up and came to stand close by me. "It's your fault, you know."

"How's it my—"

"You know," she said, threading herself through my arms and wrapping hers around me. "Why don't you love me?"

"Carmella, we've been through this bef—"

She pushed the end of the word back into my mouth with her tongue. At first, I just took it, but I was returning her kiss soon enough. When I had allowed myself to fantasize about being with her, I told myself that a second kiss would never match the first. I was right. The second kiss was better. The first kiss had been rather chaste, more a tender brush of the lips, heavy with possibility and light on passion. This kiss would not be mistaken for a chaste brush of the lips. Her slight sigh broke the spell and I pushed myself away.

"I'm not doing this," I said.

"Not that again. That was forever ago. You can't keep punishing me for what someone else did to me."

"It's never been about that."

"Then what's wrong?"

"You mean other than your being pregnant?"

That quieted her. There was chemistry between us. There always had been, but this kiss had been about distraction, not chemistry. It had done a fairly good job of distracting me as well.

"Oh, Christ, Moe, what am I gonna do?" She pulled herself close again and rested her head on my chest.

"Do you want the baby?"

"Me? I'm a thirty-five-year-old unmarried woman. What am I gonna do with a baby?"

"That's not an answer. Do you want it?"

"Yes and no."

"Now that's an answer," I said, once again stroking her hair. "How far along are you?"

"Not so far."

"Whatever you choose, you know, it's good with me."

"I know."

I reached under her chin and tilted her head so that she was looking up directly into my eyes. "Just one thing, Carm, don't think that because you're not far along that you have a lot of time. The longer you wait, the harder it will get. Whatever decision you make will be a permanent one and you'll have to live with it forever."

She smiled sadly. "Maybe not forever, but just as long as I live."

"Yeah, I guess everybody's forever is a little bit different."

Now she pushed herself away, wiping off what was left of the tears with the backs of her hands. "Come on, we got work to do. Go put that bottle away and then get your ass back in here."

By the time I returned to her office, she had completely regained her composure. I hadn't invested in this partnership because of her looks. Of the two of us, she was the professional detective. I'd only ever been in uniform. When Carmella needed to, she could be all business. You couldn't've worked homicide the way she had without the ability to check your emotions. There were times when her knack for emotional distance verged on antiseptic and, given what was going on with my family at the moment, that was probably a good thing. I was too close to it, way too close.

She slid a thick file across her desk. "That's what you asked for. You've got current addresses—home and business—phone numbers, e-mail addresses ... everything. There's only one guy, this ... Judas Wannsee, that we're having a little trouble locating."

In 1981, Judas Wannsee was the leader of the Yellow Stars, a Jewish anti-assimilationist cult headquartered in the Catskill Mountains. His group had provided cover for the woman who had started the fire that killed my high school crush. The group had attracted some national media attention in the early part of the decade, but by 1990 had fallen into the creases of history the way pocket change disappears into the furniture.

"Okay, have Devo keep looking."

"So, where do we start?"

"*We* don't. I'm flying solo. There are some people I need to talk to by myself."

"Okay, but—"

"You still have that package in the office?"

Carmella knew what I was asking for and pulled a large plastic bag out of her drawer.

"Good. Patrick and his boyfriend Jack had that tattooed on their forearms."

"So you told me, but that had to have been at least—"

"—twenty-three years ago. I know, but I want you to send some people out to tattoo parlors to see if anyone's had a tat like this done within the last few months."

"Moe, these days aren't exactly like when my dad was young and the only people who got tattoos were sailors and bikers. There are probably more than a hundred tattoo and piercing joints in Manhattan alone. Maybe double that. Never mind the boroughs."

I suppose I hadn't given it a lot of thought. "You really think there's that many?"

"Shit, everybody's got ink these days."

"I don't."

"I do."

"You do! What of? Where?"

"You should've asked me that about twenty minutes ago. There's a good chance you would have seen for yourself. But we'll talk about that some other time. I bet you Sarah got one."

"I don't think so."

Carmella just shook her head and smiled at me. "Okay, so we're going tattoo hunting. Anything else?"

"Casting calls," I said.

"Casting calls! Tattoos and casting calls, what's this about exactly?"

"At the airport ..." I hesitated.

"At the airport what?"

"Remember when Raheem pointed and said that the guy that paid him to deliver the—"

"—package looked like the guy in the painting. I remember. He fed me that same line of crap when we had our little debriefing. The kid was trying to get over is all. He was full of shit."

"No, he wasn't, Carm."

"What?"

"I saw him."

"You saw who?"

"Patrick."

"You outta your fucking mind?"

"I think maybe I am, but I know what I saw and I saw him."

"So maybe he really isn't dead," she said.

"No, he's dead."

"Wait a—"

"I didn't see an older, not a forty-year-old Patrick. I saw Patrick from when he was in college. And there's only two explanations for that. He was a ghost or a—"

"—look-a-like," she finished my sentence.

"If he wasn't a ghost, then somebody was shopping around for a replica and the best way to find one in this city is to hold auditions for a very special part."

"Okay, Moe, I can see how this would work, but I don't understand the why. Who could hate you guys this much?"

"When we find out who," I said, "the why will be self-evident."

"*If* we do."

"When we do. When!"

We discussed a few more details and I got ready to head back home. Carmella was still in her office. I stuck my head through the door.

"You gonna be all right?"

She didn't answer immediately. "Me? I guess I will be, but this isn't only about me anymore, is it?"

"I guess not."

"About before ... I ... I—"

"I won't pretend I'll be able to forget it, but don't worry about it."

"Safe home," she said, turning her chair back toward the window.

Safe home yourself, I thought, although I knew she'd be spending the night here. Would anyone walk past our offices and wonder about the light leaking through the bottom of the door?

WHEN I GOT back to Sheepshead Bay, Sarah had gone. Her note said she had decided to spend a few days with her mom. It was the right choice for all of us, especially for Katy, Folded into the note were my Patrolmen's Benevolent Association card and Carmella's Detective's Endowment Association card. The postscript read, "You were right, Dad. I was being a hypocrite. Thanks for the card and thank Carmella for hers, but I won't be needing them anymore."

Sarah really was the best of both Katy and me.

CHAPTER NINE

ALTHOUGH AARON LIVED there and our biggest moneymaker was on Long Island, the place still gave me the chills. When I was growing up and kids from the neighborhood would vanish over summer vacation, there would be whispers about their families having fled to far off places with idyllic names like Valley Stream, Stony Brook, and Amityville or to places with unpronounceable names like Ronkonkoma, Massapequa, and Patchogue. It was all Siberia to me. I lived in secret dread that one of my dad's business ventures would finally succeed and that he'd move Mom, Aaron, Miriam, and me to one of those awful places where people lived in big houses on quiet streets. My fears might have been allayed had I bothered looking at a map to see that Brooklyn and Queens were actually part of Long Island. I needn't have worried in any case. My dad's bad fortune would tie me to Brooklyn forever.

Elmont was a faceless town that was close enough to the city line to blow kisses at New York across the Queens border. It was the home of Belmont Park racetrack where the third leg of the Triple Crown, the Belmont Stakes, was held every June. If not for the track, Elmont would be notable for being on the glide path to Kennedy Airport and for its cemeteries. My parents were buried in Elmont. In the end, I guess, they had moved to Long Island, but, as yet, without Aaron, Miriam, and me. I had come to see a man in Elmont about an empty grave.

I have heard it said that concentration camp survivors sometimes pass on their torments to their children, that the victims become the victimizers. I don't know if it's true or not. People say a lot of things. What I do know is that Mr. Roth had been my friend, a second father to me, and a surrogate grandfather to Sarah. He was affectionate, warm, funny, and philosophical in spite of what he had endured, maybe because of it. Yet he, by his own admission, had been an unfaithful husband and a negligent father. I knew about some of his failings, but had come by the knowledge indirectly.

Steven Roth, on the other hand, was so utterly familiar with his dad's failings that escaping their reach seemed beyond his ability or desire. Steven was a bitter, angry man, so full of rage there wasn't room in him for anything else but alcohol. That toxic mix of bitterness, rage, and alcohol had caused his father and himself nothing but grief. He had done a long bid in prison for manslaughter—a bar fight, of course—and a second stretch for DWI. He had been in and out of marriage, jail, and rehab so frequently by the time his father passed away, it was difficult to keep count.

We'd met a few times over the years and it was never pleasant. My relationship with his dad was a constant source of irritation, an allergen from which he could not find relief. Once, a few months before he died, Mr. Roth hired me to get his son out of some trouble, big trouble. But when that trouble went away, Steven Roth treated me not with respect or gratitude, but with contempt. It all came to a very ugly head at the memorial service for his dad. Steven was lit like a roman candle and in a particularly foul mood, spouting off about how his dad should have been buried, not cremated and how *he* should have been the one to see to his dad's remains. When he shouted at Sarah that he would see to burying *her* father, I punched his lights out. Aaron tells me, I was still swinging when they pulled me off him. All I remember was that he was smiling at me. Even though I'd broken his nose and split both his lips, he was smiling.

Walking up the few steps to the front door of the neat little saltbox Cape, I had second thoughts about not bringing Carmella along. If things got ugly this time, there might not be anyone around to pull me off. I held my finger a few inches away from the bell and rechecked the address. Well-kept houses on twisty quiet streets were not usually Steven Roth's style. Not unlike my late friend Rico Tripoli, Steven Roth's taste ran to the darker edges of town, to places where the blackness of their souls blended in with the scenery. I couldn't speak to his resources or to his abilities as a schemer, but there was no doubt he hated me enough to hurt my family anyway he could. I pressed the bell and listened to the muted chimes ring inside the house.

When the door pulled back, I stood facing a very attractive woman in her mid-forties. Beyond her broad smile and positively sparkling blue-gray eyes, it was difficult to say what was so attractive about her. Her face, in fact, was rather plain and round and her hair was a mousy brown. She was thin, I guess, but her generic jeans and sweatshirt did nothing to highlight her shape. Yet there was something undeniably appealing about her.

"Good morning," she said without a hint of guile or wariness.

"Hi, my name's Moe Prager. I was wondering if Steven—"

"Moe Prager! Moe Prager. Steven will be thrilled you're here." She beamed and shouted over her shoulder, "Honey, come here, there's someone to see you."

I was sure I wasn't dreaming it, but not of much else. I was having a full out *Twilight Zone* moment. Then, when Steven Roth appeared with his right hand extended and a wide peaceful smile on his face, I thought to look for the hidden camera. When he took my hand, shook it, embraced me, I was still in shock.

"Praise Jesus, my prayers have been answered."

"Praise Jesus," the woman repeated.

"Moe, this is my wife Evelyn. Evelyn … Moe Prager."

We shook hands.

"Come on in, Moses. That is what Steven's father called you, right?" she asked, folding her arm in the crook of my elbow. "Come have some coffee with us."

"Yes, he called me that and Mr. Moe most of the time."

"Steven has told me a lot about you and his father. I want to hear it from you."

The three of us sat around the kitchen table and shared coffee in a sort of stunned silence. Then Steven, who still bore the bend in his nose from when I broke it, spoke up.

"I'm sorry, Moe, for treating you the way I did in the past. I was such an angry and empty man until I accepted the Lord Jesus Christ as my savior. When Evelyn and I found each other and God in AA, I just knew this day would come. I should've sought you out, but I was weak and afraid. Even with the Lord, I have my weaknesses and my bad days. Jesus has forgiven me, but I have prayed for the strength to come speak to you and ask your forgiveness. I can only pray for my father's forgiveness, but I can ask for yours."

"Sure, Steven, I forgive you." Then I put his alleged faith to the test. "It's what your dad would want me to do." If anything would set him off and cut through his "The New Me" veneer, it was those words.

He smiled. "You always were a clever man, Moe, but you can't rattle my cage. The pain and rage are gone. I don't blame you for not believing me. I was a pretty awful human being for a very long time. I think my dad loved how sharp you were. You were clever and quick like him. I am glad he had you to comfort him in his later years. Lord knows, I was no comfort."

"No," I said, "you weren't, but he always loved you. Your dad told me he wasn't a very good father or husband. In some ways, I think Izzy felt he deserved what you put him through."

"No one deserves what I put him through or what happened to him in the camps, but growing up, it was so hard for me to have perspective. My life was one long terrible journey of understanding, a long lonely time with a cold heart in a barren desert. Then I was saved."

Tears were pouring down Steven Roth's face. Evelyn reached across the table and clutched her husband's hand. They bowed their heads in silent prayer. After a few seconds and almost simultaneously, they looked up and said, "Amen."

I stayed for about another half hour. Steven showed Evelyn and me some old family pictures. It was good to see Israel Roth's face again. In some of the photos, he was a young man. I had never before seen him as a young man. The emotional scars from the camps were more evident, the pain much closer to the surface in those days. I told some stories about Mr. Roth and me and how well he treated us over the years. Still, Steven showed no signs of resentment whatsoever.

"I'm glad that my dad could open his heart to someone and that all the love he had to give did not die locked up inside him."

Evelyn and I said our goodbyes in the kitchen. I thanked her for her hospitality and wished her well. She assured me that as long as she followed the path that the Lord Jesus Christ had laid out for her and Steven, they would be well. Steven Roth walked me to the door.

"Thank you, Moses," he said before once again embracing me. "You've helped lift a terrible weight off my shoulders."

"Steven, I can't explain it, but seeing you and Evelyn like this … Well, it's done the same for me."

"I know you don't believe, but I also know that the Lord Jesus Christ has a place in his heart for you and can show you the way if you just look."

"I've always been good at finding things by myself," I said.

"Sometimes, it's not the finding so much as being prepared to accept what you find."

I drove around the corner and parked. My car was still, but my mind was all over the place. Hypocritical, intolerant, money-grubbing TV preachers made it kind of easy for the rest of us to turn devout Christians into cartoonish caricatures, but there was nothing remotely cartoonish about the time I'd just spent with Steven Roth and his wife. I hadn't known Evelyn before she found God. I had, however, known Steven and he truly was a changed man. He was right, I didn't believe and I was unlikely to ever believe, yet who was I to argue that Jesus Christ hadn't saved him?

Sitting there, I realized that neither Steven nor Evelyn had once asked me why I'd come. When God answers your prayers with something other than a resounding no, you don't question it. For them, my appearance on their doorstep was as much an act of God as the sun showing through the clouds or a landslide or hurricane. The appeal of turning yourself over to that kind of faith was not lost on me nor was the danger of it. The dangers of it certainly weren't lost on Israel Roth.

I thought a lot about Mr. Roth that day. I knew he would have been pleased that his son had found peace, however he'd come to it, and a woman to love who loved him back. He would also have been very pleased over his son's forgiveness. Of all the pain he took to his grave, the rift with his son troubled him most. I thought back to that long-ago day in the cemetery and his talk of spreading the ashes of the dead on the walkways at Auschwitz so the Nazis wouldn't slip on the snow and ice.

"But I've never stopped spreading the ashes," he had said.

Maybe now he could stop.

"Rest in peace, Mr. Roth," I said, the shadow of a passing 747 darkening the sky overhead. I waited for the sun to return before putting my car in drive.

WHEN I FIRST met Nancy Lustig, I didn't know or like Old Brookville or the surrounding towns very well, but for the past decade Aaron and I owned a store right on the cusp of Long Island's legendary Gold Coast. Now that I knew the area, I liked it even less than I had all those years ago. People with money, especially newfound money, have a bizarre sense of entitlement that was hard for me to take. So in spite of the fact that Red, White and You was our most profitable location, it was my least favorite. During its inaugural year, when I managed the store, I used to imagine Nancy Lustig wandering into the shop someday. I would imagine the surprise on her face and the conversations we might have. She never appeared, not while I was there.

Nancy Lustig had dated Patrick Maloney when they were at Hofstra together. She was from a rich family that owned a house—a mansion, really—less than a mile from our store. Nancy was a squatty girl back then and to have called her plain looking would've been giving her way more than the benefit of the doubt. She was an ugly girl, but so brutally honest with herself that I was awed by it. I think that's why she had always stayed with me. There's all kinds of brave. Sometimes, honesty is the hardest kind.

Frankly, I'd gotten so caught up in finding Patrick and with falling in love with his sister, that I completely lost track of Nancy.

The last I recall, she had moved out west—Northern California, I think—shortly after the debacle with Patrick, but I can't even remember if that was something I actually heard or some invention of my own that I had simply come to accept as fact. It's a funny thing about getting older. You lose a sense of how much of your past is real and how much of it is self-fabrication and filler your mind spins out in order to let you sleep nights. I'm not certain if the ratio of real to imagined was knowable, that I'd want to know it. How many of us would, I wonder?

It took me a few seconds to be certain that the woman who answered the door was Nancy Lustig. Obviously, she was older now, but that wasn't what threw me. While I wouldn't have called her a knockout, the woman in the doorway was … I don't know … attractive, I guess. Not from the inside out, the way that Evelyn Roth was attractive. It was more in the way the woman before me was put together. The thick, unflattering glasses were gone in favor of blue contacts. Her hair fell a few inches over her shoulders and was now a sort of dark blond with expertly blended highlights. The longish, lighter hair was a nice compliment to the new shape of her face. Nancy had lost at least thirty pounds, but more than diet had gone into resculpting her face. There were cheekbones, high ones, an angular jawline, fuller lips and a pert, provocative nose. Her makeup was flawless and her tennis outfit showed off a tanned, well-muscled body. The tight red polo shirt accented the shape of her new, gravity-defying breasts. Nancy crossed one leg in front of the other, tapping the floor impatiently with the tip her court shoe.

"Can I help you?"

"Moe Prager. We met back in the late '70s."

She squinted, as if she hoped squeezing her eyes together might help her see into the past. Apparently, squinting was no help with time travel.

"Sorry," she said, "I got nothing."

"Patrick Maloney."

That did the trick. She screwed up her new face as if she'd just caught a whiff of steaming hot dog shit. I didn't blame her. It hadn't exactly been a storybook romance between Patrick and Nancy. In a desperate attempt to deny his homosexuality and cope with his burgeoning OCD, Patrick engaged in a series of doomed relationships with women. With Nancy Lustig, the inevitable bad ending was particularly ugly. There was a visit to a sex club, an aborted pregnancy, and violence. He dislocated her shoulder and might've done much worse had other students not pulled him off her.

"The detective. Yes, I remember." She didn't ask me in.

"That's right. How have you been?"

"Look, what's this about, Mr. Prager?"

"Moe, please."

"Let's stay on point. What's this about?"

"Patrick."

"Sorry, not interested," she said. "What, he woke up from a coma and wants to apologize or something? He develop a conscience after twenty years?"

"Nothing like that. Patrick's dead."

"Did he remember me in his will?"

"It happens that he was murdered shortly after he disappeared."

If I thought that would shake her up, I thought wrong. She yawned. I might have told her I stepped on an ant.

"You'll have to excuse me, Mr. Prager, but I'm leaving to play tennis in a little while, so if there's nothing—"

"You sure have changed," I said, trying a new tack.

She wasn't sure how to take that. "Thank you ... I think."

"Oh, no, I meant it as a compliment," I lied. "You're quite lovely."

"Thank you," she said, flashing a satisfied smile. "It was a lot of hard work to bury dumpy old Nancy."

"I don't know, there were parts of her I kinda admired."

Nancy scowled at me like Father Blaney. I looked for clouds to move in overhead.

"Admired! What did you admire, my desperation? My willingness to take crumbs and castoffs? My—"

"Your honesty."

"Oh, that. Honesty's easy when it's all you have."

"I'm not sure it's ever easy."

"Why admire someone for something when they have nothing else? It's like admiring an amputee for still having the other leg. These," she said, running her hands over her now exquisite breasts, "are something to admire. On the whole, Mr. Prager, you can keep honesty. I'll take these. No one desires you for your honesty." She dropped her hands back to her sides.

"Why is it one or the other?"

Just then, as if on cue, a Land Rover pulled into the long driveway and beeped its horn.

"I prefer tennis to questions of metaphysics. Now, if you'll excuse me ..."

"Sorry to have bothered you," I said, and walked back to my car. I rolled out of the driveway onto Route 107 and parked. A few minutes later, the green Land Rover pulled onto the road and disappeared, heading north. I had to go north too, but I needed some time to mourn the old Nancy Lustig.

SO I WENT from money to more money, from new money to old.

In the early '80s, Constance Geary worked for Aaron and me at City On The Vine for about six months while she finished up at Juilliard. She was pleasant enough, a hard worker, good with the clientele, but we never fooled ourselves she would stay on. I had the impression she got her hands dirty with the common folk as if she were fulfilling a missionary obligation. You know, like teaching Third World children how to read. Or maybe it was just so she could say, "Hey, I had a job once." It wasn't Constance I was interested in, but her father.

It was Thomas Geary who'd hired me in 1983 to find out what had happened to Moira Heaton and to resuscitate State Senator Steven Brightman's political career. I'm not certain to this day if Geary cared for Brightman in the least or if he simply fancied himself a kingmaker. After all, what else was there for him to do besides being wealthy and playing golf? Geary was one of those men who saw golf as universal allegory. If you understood the intricacies of the game, you'd see that life and golf were just the same. *Yeah, right!* Maybe Steven Roth should have taken up golf instead of God. I mean, who needs the New Testament when you've got a copy of the USGA Rule Book.

Crocus Valley was at the WASPy heart of the Gold Coast, a place where plaid pants and Episcopal priests never went out of fashion. Don't get me wrong, the residents of Crocus Valley had made concessions to the new millennium. Some even painted the faces of their lawn jockeys white! Behind the artifice of taste and restraint, the residents of CV were as screwed up as any other bunch of rich fuckers. I would know. I was privy to their liquor bills. If they ever considered changing the town's name, Single Maltville would have been perfectly appropriate.

The Geary place was on a bluff overlooking Long Island Sound and bordered on the east by The Lonesome Piper Country Club. It was at the Lonesome Piper, during Connie's wedding reception, that I first met Thomas Geary. He took me for a stroll along the driving range. During our short walk, he managed to lecture, threaten, and bribe me. All of it done with a calm voice and unwavering smile. He was a reflection of the town in which he lived. On the outside he was all class: well-bred, well-mannered, a perfect gentleman. But beneath his well-tanned skin, Geary was as much a thug and bully as Francis Maloney ever was, only less honest about it.

The corral-type fencing that once surrounded the white country manor had been replaced by a contiguous stone wall. There was an ominous black steel gate now as well. No longer could you simply turn off the road and into the estate. Anchored by massive stone pillars, the gate was a good twelve feet high, double the height of the wall. On one pillar was a security camera, on the other a call button and speaker. Childishly, I waved hello at the camera, then pressed the call button.

"Yes, who is it?" A woman's voice asked.

"My name's Moe Prager. I was wondering if—"

"Moe! This is Connie. Come on, drive up to the house. I'll meet you out front."

The gate swung open even before I made it back to my car. Connie met me under the front portico just as her father had seventeen years before on my first and only visit to the ten-acre estate. She was very much the same as I remembered: more handsome than pretty. Looking at her now, I realized Constance was naturally what Nancy Lustig had had tried to make herself into.

"Moe, my God, look at you!" Connie grabbed both my hands and kissed me on the cheek. "You look great. How are you? Come inside."

I followed her into the house. It too was as I remembered it, at least the decor hadn't much changed. There was, however, an unmistakable medicinal tang in the air and a metal walker in the foyer next to an incongruous pair of hockey skates. Connie noticed me notice.

"The walker's Dad's. The skates are Craig Jr.'s."

"A son, *mazel tov*. Any other kids?"

"No. Craig's my pride and joy," she said.

"How's Craig's dad?"

"Fine. We're divorced almost ten years now."

"Sorry."

"Don't be. It was all very amicable. We're all better off this way. You were at the wedding, weren't you? I remember you being there. You and Katy, Aaron and Cindy, right?"

Just ask your dad. "We were indeed."

"How is Aaron? I always had a kind of crush on him, you know?"

Of course I didn't. I loved my big brother and he was a good looking man, but it was hard for me to imagine Connie falling for him.

"He'll be quite honored to hear it."

"Oh, God, please don't tell him." She turned bright red. "I'm so embarrassed."

"Don't worry, your secret's safe with me." I'm certain she had no idea how safe. "Aaron's great. You know, we own a store not too far from here?"

"Red, White and You. Yes, I've been there a few times, but no one I remember was around."

"Klaus and Kosta are still with us. They even own a part of the business now."

"Are they both still crazy?"

"As crazy as ever." I changed subjects. "The walker, you said it was for your dad."

"Used to be. He's pretty much bedridden these days. Alzheimer's," she said, as if that explained everything. I guess maybe it did. I watched Alzheimer's rob my friend and Pulitzer Prize-winning journalist, Yancy Whittle Fenn, of everything he ever had. First it erased his memory, then it erased him.

"Sorry."

"That sorry I'll accept."

"Your mom?"

"She's summering out West with some friends."

"You take care of your dad?"

"We have round the clock nursing, but I see him a lot. We can afford to keep him close to the things he loved. I'm not sure how much of him is left. We take him down to the stables when we can. He seems to still enjoy that."

"I remember he liked horses. Do you ride anymore?"

"Some."

"The piano?"

"The great love of my life, Moe. Yes, I still play. Come on, I'll get us a drink and I'll play for you."

"I could use a drink and I'd love to hear you play."

"Scotch with ice, right?"

"Good memory," I said. "Do you think I could go see your dad while you get the drinks?"

"Sure, but I don't think he'll remember you."

"That's okay, I'll remember for the both of us."

"Is that why you came, to see my dad?"

"It was, but no biggie. It wasn't that important," I lied. There was no need to add to anyone's pain. I had my answer. If he was in as bad a shape as Connie said, Thomas Geary wasn't involved in Patrick's resurrection. "Listen, Connie, does your dad ever hear from Steven Brightman?"

"Steven Brightman, now there's a name I haven't heard for a long time."

"That's a 'no' then?"

"Absolutely. Once Steven resigned, I think my dad lost interest. Until then, he was one of Dad's pet projects. He is—was a very project-oriented man, my dad. But if it's really important for you to know, I can ask Mom."

"No need. I'll just run up and see your dad and then I'll be down so I can listen to you play."

The medicinal smell was strong in Thomas Geary's room. His TV was on. He paid it as little heed as it paid him. Geary may once have been a bastard, but I could feel only pity for him now. His eyes were vacant, his mouth was twisted up into a confused smile. It was a clown smile absent the makeup and the humor. He looked so very lost, seeming to have forgotten not only who he was but what he was. I recognized the expression. Wit—Y.W. Fenn—wore it for the last year of his life.

I opened my mouth to speak to Thomas Geary, but closed it before any words came out. I might just as well have spoken to the TV. I left him as I found him.

Back downstairs, Connie handed me a glass of single malt—what a surprise—and had one herself. I expected her to play something dark and moody, but got Gershwin and show tunes instead. This way we could talk a little while she played. I told her about Sarah, about my own divorce. I didn't go into details. Connie said all the right things, cooed and sighed in the proper places in my stories, but I could tell she had built some walls of her own. The divorce, her dad's Alzheimer's were tough on her. I remembered something Mr. Roth had once said to me, "Money is a retreat not a fortress." Looking at the pain behind Connie's eyes and listening to it behind her pleasant chatter, I knew Israel Roth was right.

When I said my goodbyes, Connie held onto my hand a little longer than I would have expected and asked me if we might not go to dinner sometime. To talk about old times ... as friends, of course ... *Of course!* I thought about what had become of Nancy Lustig, how the brutal honesty had remained, but her humanity seemed to have vanished. I told Connie that I'd love to go to dinner. Who was I not to throw her a rope?

Time travel, I thought as I rode through the center of Crocus Valley, was not for the faint of heart. I had supposed, foolishly perhaps, that after my father-in-law's passing and the fallout from our shared secrets had taken its toll, that I could put the past behind me. However, the past, it seemed, was not set in granite, but rather as fluid as the future. I was as incapable of shaping one as the other. The past, *my* past, sang a siren's song to me that was beyond my ability to resist and I was forced to reach deeper and deeper into my pockets to pay the price each time I succumbed. By any measure, it had been a weird fucking day and I was off balance, way off.

Driving did nothing to restore my equilibrium. I just kept rehashing the events of the day. No one was who they used to be. They had all changed, some for better, some for worse, with no regard for my expectations.

Steven Roth, Nancy Lustig, Connie and Thomas Geary, had had time to evolve, time to ease into their new skins, but for me it was disorienting. From where I stood—*Presto change-o!*—they had morphed almost before my eyes. That was wrong, of course. It had happened during the long overnight between last meetings.

I flipped the visor down, not only to block out the sun. I pulled open the lighted mirror on the back of the visor and stared at myself. How much, I wondered, peering at my tired-looking reflection, had I changed without noticing? I thought back to philosophy class at Brooklyn College.

Essay #1: If you own a car for a number of years and over the course of those many years you replace part after part, at what point does that car cease being the original car? Does that car ever cease being what it once was? If you were to replace every part, would it cease being the old car?

I can't remember what I wrote exactly. Probably something about the essence of the car remaining unchanged. I think I argued that proximity of time and of old parts to new kept the original essence of the car intact in spite of all other factors. In conclusion, I think I wrote, unless you were to change all parts all at once, the original car remains. I wasn't so sure I believed that anymore. I wasn't sure I believed it then. What did I know in college, anyway?

If I thought today's disorientation or looking in the mirror would lead me to any brilliant new insights or deeper truths, the blare of horns, the rapid *tha-dump tha-dump tha-dump tha-dump* of my tires against the grooves at the road's edge, and the pinging of gravel in my car's wheel wells dissuaded me from that notion. I jerked the wheel left and got the car back on the road. I flipped up the visor and tried as hard as I could not to use my rearview mirror. I had enough looking back for one day, thank you very much.

My cell phone buzzed. It was Sarah. Yes, it had been a weird fucking day and it was about to get weirder.

CHAPTER TEN

THE DULL GREEN house at 22 Hanover Street was essentially unchanged from the first time I saw it in the winter of 1978. Neat, unadorned, perfectly maintained, the house had been a reflection of its owner, Francis Maloney Sr. I thought my ex-wife, a graphic designer by trade, might brighten the exterior when she moved in. Slap on a fresh coat of white paint, at the very least. Now as it was more a memorial to than a reflection of my father-in-law, I suppose Katy felt the need to keep up appearances. She claimed to hate her father and everything about him. But who knows, really? It was nearly impossible for me to figure out what she felt about anything anymore. At least she didn't feel the need to let the memorial extend past the front door. Katy had pretty much redone the interior of the house. It was more comfortable, more about her and what she'd become than preserving where she'd come from.

The first time I came, it was winter. Snowmen tipsy from the thaw had stood guard as I rolled down the street. A noisy oil truck was making a delivery at the house next door. But on a hot July night, with ice cream truck serenades in the background and the green flashes of lightning bugs filling the air, that first time seemed forever ago. Except for the sheriff's car parked in Katy's driveway, it might have been a perfect summer evening.

The TV was tuned to CNN. Larry King was breathless over the minutiae of this week's scandalous cotton candy or trial of the century. His panel of talking heads was, each in turn, louder and more hysterical than the next. Given the rapt attention of Sarah and Sheriff Vandervoort, I might have thought they were witness to the second coming.

"Hey, I hate to interrupt Larry King, but—"

"Sorry, Dad." Sarah clicked off the tube.

Pete Vandervoort stood up and came over to me, shook my hand. I didn't like the look in his eyes. "Something's up," he whispered.

"No shit?" I turned to Sarah. "Where's your mom?"

"In bed."

"In bed. It's only—"

"Sarah, maybe you better give me and your dad a few minutes."

"Sure, Sheriff Vandervoort. Thanks for coming and staying with us. Dad, I'll be in the kitchen. You want something?"

"No, kiddo, that's okay."

"Sheriff?"

"No, thanks." Vandervoort was careful to wait until Sarah was out of earshot. "We got a situation here that I don't understand. You sure you told me everything about the details concerning your brother-in-law's death?"

Of course not! "Yeah, why do you ask?"

"Come on outside a minute."

Vandervoort and I stepped out onto the little concrete stoop in front of the house. Two moths prayed at the altar of the porch light, unable to break free from the bonds of their devotion. The sheriff took a lazy swat at the faithful and refocused.

"It's not just about hearing voices anymore," he said. "She's seeing ghosts now too. That's why Katy's in bed. Took two of those pills the shrink at the hospital gave her."

"She called you?"

"No. Your kid did. Sarah's a beautiful girl ... and smart. You should be proud of her."

"I am."

"Me and the wife don't have kids. Can't. We've been to every doctor in the county. Even went to see a few in the city. My family name dies with me."

"Siblings?"

"Two big sisters."

"How about adopting?"

"We've thought about it, but it's not for us, I don't think."

"I'm sorry, but—"

"No, I'm sorry, Moe. I got sidetracked there. So your daughter phoned me a few hours ago. She said that they were in town shopping, having lunch and your wife started acting funny."

"Funny?"

"Looking over her shoulder at odd times. Apparently, while they were at Molly's having lunch, Katy practically jumped out of her seat and ran out of the diner. When she came back, she was white," he said. "Your kid asked her what was the matter and she—"

"—wouldn't say. That's Katy. In most ways, she's nothing like her dad, but she couldn't escape him totally. She can hold stuff back sometimes. So what happened?"

"They stopped at the PrimeOil Station on the way back here. When Sarah was pumping the gas, your wife ran out of the car and darted across Stuyvesant Street. FedEx truck nearly cleaned her clock. She was pretty lucky, Moe. Took quite a spill. I guess when Sarah got her back here, Katy finally confided to her that she'd been seeing Patrick here and there all day long."

"Jesus Christ!" My jaw clenched.

"There's more to it."

"More how?"

"Come over to my car a second," he said, walking toward the Crown Vic. I followed. He reached into the front seat and came out holding a video tape. "The PrimeOil's been robbed a few times since they expanded it from just a gas station to a convenience mart. They got surveillance cameras all over the place now, so I figured I'd stop by on my way over here." He handed it to me. "Get it back to me when you're done with it."

"Is there something on it?"

"Wouldn't've told you about it if there wasn't."

Without thinking, I started for the house. Vandervoort grabbed my arm.

"Not so fast. You better wait till they're both asleep," he said. "Maybe we should talk in the morning."

The first part was a suggestion, the second part wasn't.

"Okay, Pete, I'll see you in the morning."

"Until tomorrow then." Vandervoort shook my hand and, like Connie before him, was slow in letting go. "Look, Moe, I like you and your family, but I'm going to need more from you than what I've gotten so far. Your wife isn't the only one holding back. Somebody's got to have it in for you and your family to go to this much trouble. That tape in your hand is a gesture of good faith on my part, so when you come by in the morning I hope you're in a generous and sharing mood. Do we understand one another?"

"We do."

He let go of my hand and said goodnight. I watched him pull away. Then I stashed the tape in the front seat of my car.

I MADE SURE both Katy and Sarah were asleep before retrieving the cassette from my car. I watched the black and white surveillance tape over and over again. Apparently, the gas station had recorded and re- recorded over it a number of times. To say the images were muddy would be insulting to mud. Nonetheless, there was no mistaking Patrick. He knew he was on camera the whole time, giving a somber nod and salute when he came into the frame. He mouthed something that was beyond my abilities as a lip reader to decipher. The ghost wasn't taking any chances if someone thought, as Pete Vandervoort had, to retrieve the video. He arranged energy bars on the counter to spell out:

SO ALONE

The people behind this were good, very thorough. They had done their prep work, but the prep work was a blade that cut two ways. Yes, it meant they could pull off this haunting crap with great aplomb. It also meant they had done their research, the kind of research you can't do online or in libraries. That might be an opportunity for me. I rewound the tape and watched it again.

"There's something wrong."

I nearly had a heart attack. It was Sarah, standing in the dark of the hallway.

"How long have you been there?"

"Long enough. There's something about that guy that's just not right."

"Like what?"

"I'm not sure," she said, stepping into the living room. "I can't put my finger on it, but give me time."

"I don't think it's a ghost either, but it looks a lot like him."

"I guess."

"You're not the best judge, Sarah. You've only ever seen pictures of him and those are mostly ones of him before he changed."

"Changed?"

"Before he redid his hair, got the tattoo and the earring ... Just before. There aren't very many pictures of him like that."

"Yeah, Dad, but you also only know him through pictures." She knelt down by the screen and placed her right index finger on his face. "I'm telling you, something's just not kosher with this guy."

Sarah was right about one thing: I didn't actually know Patrick any better than she did. We'd never met, not face to face. It was just that Patrick, a man who was never really there, had consumed such an unnatural amount of my life that I felt as if I did know him. I shut off the VCR.

"Go back to bed, kiddo."

"I can't sleep."

"Me neither. Hey, you wanna go grab something at Molly's?"

"Sure, Dad. Just let me throw some jeans on."

"I'll check on your mom."

Katy, still fully dressed, didn't stir when I came into the room. She seemed utterly zonked. We had shared the same bed for twenty years, but I wasn't sure I recognized the woman before me. It can take a lifetime to become familiar and only seconds to become strangers again. I made to leave, but stopped. I removed the message tape from her answering machine, took one more look at Katy, then left.

I THINK I knew something was wrong even before I turned the car back onto Hanover Street. Sarah sensed it too. I could see it in her expression.

"Dad, what did you do with the security tape?"

"Oh, shit!"

Our worst fears were confirmed when we saw the flickering light through the otherwise opaque living room window. It was a bit of a blur from then on. I couldn't remember putting the car in park or closing the car door behind me or putting the key in the front door lock. The first thing that stuck was the image of Katy laying face down in a sea of broken glass, blood oozing out of the gash on her forehead, the VCR remote clenched in her right fist.

"Dad! Dad!" Sarah was screaming. It didn't register as screaming. Her panic reached me as a tiny voice at the end of a kid's string and soup can telephone. "Dad, Mom took pills, lotsa pills."

I think I said for her to grab the bottles. I was already carrying Katy to the car.

CHAPTER ELEVEN

WHEN VANDERVOORT CAME in, I jumped at him.

"This isn't funny anymore, Pete," I growled, pinning him to the wall. "This is attempted fuckin' murder."

If anyone in the emergency room waiting area hadn't heard the first part of my rant, that second part surely got their attention. I must've been pretty scary, not because Vandervoort looked frightened—frankly, I was rage blind and couldn't've described the sheriff's expression—but because a steel hand clamped down on my right shoulder.

"You okay, Sheriff?" a deep voice wanted to know.

"I'm fine. Thanks for asking. He's just a little upset is all."

Deep Voice was unconvinced. "You sure?"

"Why don't you go and sit back down," Vandervoort said. "You look like you could use some help yourself. What the hell happened to you?"

"Had to lay my hog down when some asshole in a SUV ran the light at Blyden and Van Camp."

The steel clamp eased off my shoulder and I turned. I regained the use of my right arm and my vision. Deep Voice was a big man, barrel-chested with a beer keg belly to match. He had a thick neck and thicker arms that were covered in blood and tattoos. He had a young doughy face, but was no kid. His gray beard was braided like a pirate's. It too was soaked with blood and the gash on his forehead was nastier than Katy's.

"Don't go anywhere. When I'm done with this gentleman," Vandervoort said, nodding at me, "I want to talk about your accident. Maybe we can discuss why you weren't wearing your helmet."

"Okay, Sheriff." Deep Voice was sheepish, touching his hand to the cut on his head. He went and found his seat.

I backed off Vandervoort and gave him the details as we walked outside. "She was totally asleep when we went to Molly's. I didn't think—"

"Stop beating yourself up over it. You couldn't know what she was going to do. Where's your kid?"

"She's in the treatment area with her mom."

"So that guy on the videotape with the candy bar message, he—"

"—looks an awful lot like Patrick, but the tape's so fuzzy. It would be impossible to make a positive ID from it."

"Look, Moe, don't take this the wrong way, but your ex-wife did try to … Well, she seems pretty convinced."

"So you believe in ghosts now too?"

"Nope, I'm just saying …"

"I wasn't kidding in there, Pete. This isn't funny. If I catch that motherfucker, I'll—"

"Watch what you say and do," Vandervoort cut me off. "Maybe that's what these folks want, the ones behind all this. Your ex-wife goes off the deep end, you end up killing somebody and get shitcanned for life. Your daughter, for all intents and purposes, winds up an orphan. I'd say that's playing into their hands, wouldn't you?"

"You're right. You're right. I know you're right, but you shoulda seen Katy laying there on the broken coffee table glass. I thought she was dead, for chrissakes. Sarah was freaked."

"How is she now?"

"Sarah? She seems all right, but it's hard to know."

"And Katy, what do the doctors—"

"She'll be okay. They pumped her stomach. It's a good thing we got back when we did or more of that crap might've gotten into her system. They're keeping her here for observation."

"Maybe that's a good thing," he said. "I'll keep a man posted outside her door for the duration."

"Thanks, but I doubt they'll try anything here. Too many people around."

"Let's hope so. Listen, I better go talk to that biker in there, but don't forget our appointment later this morning."

"It's a date."

We shook hands. This time he gave my hand back promptly.

Sarah was waiting for me outside the treatment cubicle when I went back inside. She'd been strong through all of this, but now that the adrenaline was wearing off, the fear and exhaustion were showing through. She was white, her eyes shot red with blood. For the first time in her life, Sarah looked old. *Welcome to adulthood.*

"Dad, you're bleeding. Your shoulder."

"Oh, that," I said, pulling my shirt around to look. "No, that's somebody else's blood. A guy who had a motorcycle accident, put his hand on my shoulder."

For some reason, that was the last straw. Sarah broke down. She fell into my arms and began sobbing.

"Shhhhh, kiddo. It's okay. Everything will be okay. Shhhhh …"

When she was a little girl and would come crying about scraping her knee or some kid in her class making fun of her red hair, those words were magic. Now when I said them, she simply cried harder. Had she finally outgrown the magic, I wondered, or was it that the magic wouldn't work if the magician no longer believed in his powers?

LATER THAT MORNING, I was quite amazed at how easily I rattled off the litany of secrets and sins to Sheriff Vandervoort. Yet, rattle them off I did. No hedging, no holding back, no compromising, no spin, just the raw, unvarnished facts. I suppose most of the people in my life knew some of the details of my involvement with the Maloneys, but drips and drabs of reality, no matter how sordid or saintly, never amount to the whole truth. And regardless of what people say, there is only ever one truth of things. There are different versions of reality, not of the truth.

Vandervoort now knew more about what had gone on between the Maloneys and me than anyone on the planet besides myself. By the look on his face, I wasn't so sure he was happy to hold the honor. It was a tossup as to whether Pete seemed more horrified by the revelation that Francis had once raped and beaten a transvestite prostitute or that he had once encouraged Patrick to commit suicide.

"Christ … I'm not sure which I want to do more, throw up or take a shower," he said. "Do Katy and Sarah know any of this?"

"Not the real details, no. I've carried this shit around with me for twenty-two years. It ruined my marriage and that's where the damage has to stop."

"I'll do what I can. The thing is, I can see why someone might hate the father. And lord knows there's plenty of people who hate fags—sorry, gays, but that doesn't explain why this is going on. This has got to be about you," he said.

"That's the assumption I've been working under since it all started."

"Any ideas?"

"Too many, unfortunately."

"Anyone from around these parts?"

"Only the longest of long shots," I said.

"Yeah, like who?"

I hemmed and hawed a little.

"Look, Moe, I've cut you way more slack than—"

"You're right. I'm sorry. Secret keeping becomes second nature."

"Names."

"There's Katy's first husband, Joey Hogan, for one. I'm going to see him right now. Unofficially, of course."

"Of course. Who else?"

"Woman used to cut hair at the Head Shop, Theresa Hickey."

"Hot blond, married to a city cop, right?" Vandervoort asked, already knowing the answer.

"That's the one."

"Forget her. My big sister Mary knew Theresa Hickey. She dumped the cop years ago and moved down to Jupiter, Florida, with some rich guy owns race horses. She hasn't been back here since."

"Tina Martell?"

Vandervoort smiled sadly at the mention of her name. "Sure I know Tina. She owns Henry's Hog over—"

"I know the place. Outside of town, over the tracks, right?"

"That's the one."

"She owns it?" I asked.

"Her old man left it to her. What's old Tina got to do with this?"

"Probably nothing," I said, "but remember when I was telling you about how Patrick had gotten a few girls pregnant?"

"Tina?"

"Yeah, Tina."

"Well, fuck me. I can't quite picture old Tina and Patrick. You know, Moe, for a—for a gay guy, this kid got a lot of—"

"It's testament to how hard it was for him to come to terms with who and what he was."

"I guess."

"I gotta get to the hospital. They've moved Katy into a room and I want to make sure all the bases are covered."

"Room 402," he said. "You'll find a deputy outside her door."

"Thanks, Pete."

"Remember, Moe, keep me posted."

JUST AS VANDERVOORT had promised, there was a deputy outside Katy's door. It was Robby, the young deputy who had stood out in the rain with me at the Maloney family gravesite. He smiled at noticing me and, I suppose, at the chance of conversation. There are aspects of police work that can be mind-numbingly dull. None duller than guard duty. The deputy assured me that everything had been quiet, that the only people to enter the room were nurses and doctors and not too many of them. As a matter of courtesy, I asked the deputy if I might not take a look myself. He liked that I asked.

Katy was asleep, but unnaturally still. I don't know, maybe that was my brain talking and not my eyes. Her attempted suicide had changed everything. For all our years together, I had assumed Katy was a rock, that she could bear anything. Only once, when she miscarried, did she break down. Even then, I thought she recovered well and had gotten back to the business of life quicker than most. But now I wasn't so sure I knew who my ex-wife had been all those years. Had she misled me or had I misled myself? Did I see who she wanted me to see or did I see who I wanted to see? Had she hidden the pain from me or had I blinded myself to it?

I thought about lifting the sheets to see if her wrists were restrained, considered consulting the attending psychiatrist to find out if Katy was sedated or if her sleep was a natural reaction to the trauma. I did neither. It was all I could do to swallow up the guilt I was already feeling. I knew I couldn't handle anymore revelations about the myths of our marriage, not now, not yet. When I walked back past Robby, he called out to me. Something about last night's Mets score, I think. For some reason it just made me angry, really angry, but not at him.

I started toward Joey Hogan's house. *Joey, what kind of name is that for a grown man, for chrissakes?* Joey was Katy's ex. Now, I suppose, first ex is more accurate. Not that I had anything against him. On the few occasions fate had thrown us together, he had been more than cordial, friendly really. He was a stand-up guy who cared so deeply for Katy that if another man made her happy, well then, that was okay with him. They had been high school sweethearts. Katy grew out of it, but Joey never did. As Katy said, she agreed to marry him for all the wrong reasons. He was loving. He was handsome. He was a good provider. It was time.

"You don't marry a man because he scores well on some stupid test," Katy had said many times. "Marriage isn't about a checklist. It's about passion."

I wondered if she would still feel that way when she got out of the hospital and took stock of the last twenty years of her life. In any case, there wasn't any passion left between Katy and Joey by the time they took their vows before Father Blaney. And moving into his parents' house right after the wedding hadn't exactly enhanced the chances of their rekindling any dormant high school sparks. Their divorce had been relatively painless, at least for Katy, and had come as a relief for the both of them.

Francis Maloney loved to use Joey to get under my skin.

"He still loves my daughter, you know," my father-in-law jabbed at a family barbecue, Katy and Joey chatting happily at the opposite end of the backyard. "All she'd have to do is say the word and that boy would take her back, no questions asked."

"Except she's never going to say the word."

Then Francis would smile that smile at me, raising his glass of Irish. "Ah, don't be so sure, lad. Do you believe in ghosts?"

He'd always find some excuse to ask me that fucking question. I never quite understood what he meant by it. I did now, of course. Back then, when I didn't answer, Francis would have a private little laugh at my expense. It was a laugh with red fangs and talons.

"Are you laughing now, you prick?" I shouted out the window.

Joey Hogan's impeccably restored Victorian put a lie to the adage about the contractor owning the worst house on the block. Man, with the spindle work, wrap-around porch, clapboards, rows and rows of fish scale and diamond siding, a lot of trees had given their lives to let that house live again. Between the turrets and gables, between the asymmetry and compound angles, there was enough visual noise to keep my eyes busy for a week. And forget about the color scheme. Only on a Victorian could you use twelve different colors—including lavender or purple—without getting arrested. But I guess maybe that's why I liked Victorians. They could break all the modern rules and still look beautiful.

I halfway pulled into the driveway and stopped, the ass end of my car sticking out into the street. Around here you could get away with that without getting the rear of your car sheared off. Truthfully, I didn't think Joey had a thing to do with what had happened at the gravesite or with torturing Katy. Even if he wasn't as comfortable with another man having his ex-wife as he let on, I knew as surely as I knew anything that he could never hurt Katy. I guess it was possible that he might hurt me, but he wouldn't use Katy to do it. Nor did I think he had much in the way of information that could shed light on who might actually be hurting my family, but based on proximity alone—his home was less than a quarter mile from the entrance to the cemetery—I had to talk to the man. Yet, for some reason, I couldn't quite bring myself to pull all the way down the driveway.

I was afraid. I was afraid that Joey Hogan might accuse me of fucking up Katy's life. I was afraid that he was right. But it wasn't Joey Hogan who accused me. Christ, I wasn't even fully into the man's driveway. My own guilt accused. Guilt and me were usually strangers. Like jealousy, guilt was a cancerous waste of time. The world was only too happy to beat you up, so why do it to yourself? Anyway, I was suspicious of the eagerly guilty. They stank of martyrdom.

"Responsibility and guilt are not the same things, Mr. Moe," Israel Roth used to say. "We all do wrong things for all kinds of reasons, mostly they're not worth losing sleep over. Besides, what does guilt change? A real man, a *mensch*, he knows when to feel guilt. When you've done what I had to do to survive, you know guilt. I can see in your eyes, Moses, that you too know guilt. For this you have my pity and my respect."

Because guilt and I were usually estranged, because it was not my first instinct, I knew when I felt it, that it was right. I felt it now and it was right. It was to laugh, no? One lie, a lie that wasn't even mine to begin with, still impacted lives in ways I could never have anticipated. I thought of Katy lying in the blood and broken glass. I thought of her lying so still in bed and imagined Joey Hogan's face as I tried explaining myself to him. I backed out of his driveway and drove away as quickly as I could.

Located several miles outside Janus in sort of a municipal no man's land, Henry's Hog was on the wrongest side of the tracks. When my tires crossed the pair of tracks on Industry Avenue, I could swear that the sun's light became more diffuse and the air got thicker and smelled of burning oil. The dust and decay, however, were not products of my imagination. Industry Avenue, once a meaningful designation, had long since given way to irony. Even before my first and only visit here, the area factories had already been abandoned. Now the only industry around here was of the cottage variety: meth labs and warehouse marijuana farms.

Henry's Hog, an old wood frame house that had been converted into a bar, hadn't much changed. The joint was as welcoming as a stuffed toilet and its windows were as yellow as a smoker's fingers. The desolate paint factory and auto body shop that had once bookended the place were now masquerading as empty lots. There weren't any bikes parked outside, but I tried the doors anyway. Pessimistic about success, I nearly fell inside when the door swung open.

Age hadn't much improved the interior of Henry's Hog either. The aroma was a vintage blend of black lung and beer piss. I wondered if the lazy fly that buzzed me as I stepped in wore a nicotine patch. A broad-shouldered woman in a Harley tee and black leather vest leaned over the bar, reading the *New York Post*. Her body jiggled as if she were laughing, but I can't say she made any sounds that I recognized as laughter. And because she had her head down, I couldn't see much of anything but the top of her short gray hair.

"Excuse me, I'm looking for Tina Martell."

When she raised up to face me, I knew I had found who I was looking for, but not all of her. Tina Martell had once been the girl most likely to fuck you because she felt like it. She liked sex and didn't dose it out like saffron or gold dust the way the other girls in town had. That hadn't won her a lot of close girlfriends back in high school, but it made her pretty popular with the boys. When I met her, she was thick-bodied and big-breasted, but she had a cute face with a friendly mouth. She was tattooed and pierced a good two decades before every suburban kid came with a nose ring and ink as standard equipment.

Now part of her neck and throat were missing and ugly scars obscured her tattoos. A flap of white material covered the front of her throat above her collar bone. She sort of resembled a Salvador Dali painting, the entire left side of her face drooping down toward the scarring. Although her shoulders were still broad, Tina's breasts were much smaller. Seeing her this way, I understood Vandervoort's sad smile and his confusion over Patrick and Tina. She raised a clenched right hand to her throat.

"Who is … looking?" she asked in a robot voice, pressing her other hand to the white flap of cloth.

"Throat cancer?"

"Breast cancer … too," she said, with an unexpected smile. "I'm thinking of getting … skin cancer and going … for … the trifecta. Wait, you look … familiar."

I explained that we had met once, many years before. She remembered.

"You bought me a … beer."

"That's right. You told me to go fuck myself."

She liked that, giving herself the thumbs up.

I explained about what I was doing there. The last time we'd spoken, Tina Martell hadn't been particularly sympathetic to Patrick's plight or mine. Not that I blamed her. Patrick had gotten her pregnant and asked her to marry him just as he had later done with Nancy Lustig. For all I knew, there were other women with whom Patrick had danced that dance.

She shook her head a little bit, eyes looking into the past. "I don't know what to … tell you. I never wished no harm to … come to him. Wished harm on some, but not … him. Lotta tragedy in that family … lotta tragedy. Too bad about Frank Jr., he was … hot."

"So you don't know anything about the desecration of the graves or about—"

"I got my own … problems, mister. Don't need to cause none for … others."

"You know anyone else who might have it in for the Maloneys?"

"The old man … maybe. Someone might've had it in … for him. He was a bona fide … cocksucker."

"Amen to that."

"But I can't think of no one who'd want to hurt … the daughter. Hey, you want a … beer?"

"It's kinda early."

"Early's a matter of … interpretation."

"Sure. Fuck it!"

She put a Bud up on the bar and went back to her paper. I tried searching for some follow-up questions, but came up empty. When the bottle was likewise empty, I said my goodbyes and headed for the door. Before I got halfway there, a familiar figure came strolling on in. It was Deep Voice, the biker who'd been in the ER. The doctors had patched up his head, bandaged the nasty road burns and scrapes on his arms, washed the blood off his face and beard, but he was still wearing the shreds of the clothing he'd worn last night. He stared at me without recognition. I realized I still had trace amounts of cop vibe and that didn't work for him.

I put my hands up in submission. "Haven't been a cop for a long time," I said. "Besides, I'm kinda hurt you don't recognize me."

The light went on behind his eyes. "Last night in the hospital. You were all up in the sheriff's face. What was that about?"

I should have told him it was none of his business and walked out, but I didn't. For reasons I was only vaguely conscious of, I wanted to talk to this guy. I wasn't at all sure why. I suppose I figured the why would come to me eventually.

"Let me buy you a beer." He was thinking about it when I made the decision for him. "Tina, two Buds over here, please."

We sat down at a nearby table and waited for Tina.

"How you know Tina?" he asked in that low rumble of a voice.

"We're old acquaintances is all. So," I asked, "how are you feeling?"

"Sore as shit, but they sewed me together okay. I'll live. It's not the first time I've had to lay a bike down."

"I don't doubt it. You got a name?"

"Crank."

Great, I was buying beer for a meth cooker, but I didn't react other than to reach my hand across the table to him. "Moe."

Tina brought the beers over and I paid her. "Hey, Crank."

"Hey yourself, Tina."

She walked away shaking her head at the odd pair of us.

"So what about last night?"

"My ex-wife tried to kill herself." He stopped mid-sip, eyes wide. "That's why I was so agitated. It's a long story."

"Always is. Your old lady okay now?"

"She'll live, but she isn't okay."

"Here's to her," he said.

We clinked bottles. A question was wiggling around in the back of my head. I thought it might be about something Crank had said last night. I tried recalling what he had said to Vandervoort about his accident. Just as words started to come out of my mouth, my cell phone vibrated. The question vanished.

"Hey, I gotta take this," I said waving the phone at him. "Feel better. Enjoy the brew."

I walked outside in a near panic. "Hello."

"Moe, where are you at?" It was Carmella.

"You wouldn't believe me if I told you."

"Try me."

"Sharing a beer with a meth cooker named Crank."

"You're right, I think you're fulla shit."

"I'm up in Janus. Katy tried to kill herself last night."

"Oh, my God! Is she—"

"She'll live. We can talk about it later. What's up?"

"Can you get into the office? We got something."

"I got something too," I said. "Let me check in with Sarah and then I'll be down. Make sure Devo's around."

"Okay."

"How are you and … I mean—"

"I'm still pregnant, if that's what you're asking."

"It is."

"Don't let's start that now. I need to keep things together when I'm here."

"Fair enough."

I got in my car, crossed back over the tracks and out of un-Wonderland, but fragments of that question I had for Crank were still scratching around the back of my head. By the time I hit the interstate, they were gone.

It seemed to me that this was one case being played out in two worlds: one up here and one back in the city. The weird thing was that in spite of it all playing out with my family and me at center stage, I felt more like a spectator than a participant. I sensed Katy slipping completely out of my life and I was helpless to prevent it. Maybe that was best for both of us, but I couldn't let her slip out of my life and straight into hell. No, I owed her to make this right.

CHAPTER TWELVE

CARMELLA WAS OUT of the office when I got back into Brooklyn.

"Is she taking a late lunch or what?" I asked Brian.

"She don't report to me, boss. She just ran outta here"—he checked his watch—"like forty minutes ago."

Brian Doyle was a project of ours. He was NYPD for about fifteen years. That he lasted so long was proof of God. Rough around the edges and a bit too quick with his fists, he was an old school cop three generations of cops too late. But Brian was perfect for us or would be, once he learned to listen. He knew the street and had a knack for getting information out of the most reluctant people. Brian had never had to rough anyone up while in our employ, at least not that we knew of. People could see the potential for violence in his eyes and that was enough. The whiff of violence usually is.

"How did she seem to you?"

"She seemed like the hottest fuckin' detective I ever seen."

"That's not what I meant."

"How the hell should I know how she seemed?"

"*Oy vey iz mir.* Forget it," I said, rubbing my eyes in frustration. "Carmella said she had something for me."

"She did?"

"Oh, for chrissakes! Doesn't anybody in this fucking place—"

Doyle was laughing so hard, he started gasping for air. Even Devo came out of his office with a wide grin on his face.

"Okay, gentlemen, you got me. Now can someone around here tell me what the fuck is going on?"

Brian and Devo looked at each other.

"You first, Devo," Brian said, still wiping tears from his eyes.

Devo's office looked like a cross between a recording studio and the cockpit of a B2 bomber. I had been wise enough never to ask who paid for all the equipment.

"Before we get started, take these." I handed him the surveillance tape from the PrimeOil station and the little cassette from Katy's answering machine. "Once you've had a look and a listen, you'll know what I want from you."

He took the tapes, laid them down on a shelf, and asked me to take a seat in front of a computer monitor.

"Here," he said, a newspaper ad flashing up on the screen, "is a notice for an audition that appeared in the *New York Minute* six months ago."

CASTING CALL
Male Caucasians between the ages of 18-22,
150-160 lbs., 5'8" to 5'10". For leading
role in an indie docu-drama. Experience a
plus, but not required. Must be willing
to travel. February 16th, 11:00 AM.
LaGuardia Runway Inn, Ballroom B.
Tilliston Casting.

"The *New York Minute*? Never heard of it."

"It is one of those free weeklies you can pick up in newspaper boxes on corners around the city. Very popular for advertising bands, selling cars, subletting apartments, promoting clubs and such."

"Yeah, okay, but what's the big deal about this ad? I don't know shit about casting calls, but there's got to be notices like this all the time."

"Look at the screen." He clicked the mouse. "This is that same notice in the *LA Freeway*. He clicked again. "In the *Second City Loop*. I found this notice in about twenty places in publications of this type dating back six to eight months. Only the location of the auditions is different."

"Someone was casting a wide net, so what?"

"Yes, a wide net, but a shallow one. One notice in *Variety* would get more turnout than one hundred of these type ads in smaller free presses. My supposition is that they were looking for a non-union, inexperienced actor. In fact, they weren't necessarily even looking for an actor. If one reads carefully between the lines, one might conclude they were looking for someone they might be able to manipulate."

"One might. Good points."

He bowed slightly. "Also, I did some checking. I found someone who went for the audition at LaGuardia."

"How'd you manage that?"

Devo smiled slyly. "Come now, Moe, need you ask?"

"I know, I know, that's why we pay you the big money. So what did this guy you found have to say?"

"He said it was the oddest audition he ever attended. They didn't ask him to run lines, to do a scene or to discuss his training or experience. Apparently, it truly was like a cattle call. Appearance ... everything was about appearance. They had a very specific set of parameters even beyond what was listed in the ad. You had to have a certain type of complexion and visible tattoos were strictly verboten."

"That's odd," I said. "I thought movie makeup could cover anything."

"It can ... on film, but what if the role required—"

"—live appearances?"

"Precisely."

"Moe, pick up line two. It's your daughter." Brian's voice came loud over the intercom.

"Excuse me a second, Devo." I picked up. "Is everything okay with—"

"Mom's fine, Dad. I mean, as fine as can be expected. I just saw her and I think she's more embarrassed than anything else."

"Good. I'll be coming back up there tonight to check on you guys. Is the deputy still outside the door?"

"The cute one, Robby? Yeah, he's still there."

"Too much information, kiddo. Way too much."

"Oh, Dad, grow up. Besides, I have something I want to tell you."

"What?"

"Remember when we were watching that video of Uncle Pat—I mean, of the guy posing as Uncle Patrick?"

"I remember."

"I said something wasn't right about him even though he looked just like the pictures of Uncle Patrick."

"Yeah."

"I know what it is," she said. "He was too comfortable on camera, too much at ease."

"I'm not sure I'm getting you."

"Look, Dad, think about those old pictures of your family from Russia. You know how they're all so stiff and unsmiling and their eyes have that deer in the headlights thing going on. Then think about your folks' generation and then yours. People got more and more comfortable with having their pictures taken, but not necessarily with being videotaped. My generation is really the first generation that's grown up on video. Births, our first steps, first baths, birthday parties, bat mitzvahs, weddings, sweet sixteens, baseball games, dance recitals, almost everything my generation has done our parents taped. We're really used to being in front of the camera. We like it. Being on tape is … for us, it's affirmation. All the people I go to college with have cameras on their computers. And Uncle Patrick was killed in what, nineteen seventy-sev—"

"—seventy-eight," I corrected.

"But you get my point. That was way before the ever present, all-seeing eye. That guy on the tape is no ghost, he's my age."

"Funny you should say that. I think Devo's arrived at the same conclusion. Thanks for the assist, I'll see you later." That was met with a very loud silence from the other end of the phone. "Okay, Sarah, what is it?"

"I think you should leave Mom alone for a little while. Like I said, she's pretty embarrassed and feeling kinda stupid about this. If she feels you're there to judge her or … I just think you should give her some time. I can look after her for now."

It bugged me that Sarah twice mentioned Katy being embarrassed, but I couldn't say why exactly. There seemed to be a lot of things I didn't have answers for just lately. In any case, I didn't pursue it.

"I'm very proud of you, Sarah. I think I'll take your advice, at least for a day or two. But I want to know if anything happens with your mother. I mean anything. Deal?"

"Deal."

"Love ya."

"Love you too, Dad."

I put down the phone and recounted Sarah's theory to Devo, after first explaining what was on the videotape I had given him.

"My guess," I said, "is that the guy you'll see on that tape is the guy who got the part."

"Yes, personal appearances and all. Why don't you go talk to Brian while I get started with the tapes?"

I hesitated. "Just one more thing. This Tilliston Casting, they legit?"

"I am afraid not. They were a post office box and a phone number. The phone number has been disconnected and the P.O. box closed."

I made a move for the door. Devo called after me.

"One last thing, Moe. Judas Wannsee."

"What about him?"

"Here." Devo handed me a folder. "I have tracked him down, He was a difficult man to find."

"He would be."

"He has changed his name several times in the past decade, but you should be able to contact him there."

"Thanks."

When I stepped back out into the main office, Brian nodded at Carmella's office.

"She's back, in case you're interested."

"Okay, but first, show me what you got."

Brian slid a Polaroid across the desk to me. It was of a freshly done tattoo. The tattoo was of a rose threaded through the Chinese character for eternity, and 4/7/00 was written neatly across the bottom in black marker.

"By the way, boss, that ain't one Chinese character, but two that have been superimposed on each other. My bud tells me that even that's a sorta shorthand and that this one here means," he said, pointing at the back of one of his business cards, "long or no change. This one here means never eroding." He showed me the back of two more business cards. "The proper way to write it is like this or this here. These four mean forever and those four there stand for eternity."

"Thanks for the Chinese lesson. I don't know, Doyle, maybe we should can your ass and hire your friend."

"Maybe, but he ain't half as charmin' as me."

"I'd like to meet him. I've never met anyone completely devoid of charm before."

"Huh?"

"Forget it. Who'd you get the Polaroid from?"

"Mira Mira," he said, as if that were explanation enough.

It wasn't. "I'm listening."

"She's a tattoo artist. Works by appointment only and charges an arm and a fuckin' leg."

"Nice pun."

"Pun?"

"Never mind."

"Anyways, an old snitch of mine turned me onto her. When I showed this Mira Mira what I was lookin' for, she pulled that Polaroid right out of her … whachumacallit … her—"

"—portfolio."

"Yeah, her portfolio. She does Polaroids of every one of her creations. She even has photo portraits done of some of her work. She says those photos sell in galleries for thousands of bucks. Me myself, I don't see it, paying for a picture of a fuckin' tattoo."

"I don't think you're her target audience, Doyle. She tell you anything about the client?"

"White kid, twenty, maybe younger. Came in with a heavyset guy in his late sixties."

"Did she think they were lovers?" I asked.

Doyle cringed. "I didn't ask. She did say that the old guy had an eye patch over his left eye. Here's her contact info. I told her you might wanna talk to her."

I slid the Polaroid and the contact info into my jacket pocket. "I'm curious. Why'd she give you the Polaroid?"

"Because she said she was embarrassed that she had even done the job and …" He hemmed and hawed.

"And … I'm waiting."

"I paid her for it."

"Don't tell me how much. I don't want to know, not now, not when I'm thinking of telling you you did good. Just put in your reimbursement request to Carmella."

"Thanks, boss."

"And Brian …"

"Yeah?"

"Don't pad the request because I'm going to ask this woman how much she charged you."

He opened his mouth to say something and thought better of it.

Carmella was once again sitting and staring out the office window. Only this time there was fire in her eyes and no tears to contain the flames.

"What an asshole!" she growled.

"Which one?"

"Me. The father. Take your pick."

"The father?"

"The baby's father. I told him that I was pregnant. That's where I was, meeting him for a drink. He didn't even ask me why I wasn't drinking. When I explained it to him anyway, you know what he asked me?" She didn't wait for my answer. "He asked if I was sure it was his. Like I'm out there soliciting sperm donations. What an idiot!"

"Him?"

"No, me. I sure as hell can pick 'em, can't I, Moe? What am I gonna do?"

"Just tell me who he is and I'll show him the error of his—"

"No. I wouldn't let him within fifty yards of this baby, the selfish, self-centered prick. Not now."

"Isn't there anybody you can talk to?"

"I'm talkin' to him."

"I mean a girlfriend, someone in your family."

"Someone in my family! Are you nuts? You know what they would tell me? Go talk to the priest. Yeah, like a priest's gonna help me make a decision about an abortion. After … you know, after what happened to me as a girl, my mother took me to a priest to have him bathe me in holy water, to wash away the stink and shame. You know what the priest said? He said that my mother should pray for God to forgive me. Forgive *me*, a little girl! What did *I* do wrong, Moe?"

"Nothing. Your mother was a foolish woman. And priests ... What can I say? But I'm sure your brothers and sisters would—"

"No, they wouldn't. I hate this fuckin' baby," she hissed, her face belying her words.

"Sure you do, that's why you're so torn up about it. That's why you said you wouldn't let the father get near it."

"Who asked you?"

"You did."

"I shouldn't've."

"Would you think about giving the baby up?"

That stunned Carmella, the air going out of her as if I had caught her solid in the solar plexus. I don't think the notion of giving the baby up was a possibility she had ever wanted to consider. It was the hardest option for a reluctant mother. Though I believe the concept of closure is complete bullshit, I have to think that carrying a baby to term and delivering it only to hand it over to strangers has got to be a vicious form of living hell. I'm not sure I could handle the uncertainty of it or the second guessing.

"I couldn't do that, Moe. How could I do that?"

Now the tears came. The fire was out. I took a step toward her.

"Leave me alone. Just leave me alone to think, okay?"

"Sure."

IN CONTRAST TO her name, Mira Mira was as exotic as whole wheat toast. Oh, she was pretty enough—Italian, early thirties, svelte and dark— but with a Brooklyn accent that made mine seem minted on the Thames. And if her loft in SoHo was indicative of how lucrative tattoo artistry was, I was going to tell Sarah—a gifted painter—to lose the brush and oils in favor of the ink and needle. You could have played full-court basketball in the place and have had room for bleachers and concession stands. The exposed brick walls were covered in enormous photographs of body art. Some were rather stunning and done in colors you were more apt to find in a Klimt than on a teenager's bicep.

"So, you wanna to tawk about an original Mira Mira creation."

"Not original, really," I said, sliding my business card and the Polaroid across the table to her. "I believe you already spoke to my employee about it."

"That Brian Doyle works for you, huh? A real freakin' charma, that guy."

"Charm is a funny thing. Depends on taste."

"Yeah, well, just because some assholes who are drownin' think they're just slow swimmers, don't make it so. You know what I mean?"

I didn't, but I wasn't here to argue with her. "Exactly. So what can you tell me about that tattoo?"

"Nothin'. I mean, nothin' I didn't already tell Prince Charmin'."

"Amuse me, okay?"

"Sure. Whaddya wanna know?"

"Everything. Anything. How were you contacted? Who did you deal with? Did they leave a contact number or address? What was the kid like and the guy with him?"

"Nothin' unusual in how he got in touch. Got a call from a guy sayin' he's seen my work and that he's got a friend that he wants to get inked. I asked him if him or his friend wanna come in to tawk about what kinda design they're lookin' for, but he says they already got somethin' specific in mind. I told him I didn't do crap. No Christ heads or hearts or dragons, you know, that kinda crap and that I don't negotiate price. He says that ain't no problem and when can he come in."

"So you spoke to the older man, the one with the eye patch."

"Yeah, it was Cyclops I tawked to."

"Do you have names, addresses, phone numbers?"

"Sure do, for what it's worth. I mean, I don't like check references or nothin', but I make people sign all kinda fuckin' releases before I put ink to skin. You have buyer's remorse with a house, you can sell it. Body art, the way I do it, it's kinda hard to give back."

"Could I see the paperwork?"

"Nope."

"Why not?"

"My studio got busted into in May. All the files got trashed."

"Any other damage?" I asked.

"Some. Nothin' that couldn't get fixed."

"You remember any names?"

"Nah. I don't remember what they wrote on the release forms and when they tawked to each other, I don't even think they used names. Cyclops called the kid Kid. I don't remember the kid callin' Cyclops anything, but his expression called him Asshole. I don't guess that's what you're lookin' for."

It wasn't, but I didn't want to lose the momentum. "So they make an appointment and …"

"Yeah, at first when I see 'em I'm thinkin' it's the man-boy love thing and that sugar daddy is buyin' his boy toy a little art as a token of his appreciation. It wouldn't be the first time. But as things went on, I changed my mind. It was more like boss and employee kinda situation. In fact, the kid didn't seem very into the whole tattoo thing at all. Kept whinin' about not likin' needles and shit like that. Cyclops told him to shut up and take it like a man."

"Nice guy, huh?"

"A typical cop."

I nearly swallowed my tongue. "What?"

"I'm pretty sure he was a cop. My dad, my uncles, my little brothers are all on the job. Just like you and Prince Charmin'."

"Well, Mira, you wouldn't have to be Kreskin to figure out that Brian and I were once cops."

"I guess not, but Cyclops was once a cop. I'm tellin' ya. And then when he pulls out that picture and shows me what he wants me to put on the kid, I almost threw them both out on their freakin' asses."

"The rose and Chinese characters?"

"Yeah," she said, tapping her finger on the Polaroid. "It was an enlargement of an old photo, all grainy and shit, but clear enough so's I could copy it."

"The person in the photo, was he a—"

"Tell you the truth, I just looked at the tat. It was a man's arm. That much I could tell."

"Why'd you want to throw them out?"

"'Cause it was a bullshit job. Any hack coulda done the work and I didn't wanna waste my time."

"If it was a bullshit job, why come to you?"

"You're askin' the wrong party here," she said. "I don't know. Some people they think like expense equals quality. So for what I charged 'em, they got lotsa quality."

"You mind me asking how much quality they received?"

"Three large cash."

"He paid you three grand for—"

"That's where my prices start, not where they finish. And he tipped me an extra few c-notes on top."

"Nice work if you can get it."

She pointed at an eight foot by ten foot photo on the wall behind me. It was a tattoo of a peacock, its tail feathers fanned across a woman's upper thigh and right cheek. The colors were incredibly vivid, the iridescent blues and greens fairly jumped off the subject's flesh, but it was the subtle shadings, the gold and beige, the darker browns and black that were the real trick of her art.

"You do that, you can charge what I charge," she said. "Until then …"

"I see your point. You're good."

"Good. *Pfffffff*. Fuck that!" She made a face like she'd bitten into a bad nut. "I'm the best."

"So what about the kid?" I asked. "I mean beside the fact that he was whining."

"He was handsome enough if you like the type. Kinda a young Travolta without the charisma."

Bingo! I thought back to when I first got involved with Patrick. The Maloney family had plastered the kid's high school prom picture all over the city. I remembered thinking that he reminded me of Travolta. But that was before Patrick had colored his hair and gotten his ears pierced, before he had gotten his tattoo.

I stood to go. "Thanks for your time. Here's my card if you think of anything else."

"So what neighborhood you from?"

"Sheepshead Bay via Coney Island."

"I went to Lafayette. You went to Lincoln, huh?"

"I did."

"Well, screw that, I like you anyway," she said.

"Oh, yeah, why's that?"

"'Cause most people walk in here or my studio and within thirty seconds say 'Mira Mira on the wall,' or some stupid shit like that. Not you."

I wished she hadn't said that last part, because now I couldn't get it out of my head. *Mira Mira on the wall, who's the fairest of them all? Mira Mira on the wall, who's the fairest of them all? Mira Mira on the …* At least when a song gets stuck in your head, there's a melody to mitigate the annoyance. Like I didn't already have enough crap to drive me nuts.

CHAPTER THIRTEEN

I HAD SURELY disappointed Sarah a thousand times over the years in ways both large and small. Nothing hurt more than seeing disappointment in my kid's eyes, but letting your kid down is an inevitable and likely beneficial part of parenting. You can't pick kids up every time they fall, you can't and shouldn't give them everything they want, nor is it in your power to come close to living up to their image of you. Yet, in spite of my myriad foibles, missteps, and mistakes with Sarah, there was one way in which I couldn't recall letting her down. I had always kept my word to her. It was in my nature to keep my word even when it worked to my detriment. You need only survey the shambles I'd made of my marriage to know the truth of that.

Had I walked out of Jack's apartment in the West Village twenty-two Februaries ago and called Katy to tell her that I had found Patrick … Sometimes in my blackest moments, I think about what might have been had I, just that once, broken my word. I mean who the fuck was Jack White to me? And Patrick, what had he done to earn my trust? If anything, his behavior had earned my scorn. All those times my father-in-law asked me about ghosts, he was off target. He should have asked me about being haunted. For while I still didn't believe in ghosts, I did believe in hauntings. Who needs ghosts when questions will suffice? Ghosts, one in particular, were the reason I was heading back upstate and why I was about to break my word to Sarah.

Pete Vandervoort had taken up the post outside Katy's door. When he saw me approaching, a series of expressions washed over his face in rapid succession. He smiled, squinted, frowned, and snarled before settling on the world-weary cop smirk. Instead of shaking his extended hand, I placed the Polaroid in it.

"What's this?"

"A ghost with a freshly inked tattoo," I said.

"Nice trick, a ghost with a new tattoo. Where'd you get this?"

"My people tracked the tattoo artist down and she gave that to us. I'll give you all her info after I talk with Katy. I think she needs to see that Polaroid."

"Good timing. She's up. Her shrink was in there checking on her about fifteen minutes ago. He said she seemed more stable. Whatever that's supposed to mean. More stable than what?"

"It's cover-your-ass-speak. Have you seen Sarah? I tried to get her on my way up, but kept getting her voice mail."

"Nope. Haven't seen her today. Why, is something wrong?" he asked.

"I promised her that I would back off for a few days, so Katy could catch her breath."

"I see, but they'll understand when they get a look at this. I mean, Christ, you can't sit on this. It proves that this has all been a setup." He handed the Polaroid back. "Go on in and show her."

I knocked before stepping in. My ex's expression was less ambiguous than the sheriff's had been. Disappointment was writ large in every fold of her face and her first words didn't leave much room for interpretation.

"What the hell are you doing here?"

"I—"

"Sarah told me you promised to—"

"I *did* promise and I meant to keep my word, but something came up that I couldn't keep a lid on."

"You're full of shit, Moe! Do you even believe half the things you say? You kept a lid on things for twenty years."

Her anger, it was like a separate entity. There were times I fooled myself that it was at an end, that Katy had gotten past it. No, it was metastatic, laying dormant for months at a time and then ... *Bang!* Like today, something I would say or do would set her off. That's why our early attempts at reconciliation were short-lived. Our mutual despair or old hungers could keep it at bay or out of the bedroom for a few hours at a time. Then it would flare up. The odd thing was that I knew at least a part of the anger wasn't even meant for me, but rather for my father-in-law. When Francis died, I was left the only available target.

"Look, I didn't come here to fight, but to show you this," I said, holding out the Polaroid. She took it. "Brian Doyle tracked down the tattoo artist who did that back in April and Devo found more than twenty casting calls for young men who would meet Patrick's physical description."

I felt myself wince, waiting for that second wave of anger. It didn't come.

"Who is he?" she whispered.

"I don't know. Some kid desperate for an acting job, I guess."

"You don't know his name or anything?"

"Give us a little time."

"I want to see him again."

"What?"

"I want to see my brother again."

"He's not your brother."

"I don't ... care. I ... I ..." Katy tried choking back the tears, but it was no good. She was sobbing now so that her whole body shook. "I want ... I want to see ... him. I want to know ... why he—"

"He's not your brother, for chrissakes."

She crumpled up the Polaroid and threw it at me. "I hate you! I hate you! I hate you! You've taken everything away from me."

"But Katy, I—"

"Get out of here! Get the fuck out of here." She was squeezing the life out of the call button. Even before the staff could respond, Vandervoort and Sarah came rushing into the room. "Get him out of here. I want him to leave. Get him out of here. Get him out—"

With little effort, Pete Vandervoort ferried me out of the room, but I could still hear Katy screaming and Sarah trying to calm her down. A roly-poly Filipino nurse and a psychiatric aide flew past us and almost immediately some coded message went out over the loudspeaker.

"What happened in there?" the sheriff asked.

"I'm not really sure. I showed Katy the Polaroid and she went batshit on me. When did Sarah get here?"

"Just after you walked in there. She was none too pleased."

"Figures. I seem to be having that effect on the Prager women today."

Just then, Dr. Rauch, the shrink who had seen Katy on her initial visit, came charging down the hail. He looked less pleased to see me than Katy and Sarah, but didn't stop to elaborate.

"Shit," Vandervoort said, "you're just making everybody's day."

"Yeah, you noticed that look too, huh?"

"Hard to miss."

A few seconds after Dr. Rauch went into the room, Sarah came out glaring.

"Dad, I thought you said you were going to give Mom some time. Now look at her."

"But we found proof that there is no ghost and that it's just some actor parading around out there like—"

"And you thought, what, that Mommy was going to be thrilled about that? You know, for the world's smartest dad, I think you're just totally lost sometimes."

"Look, kiddo, I know I broke my word to you about coming up, but I had to show Mommy what I found. What was I supposed to do, sit on it? What if she found out that I was keeping it from her? Can you imagine how she would've reacted to that? Either way, I was screwed."

"I guess you have a point, but still, you should've warned me, us. Her doctor's pissed."

"Your mother is my concern, not her doctor. Besides, I tried, to call ahead, but I kept getting your voice mail. Where were you anyway?"

"The movies. I needed a break."

The door to Katy's room opened again. Dr. Rauch held it open for the nurse and the aide. He told them he'd be up at the desk in just a moment. When they were out of earshot, he pointed his finger at me.

"Listen very carefully, Mr. Prager, I—"

"Doc, you want me to listen, I suggest you get that finger out of my face."

He looked at his finger like it didn't belong to him, shrugged his shoulders, and put his hand in his pants pocket.

"Very well, Mr. Prager. Why don't you and your daughter meet me in my office in …"—he checked his watch—"… ten minutes?"

"That'll be fine, Dr. Rauch," Sarah answered. "I know where it is."

He didn't wait for my response before heading to the nurses' station.

RAUCH'S OFFICE WAS like a movie set of a doctor's office. The carpeting was high end industrial in a sort of speckled sage green, a few shades darker than the matte finished walls. The shrink's desk was large but non-descript and cluttered with patient files, pharmaceutical company doo-dads and note pads, a phone, an engraved pen and pencil set and a plastic model of a human brain. His chair was the standard issue high back, black leather swivel. One wall was dedicated to enlargements of family vacation photos and a goofy *My Brother the Psychiatrist* needlepoint, one to overstuffed bookcases, and one to degrees and decrees of board certifications. It seemed that Rauch was certified to perform neurosurgery and sell real estate.

It took Dr. Rauch quite a bit longer than ten minutes to make his way to his office. Good thing he got there when he did. Sarah and I had already exhausted sports talk and small talk and were about to move on to thumb wrestling.

"I'm sorry for taking so long," he said. "But I stopped to have a conversation with Sheriff Vandervoort. He briefly explained to me what the two of you have been up to."

"Look, doc, I didn't mean to upset Katy, but I had proof positive that what's been going on has been a total setup. And given our history, I didn't feel like I could keep it from her."

He made a show of rubbing his chin and sighing. "I'm certain you had only the best intentions, Mr. Prager, and that you were acting in what you considered to be a reasonable manner. It may well be that under most circumstances, your actions today would have been completely within the realm of acceptable behavior. However, I feel duty bound to remind you that Katy just made a serious attempt to take her own life and that she is in a fragile state of mind. Your presence here today may have caused a serious setback."

"I'm sorry, doc, but like I said, I had proof that I needed to show my wife."

"Nonetheless, Mr. Prager, I am alarmed at how you simply disregarded my prohibition against your visiting Katy without my prior consent."

"Prohibition?"

"Yes, your daughter assured me that she discussed it with—"

What the fuck are you talking about? "Oh, that! Yeah, we discussed it. Like I said, I'm sorry. It won't happen again."

Dr. Rauch looked from me to Sarah and back again. "Yes, I see. Make sure that it doesn't. Sarah, could you please give me a minute alone with your father? He'll be right out."

When Sarah closed the door behind her, I nodded across the desk. "You first, doc."

"So I assume your daughter didn't discuss it with you."

"Not in so many words. She asked me to give her and her mom a few days. I guess she didn't think I'd react well to being ordered not to visit."

"Was she correct?"

"Probably."

"Look, Mr. Prager, Katy is my patient and therefore necessarily the focus of my efforts. That doesn't mean, however, that I am unconcerned about you. So I am going to give you some free advice that I have come by honestly. We can't escape our pasts. We can neither undo them nor make up for them, but ultimately they must be dealt with. Not everyone pays the same prices for their perceived transgressions. In a very real sense, the prices we each pay are dependent upon how we choose to pay them. Take a long hard look at the price Katy is paying. Know this, that regardless of how you may have contributed to her difficulties, the bill is hers to deal with, Mr. Prager, not yours. And no grand or sweeping gesture on your part can change that."

"Thanks, doc. I know Katy's your patient and you can't really discuss too much with me, but why did she freak out like that before? I would've thought she'd be relieved to know she wasn't seeing things."

"Part of her was relieved, but part of her was also disappointed. Can you understand that?"

"Yeah, I guess I can."

"You must also understand that logic and reason will not just make Katy's issues vanish. You can't argue her out of her depression. You can't just say, 'Snap out of it.' So no matter what proof or evidence or whatever you and the sheriff come across, you mustn't ever repeat today's episode. Please, if you want to see Katy, you must clear it with me beforehand."

"I give you my word." I stood. We shook hands on it. "One more thing, Dr. Rauch, if you don't mind."

"Yes."

"Is there anything else my daughter conveniently neglected to mention to me in her attempt to manage the situation?"

"It would be difficult for me to know what she didn't tell you as I don't know what she *did* tell you."

"Well, on the phone earlier, she kept saying Katy was embarrassed. I'm a pretty smart guy and I can understand why a person who survives a suicide attempt might be ashamed, but Sarah didn't say ashamed. She said embarrassed and my kid chooses her words pretty carefully."

"I'm not sure. I suppose it could be a reference to what she says drove her to overdose."

"The videotape?"

"That, and seeing her brother looking through the front window."

"What?"

"I thought you knew. While she was watching the videotape, she saw who she thought was her brother staring at her through the window. Given Katy's fragile state of mind and her serendipitous viewing of the security tape, it's easily understandable how his appearance, imagined or otherwise, might have been the precipitating event …"

But I had stopped listening. "Fuck me! Now I gotcha."

I ran out of the office without saying goodbye. Sarah was pacing circles in the hall outside the office. She called after me, but I didn't hear a word.

CHAPTER FOURTEEN

DRAMATIC AS THE image might be, it wasn't like Day-Glo puzzle pieces assembling themselves on a black felt backdrop in the void. Things are apart. Things come together. It's not there, then it is. You can only see pieces come together in retrospect. As Dr. Rauch spoke, it wasn't his words I heard. I was transported back to the ER the night of Katy's attempted suicide.

"Had to lay my hog down when some asshole in a SUV ran the light at Blyden and Van Camp."

That was Crank's exact quote to Sheriff Vandervoort in the ER waiting area. What he said registered with me, but not in any way my brain was prepared to handle at the time. I was too agitated about Katy to grasp the implications of what a bloody-faced biker said about some minor motorcycle accident. When I saw Crank the following day, something about the time and place of the accident made more of an impact. Still, I couldn't quite pull it all together. But now that I knew the kid in the videotape had been snooping around the Hanover Street house, I had the questions to ask and, more importantly, some of the answers. To access Hanover Street, you needed to turn off Van Camp. To get out of Janus and head toward New York City, you had to go through the intersection of Blyden and Van Camp.

"That biker, the one we saw in the ER."

"What about him?" Vandervoort asked, his eyes skeptical.

"Did he come in the next day to talk about the accident like you asked?"

"Hell, with all the excitement, I forgot about him."

"Shit!"

"Why, is he important?"

"Could be. I gotta go find him. In the meantime, do us both a favor."

"What?"

"Go back to the PrimeOil station and look over *all* their security tapes, inside and out, for the day that Katy tried—for the day Katy saw her brother in town. Look for any SUVs and try and get their tag numbers. Also, go back over the station's credit card receipts for that day and try to match it to the SUVs."

"Why?"

"Because I think our ghost drives a SUV."

DUSK HAD JUST passed the *baton noir* to the night when I pulled up outside Henry's Hog. I'll tell you what, the joint wasn't a damned thing like red wine. It didn't grow on you with repeated exposure and it sure as shit didn't improve with age. Jesus, maybe I had been in the fucking wine business too long.

Unlike my two previous visits, when horse flies outnumbered patrons, the place was buzzing with more than beating wings. There were a good fifty motorcycles parked out in front of the roadhouse, but the machines were all of a type. Ducatis, Moto Guzzis, BMWs, and Suzuki dirt bikes need not apply. These were Harleys, Indians, and custom choppers. There was the occasional Japanese faux hog mixed in with the odd classic Norton and Triumph as well.

I could almost smell the sweat, black leather, and cigarette smoke as I got out of my car. That "Born to be Wild" wasn't blaring on the juke was the only missing part of the cliché. I felt for the familiar bulge at the small of my back. My snub-nosed .38 was now as old and as much a classic as a Norton or Triumph: a museum piece, just like me. Currently, Glocks, and Sigs were the rage. It was all about rates of fire and walls of lead, but sometimes it came down to a single bullet. My hopes were to never find out and for my revolver to stay holstered until the next time I cleaned it.

I had worn it nearly every day for the last thirty-three years. First it was my off-duty piece. Then it was my insurance when I worked my cases as a PI. Eventually, although I was loath to admit it to myself, the little .38 had morphed into a shopkeeper's gun, something to keep me safe when I made bank drops or closed one of our stores late at night. *A shopkeeper!* I mean, who says I wanna be a shopkeeper when I grow up? But that's what I was, a goddamned shopkeeper.

Some old Lynyrd Skynyrd was blasting when I walked into the noisy bar, my entrance seeming to cramp everybody's style. Except for the dead man singing on the juke, most all the patrons stopped what they were doing. If my cop vibe revealed itself a bit on my first two visits here, it was fairly screaming this time. I blended in like Neil Diamond at a hip hop show. I might just as well have yelled *Fore!* and asked to play through. Actually, if not for all the hostile facial expressions, I would have gotten a kick out of it. But I walked through the crowd as my namesake through the Red Sea and straight up to Tina at the corner of the bar. As I passed, the sea filled in behind me and the noise started back up.

"You again," she said, pressing her hand to the flap on her throat.

"Is there someplace we can talk?"

"Sure. Come … on. Butchie, keep an eye … on things."

I followed Tina into the back room and down the stairs into her office. It might have been a biker bar on the upper level, but down here it looked like any other basement office. It was a business. There were bills to pay, a payroll to meet, and taxes to evade.

"So," she said.

"Crank."

"What about … him?"

"I need to find him."

I didn't wait for her to ask why or to do the Bribe-me-first Cha-cha. I took out a roll of money and explained to her why I needed to find him.

"He's that important … to you … to find, huh?"

I shook my head yes.

"Put your money … away," she said, closing the door behind her, "and … fuck me."

I didn't have to say *what*. My face said it for me.

"You heard … me." Tina unbuckled her belt, unhitched her leather pants, and made a show of slowly undoing her zipper. She reached up with her free hand. "You don't even have to … look at … me. I'll bend over or … you can shut the … lights."

I didn't flinch. My father-in-law and I had played a game of chicken that lasted two decades. If I hadn't flinched for him, I wasn't going to for Tina Martell. I'd also learned that chicken was a two-team sport and that it worked both ways.

"You know, Tina, I didn't think you were ugly till right now," I said, starting for the office door. "I can find out what I need to know without Crank. But remember this, anything happens to my family because it took longer than it had to, I'll come back and burn this shithole down."

She stopped tugging on her zipper. "Once, I coulda had any man … I wanted. I did and … women too … sometimes. Now look at … me. I can't even suck—"

I kissed her hard on the mouth, running my hand through her short-cut hair. She didn't exactly resist, but she didn't quite melt either. She stepped back after a moment.

"You must really ... need Crank," she said, looking anywhere but at me.

"Yeah, I do."

"A cabin back in the woods ... off Dunbar Road and ... Limehouse Creek Way in Craterskill."

"By the lake?"

She nodded. "Be careful ... out there."

Before I left, I stuck my head back into the office. "No one's ever accused me of doing things I didn't want to."

STROLLING INTO HENRY'S Hog was one thing. Driving up on a meth lab out in the woods in the middle of the night was something else. The cop vibe at the roadhouse earned me a few nasty stares. Here, nasty stares would be the very least of my worries. Meth was big business and these guys didn't fuck around. Shooting first and asking questions later was what they did with their friends. In my case, the questions would come after they had chopped me up and fed me to the local porcine population. As I rolled down Dunbar to the gravel road that was Limestone Creek Way, I thought that I might have asked Tina's advice on how to approach Crank without getting a shotgun stuck up my ass. It was a wee bit late for that now.

I had three options, none of them any good, but some more dangerous than others. I could have left my car where it was and tried to work my way through the woods to the cabin on foot. That was my 'if' option: If I was twenty pounds lighter ... If I was twenty years younger ... If my knees worked ... Even then, I'm not sure I would have tried it. The woods around the cabin were probably full of eyes and ears and booby traps. Call me a worrier, but I didn't much feel like stepping into a steel trap or wire snare. I could have tried to sneak up on one of the lookouts and have my .38 convince him to take me to Crank. Again, I wasn't sure I could pull it off nor did I want to create any more ill will than my unexpected visit was apt to generate. I needed Crank's help, not his animosity. I went with option three. I restarted my car, put on the brights, rolled down my windows, blasted the radio, and headed straight for the cabin. I might be accused of stupidity, but nobody was going to accuse me of trying to sneak up on anyone.

That was all well and good until the front end of my car plowed into a log placed across Limestone. I didn't hit it hard enough to have the air bag deploy, but the seat belt tightened up and gave me a pretty good jolt.

Before my head had fully cleared, someone reached out of the darkness and stuck a cold hunk of metal into my neck just under my jaw.

"Shut the car off, asshole. Put your hands on the back of your head, and get out easy," the man said, slowly pulling back the car door and guiding me with the end of his sawed-off. I still couldn't quite make him out, but the rifle caught enough light for me to see. "Walk. That way. Slow." He indicated which way with the gun barrel and moved it from my neck to my back.

If I had ever been more frightened, I couldn't remember when. I'd been involved in a few shootings, but they had just sort of happened. One minute there wasn't shooting and the next minute there was. The first time happened up in the Cat-skills. I was in the room when a crooked town cop blew the head off his fellow blackmailer. The next time was a setup. I'd been lured to a meeting at a shuttered Miami Beach hotel during the Moira Heaton/Steven Brightman investigation. When I showed, an ex-U.S. marshal named Barto tried to kill me. I fired back. I think I hit him, but didn't stick around to make sure. Then there was the shooting at Crispo's bar in Red Hook when Carmella's partner was killed and she took that bullet in her shoulder. At Frankie Motta's house in Mill Basin, there were a few minutes of calm before the old mob capo and his former henchmen shot each other.

Being marched to your own execution was more than a little bit different. The string was going out of my legs and I didn't think I had the strength to walk much further. A thousand things to say went through my head, but my mouth just didn't seem capable of forming any words. On the other hand, the little voice, the one that never leaves me, had no trouble with words. *Be a man. Don't beg. Don't shit your pants. Be a man.*

I was so angry at myself for worrying not about my family, but about how I would look to strangers when they blew the back of my head off, that I nearly turned around and charged the guy holding the shotgun on me. Given another few seconds, I think that's just what I would have done. Luckily, I didn't get a chance to find out.

"Pull his car off the road. I'll take it from here," someone said, stepping out of the darkness in front of me.

"Crank, is that you?" I said, my voice cracking.

"That was awfully fucking stupid, coming up here like that. Good thing Tina called ahead."

"Good thing," I agreed.

"Come on inside."

The cabin in the woods was just that, a cabin in the woods. There was a stone fireplace, a futon, a TV, a stereo, a small kitchen with a table and chairs, a bathroom, and not much else. There wasn't any lab equipment that I could see and I hadn't spotted any chemical drums on the walk up. Crank followed my eyes and smiled.

"We don't cook the shit here, man. Biker don't equate to moron, you know."

"Glad to hear it."

"Tina says you wanna talk, so talk. You wanna beer?"

"Sure."

He handed me a Coors. Panic makes your pants wet and your throat dry. I hadn't realized how dry until the first sip of beer went down smooth as silk and cold as ice. From now on, Coors would definitely be my post-shotgun beer of choice. I wondered if they could work up an advertising campaign around that slogan.

"How you feeling?" I asked.

"Okay. You risked getting your ass shot off to check on my health?"

"That night at the ER, you said you had to lay your bike down when an SUV ran the light at Blyden and Van Camp, right?"

"Asshole blew right through the intersection without hesitating and didn't even tap his brakes after I went down. Good thing I was paying attention."

"Can you remember anything about the SUV? Color? What state the tags were from, how many people were in—"

"Pretty sure it was a pewter Yukon. New, I think. At least two people, men up front. New York plates. Sorry, but I was a little too busy to get the number."

"That's good, but how do you know there were two men up front?"

"Dome light was on. I can't tell you anything about them. Everything happened so fucking fast, you know? Does that help?"

"More than you can know. Thanks a lot, Crank."

I shook his hand. When I did, he pulled me close and whispered in my ear, "Don't come back here no more, bud. Makes the boys nervous to have cop types around and that don't do me no kinda good. We understand one another?"

"We do."

I turned to go and then the world shook. *Baboom!* The explosion wasn't in the cabin, but it was close enough to shake the place and blow out the windows. I bounced off the wall and saw the fireball rising up out of the woods about a hundred yards away. I thought I could feel the heat on my face, but I was probably imagining that. I ran over and helped Crank up off the floor.

"You gotta get outta here," he barked. "The timing don't look so good for you."

"I didn't—"

"I know you didn't, but they're not gonna believe that. Keep your head down by the door and listen. You'll know what to do."

Crank waited till I crouched down and then ran out the front door screaming, "He jumped out the window and headed toward the lake. Hammer, you get Blade and Cutter and get to the lake. Skank, you go check on the kitchen to see if anything's left of Skinny and the equipment. I'll check the woods to make sure he don't double back."

"Shit, Crank, ain't nothin' gonna be left a Skinny, not after—"

"Listen, Skank, get the fuck over there and check on Skinny or—"

"Okay, Crank. Jesus, fuckin' Christ, who the fuck died and left you God?"

I listened to all the footsteps heading away from the cabin and the road where my car was parked.

Crank kicked the door with his heel. "Go now. Fire your gun when you get to your car."

I didn't hesitate. Taking off, I kept low as I could and close to the trees. My car wasn't too far from where I left it. I didn't bother checking the damage to the front end. As Crank asked, I fired off a few rounds. He didn't have to explain. I was giving him cover for when his crew got curious about how I had escaped.

As I drove back into Janus, I thought about what Crank had said about the timing of the explosion. It was one hell of a coincidence that his meth lab just happened to blow up during my visit. I didn't like it, not even a little. I called Pete Vandervoort. He was asleep, but when I told him about Crank's lab being launched into low Earth orbit, he agreed to meet me in his office.

Given the sheriff's looks, I was glad I'd avoided mirrors. And he was just tired. I'd crashed a car, had a shotgun stuck in my throat, and witnessed a recreation of the Trinity test. I had just about used up my yearly allowance of adrenaline and was now paying the price. I could literally feel myself crashing and unless he was hiding a fifty-five gallon drum of coffee somewhere, I wasn't going to last much longer.

I described the SUV to him that Crank described it to me.

"We've got a winner!" I think I remember him saying.

I recall his mouth moving some more after that, but I had already retreated behind a wall of sleep.

YOU REACH A certain age in life and you've woken up in a few strange beds, Even so, it can be a pretty jarring experience. Waking up in a jail cell kicked that jarring thing up to a whole different level. The bed wasn't too terribly uncomfortable and the bleach and pine disinfectant aroma wasn't quite as pleasant as my dad's Old Spice aftershave, but I guess it had its charms. On the other hand, I didn't find the cold metal toilet hanging off the wall very welcoming. I kind of felt like Otis the town drunk on the old *Andy Griffith Show*. I think I half-expected Barney Fife or Aunt Bee to show up with my breakfast.

My watch said it was 8:22 a.m., but the florescent lighting and lack of windows kept the place in a kind of perpetual dusk. I threw some cold water on my face. I might have dunked my head into the water had the sink been larger than the ones in aircraft rest rooms. I was about to try the door to make sure the sheriff didn't have a frat house sense of humor. Just then he walked in and swung the door back open.

"Where's Opie?" I said.

"Huh?"

"Forget it, Pete. Thanks for putting me up. I was pretty zonked."

"I'd say. I've been checking on you every hour," he said, pointing at the security camera mounted on the ceiling outside the cell, "and you've been in one position for most of the night. Come on, I got some coffee for you out here."

We stepped into the offices. Here, the sun streaming through the windows confirmed that my watch was telling the truth. Vandervoort handed me a cup of coffee and motioned for me to sit down in front of his desk. Although his expression was neutral, I could tell that the news he had for me wasn't good.

"It's a dead end, Moe. We got your Yukon on one of the tapes and we got the kid walking into the convenience store at the station, but it's impossible to read the tags. The driver never got out of the vehicle to buy gas or anything and he drove off right after dropping the kid."

"Shit!"

"I know it's not what you wanted to hear, but it totally confirms that this is a setup. You got that much, anyway."

"Tape show anything about the driver?" I asked.

"Well, the good thing is that this tape was brand new, so it's much cleaner than the other one I gave you. No murky images on this one."

"But …"

"But you can't tell anything about the driver. The windows are slightly tinted and there's some sun glare."

"Can I have the tape?"

"I knew you'd ask that." He shoved a plastic evidence bag across the desk. "Here you go."

"Any news on the lab?"

He started laughing. "The damned explosion registered on earthquake sensors. That was no small operation there, my friend. Somebody's not going to be happy about it going boom."

"I don't suppose they're going to file any insurance claims."

"I suspect not."

I got up. "Thanks for the tape and for the accommodations, Pete. I better get back down to the city and see if I can figure out how to come at this from another angle."

"Sorry the SUV thing didn't work out for you."

"Me too. Later."

CHAPTER FIFTEEN

THERE ARE TIMES when Brooklyn feels more like home than others. This was one of those times. I considered stopping at the office, but decided against it. I'd stop by later and drop off the new videotape and see if Devo had made anything of the answering machine tape and the original security video. Without tag numbers, it was a waste of time to put people on tracking down the Yukon. There were probably hundreds, if not thousands, of Yukons registered in New York State. Crank and the SUV had been worth a shot, but the sheriff was right, it was a dead end. Dead ends, unlike closing doors, are not very Zen. When one door closes, it's said, another opens. When you hit a dead end, you make a U-turn. I needed to clear my head and think. I used to do my best thinking in Coney Island.

I strolled down the boardwalk toward the looming monster that was the Parachute Jump: its orange-painted girders rising like dinosaur bones two hundred and fifty feet off the grounds of Steeplechase Park. What a silly beast it was, after all, serving no purpose but to remind the world of its impotence. It might just as well have been a severed limb. Besides the salt air, the boardwalk smelled of Nathan's Famous hot dogs, Italian sausages frying with sweet peppers and onions: the fat from the sausages hissing and spitting on the grill. It smelled of sun block too. The beaches were crowded, but not so crowded as when I was a kid. The beaches weren't as much of a magnet for city kids as they once had been.

With Sarah fully grown and nearly all my old precinct brothers moved or dead, I didn't find much cause to come back here as I used to. I still loved the wretched place. How could I not, but it had never been the same after Larry McDonald's suicide. This is where I saw him alive that last time in '89, the ambitious prick. He had been a murderer too, though I didn't know it then. I guess it broke my heart a little to find that out about Larry. That day back in '89, Larry and I stood on the boardwalk directly over where his victim had been found. Larry threatened me and my family. He said he was desperate. Maybe he was. Somehow his words and deeds had tainted the place a little. It was the divorce too. Divorce does more than split things apart. It taints things, all things, especially the good ones.

As I walked I thought back to my chat with Mira Mira and how she said the older guy with the eye patch was a cop. Maybe there was an angle in that, but intuition didn't usually stand up under scrutiny. It had been my experience that people who insisted they knew things for sure didn't necessarily know shit. I don't care if every one of the tattoo artist's relatives was a cop. Just because a man is a chef doesn't mean his kid can cook.

I thought about how much money was involved in arranging for the audition ads, for paying the kid and fixing him up to look just like Patrick. I thought about what it had cost to fly around the country for the auditions and to have arranged for the roses and the dramatics at Jack's grave. I estimated it had cost between ten and thirty grand, maybe a little bit more, to stage this little charade. A nice chunk of change, yes, but not big money. Any regular schmo, if he was motivated enough, could come up with that kind of scratch, so the money was another dead end. It all led back to the motivation. In the end, it was the only way I could figure to come at this. There was someone out there who wanted to hurt me and wanted to use my family to do it. For now, I had to go back to stumbling around in the dark, to interviewing everyone I could think of who might have a reason to want to hurt me.

IT WAS NO wonder that Devo'd had trouble tracking down Judas Wannsee. First off, the name was an obvious alias, a construct of the most hated Jew in history, Judas Iscariot, and of the Wannsee Conference at which the Nazis worked out the details for the Final Solution. Headquartered in the Catskill Mountains, his cult, the Yellow Stars, rejected the concept of assimilation and believed that the only way to avoid Jewish self-hatred was to announce your Jewishness to the world, to brand yourself a Jew, and to avoid the false comforts of fitting in. Most of the members did this by wearing the eponymous yellow star on their clothing to mark themselves as the Nazis had marked the Jews of Europe. Some went so far as to shave their heads and don the striped pajamas of those herded into concentration camps. In a few extreme cases, they had numbers tattooed on their forearms and ate a meager diet of stale black bread and potato soup.

If Karen Rosen had sought refuge from any other group, cult, or religion, Judas Wannsee and I might never have crossed paths. Karen was one of the three girls from my high school who had allegedly perished in a Catskill Mountain hotel fire in the summer of 1965, so you can imagine my response when her lunatic older brother Arthur came to me in 1981 claiming not only that the fire was no accident, but intimating that one of the dead girls wasn't dead at all. As it happened, he was right on both counts. Not only had his sister survived the fire, she started it. Exhausted from guilt and years of hiding, she found her way back to the Catskills and joined the Yellow Stars. Why she joined them is hard to say. Maybe she thought she could fashion her own murderous self-loathing into something that could be exorcised by slapping on the yellow *Juden* star. Maybe it was proximity to the scene of the original crime. By the time I found Karen Rosen at the Yellow Star compound and got to discuss it with her, liver cancer had since rendered her more dead than alive. When we spoke, she wanted from me something not in my heart to deliver: forgiveness.

Years later, I read an interview with Wannsee in a magazine. Although he gave no specifics, he discussed the issue of giving refuge and how the sins of those he had harbored over the years had come to weigh heavily upon him. *Yeah, tell me about it.* Shortly after the interview appeared, buzz over the group faded. Then the Yellow Stars went the way of their buzz. It was a stretch, I know, but I wondered even then if he blamed me for pulling the first stone from the foundation upon which his little semi-secular temple had rested. Back then, it hadn't interested me enough to bother tracking him down. It did now.

Given his fanatical rantings against assimilation, there was a kind of perverse symmetry in his latest incarnation. Judas Wannsee had gone from the ultimate outsider and gadfly to faceless bureaucrat, from messianic to mundane, from bright yellow stars to grays and inspection stickers. The Department of Motor Vehicles office on Route 112 in Medford on Long Island was the perfect physical manifestation of the anonymous new life Wannsee had chosen for himself. It was tucked neatly into the corner of one of the gazillion strip malls and shopping centers that scarred the island. Long Island had been transformed from a place of endless trees and beaches to a land of ugly, mind-numbing repetition. Deli. Chinese take-out. Dojo. Pizzeria. Card store. Phone store. Deli. Chinese take-out. Dojo. Card store. Phone store. Deli. Chinese take-out ...

As I stood on the information line and listened to the beige woman at the desk endlessly repeat *How can I help you?* I had to snicker. There were several layers of irony in Judas Wannsee's transformation.

"Yes," I said, "I'd like to speak to your supervisor, please."

"What's this in reference to?"

"Just tell him it's about Bungalow number eight. He'll understand."

She hesitated and shook her head. Apparently, this situation had not been covered in *Information Desk 101*, so she handled it as she would if I'd come in to surrender some old license plates. She hit a button that generated a white numbered chit—A 322—and handed it to me.

"Take a seat. *Next!*"

I did as she asked, taking a seat on a long pew. The pews faced numbered stations where bored-looking clerks did what clerks do. The pews also faced big electronic boards that posted chit numbers and stations in red lights:

F121 12

D453 10

A320 08

And whenever new numbers were posted, a bell would ring. The place seemed to have been designed by a bingo-playing priest heavily influenced by Pavlov. A322 12 flashed up on the screen quickly enough. The woman at window 12 directed me to walk over to a door. When I reached it, she buzzed me in.

"Down the hall," she yelled to me as I closed the door behind me.

The man I had known as Judas Wannsee sat behind a metal desk, shuffling and scribbling on papers. The walls were white and blank except for the mandatory notices about sexual harassment, emergency procedures, and handwashing when leaving the rest rooms. They were devoid of pictures, posters, of anything that might have given a visitor insight into the man who occupied the office. He was twenty years older and it showed. He had thinned, as had his hair. He was stooped somewhat and gravity had taken its toll on his face, but the eyes still burned bright.

"Mr. Prager," he said without looking up. "Bungalow number eight, indeed."

I knew he would remember. Bungalow 8 was where Karen Rosen had spent her last days, where we spoke that final time.

"I figured it was better than asking for Judas Wannsee or throwing a felt star on the counter."

"I suppose," he said, rubbing his chin. "Or you might simply have asked for Howard Bland. But no, as I recall, the simple way was not your way. You have a weakness for the dramatic turn. Please sit."

I sat.

"How did you find me?" he asked.

"I'm a detective."

"Lost is what you are, Mr. Prager. You always have been and I sense you will always be so."

That stung some. I didn't try to hide it. "And you're a hypocrite. What happened to all your speeches about not fitting in and showing yourself to the world as a Jew as a black man shows the world he is black? Look where you are now. You're a glorified clerk: faceless, pointless, invisible. Polonius too was full of high sentence, but at least he moved the plot along."

"The lost detective ... who quotes from Prufrock, no less."

The less I liked his attitude, the more I liked him for what had happened to Katy.

"I was paraphrasing, not quoting."

"Polonius? I think not. My speeches are like the soft tissue of dinosaurs, lost to history."

"Talk about a flare for the dramatic. Besides, that's no answer."

"And why should I be obliged to answer your questions at all?"

I suppose I could have grabbed him by the collar and twisted. It might have given me some short-term satisfaction, but would've ultimately proven counterproductive.

"You're not obliged, but I might tell you how I tracked you down if you cooperate."

"You know, Mr. Prager, upon brief reflection, I find I'm not really so interested in how you found me. In fact, maybe how is beside the point. Let me ask, why?"

Again, I had a choice. I chose the non-violent option and explained. He never took his eyes off me as I spoke. He still had that ability to make you feel as if he could see right into you, into the darkest places, places where you stored your most shameful thoughts and unshared secrets. I was convinced he could detect the slightest hint of pose or artifice. When I finished, he considered what I had said before speaking. He still had it, the charisma. A lot of people want it. Some think they have it and don't. He had it in abundance.

"I can understand why you might have suspected me," he said, "but I'm sorry to disappoint you. I have nothing to do with the crimes perpetrated against your family."

I didn't want to believe him, yet I did, instantly. "Fair enough."

"I was quite piqued at you there for a time, I must confess. Your stumbling onto Karen did disrupt things for me. The group went on, even grew larger. I still believed in what I preached, but your presence caused me to have to look beyond my own belief system and motivations and to examine more carefully those who would follow my lead or, like Karen, seek refuge with us. You'd planted the seed. You see, I began the group because I believed in a set of values, not because I had a need to lead or a lust for power. Leadership and power are onerous, heavy yokes, not pleasures. Yet they were burdens I was glad to take on if it helped the misguided Jews of this great country.

"What I discovered, Mr. Prager, was that you could worship watermelon pits or sacks of gray pebbles or anything else for that matter and people would follow. Sadly, the world is populated by a lot of lonely, hungry, and lost souls. They all want to belong, to be loved, to be fed, to be anchored. Beliefs, unfortunately, are cold cold things. They give no comfort, no acceptance, no sustenance. Only other people can minister to those needs. Beliefs may inspire the founding of a group, but yearnings are the fuel that drives its growth engine. After years of self-exploration, of denial, and of rationalization, I knew what I had to do.

"I had already made my initial journey and come out the other side. I was a proud Jew by the time you and I had met that first time. I realized that if the group had true strength, it would survive and prosper without me at its center. If, however, I left and it collapsed, then my cause was folly. In the end, my decision to leave was set in motion by Karen's impending death and your arrival, Mr. Prager. It took me years to build a new identity into which Judas Wannsee might vanish. Even then, it wasn't as easy to let go as you might expect. No man wants to feel that what he's lived for has all been an illusion, a heat mirage on the asphalt in summer. Yet, eventually, Judas Wannsee faded slowly into the backdrop. So you see, I owe you not antipathy, but thanks. Just as my brother soldiers had inspired my first journey of self-exploration, you sparked my second."

"But this …" I said, gesturing at the generic office. "Why the anonymity?"

"My first journey required the participation of others. I needed the rest of the world to react to my declarations of proud Judaism. The star, the tattoo, the pajamas, the name were all props meant to elicit responses. My growth, my self-discovery was a function of my reactions to those responses. And by confronting that daily friction, I was conditioning myself out of the shame and self-hatred of the assimilated Jew.

"This second journey has been a purely internal and personal struggle: Could I sustain my transformation without the participation of another soul? Could I be a proud Jew even if the rest of the world didn't know I existed? Could I remain unassimilated in the midst of utter assimilation? We have all heard the cliché, 'What a man believes in his heart, is what matters.' That was what I needed to discover, what I believed in my heart. For this question to be answered, I needed to remove all external things from my life that might serve to give me reinforcement, that might elicit response. Until the moment you walked through my office door, I had been remarkably successful."

"Hasn't it been long enough for you to get your answer?"

"Yes and no, Mr. Prager. What I have come to realize is that the answer requires one last journey. At the instant of my death, I will know for sure."

"A little late in the game, don't you think?"

"It's always late in the game for everyone. We're all of us on several journeys at once, different journeys, yes, but we all get the answer to the same question at the same time. I am ready for that answer whenever it may come."

"Goodbye, Mr. Bland." I nodded, standing. "Be well."

"And you, Mr. Prager. Although there is great value in being lost, try and find something in the meantime. There is no shame in comfort."

As I walked back down the hallway toward the bingo parlor, his words rang in my head. Just as his words had stayed with me for the last twenty years, these would stay with me until the day I died. But unlike Mr. Bland nee Wannsee, I was not ready for that answer, whatever it was and whomever its deliverer might be.

Right now I had to focus on closing chapters in my life. And with the exception of Judas Wannsee, all the significant people connected to my time in the Catskills were dead. Karen Rosen and Andrea Cotter, my high school crush, were gone. Everyone from R.B. Carter—Andrea Cotter's billionaire brother—to Anton Harder—the leader of the white supremacists—was gone.

Closing chapters, that's what I was trying to do now, at least until I could think of a more inspired approach. When I was done reconciling the books, I'd take a look at the landscape and see who remained standing. One of them would be the man or woman behind the grave desecrations and the appearance of Patrick Michael Maloney's ghost. And since I was already on Long Island, I decided to make one more stop. It would no doubt be an unpleasant one.

A MIDDLE-CLASS hamlet with pretensions, Great River was tucked neatly between East Islip and Oakdale on Long Island's south shore. For many years Great River had resisted the Gaudy-is-Great infection spreading wildly across the rest of the island, but just lately its ability to fend off the disease had weakened. Acre lots that had once sported comfortable colonials and solid split ranches had begun sprouting giant "statement" houses, beasts that featured design elements from styles as disparate as Bauhaus and French Provincial. But the house that had to have won the Good Housekeeping's seal of disapproval boasted minarets, a faux moat, and scale model marble mailbox sculpted like the *Pieta*. In place of Michelangelo's name, it read—in gold leaf I might add—Mr. Michael Angelos and Family. Visitors to the home were probably confused as to whether they should purchase a theme park pass or prayer cards.

A little further on, I turned right before the gates of Timber Point Country Club and parked across from the expanded L-shaped ranch that I'd visited once, eleven years earlier. The Martello house looked much the same now as it had then, but things had changed. Currently, the house belonged to Raymond Martello Jr., a Suffolk County Police sergeant. The house had once belonged to his dad. The father had been a cop too, NYPD, the captain in command of the 60th Precinct: my old house in Coney Island. I was ten years off the job by the time he was posted to the Six-O. Ray Sr. and me might not have known each other as cops, but we made up for lost time and got real well acquainted back in the late '80s.

I strolled across the street to talk to the tanned, shirtless man kneeling to adjust an in-ground sprinkler head on his front lawn.

"You Ray Jr.?" I asked.

"Why? Who wants to know?"

"No fair. You asked two questions. I only asked one."

He stopped what he was doing, gazed up at me, and got to his feet. Whereas Ray Martello Sr. had been a small, compact man, this guy was eye to eye with me. He was square-shouldered and ripped. He did the cop thing of getting in close to me—his nose nearly touching mine—and staring through me. He was checking me out and trying to intimidate me all at once. A sly, arrogant smile worked its way onto his face. I figured him for Martello's kid. Had to be. Had the father's looks and the same impudent style. I was feeling guilty about trying to get a rise out of him until I saw that fucking smile.

I noticed some rather intricate and unusually colored tattoos on his forearms, biceps, and delts. There were a series of Chinese characters on his left forearm done in bright red, not the usual dull blue. Both biceps were encircled by bands of blue-green barbed wire highlighted with that same bright red, but the tat that caught my attention was on his right delt. It was the head of a Peregrine falcon done in vibrant shades of black, dark and light brown, off-white, and hints of blue. The yellow around the beak and eyes was so real, I could almost imagine pricking my finger on the tip of its hooked bill. I shifted position slightly and observed that the falcon's body and talons continued down his back. Here the work was even more skillfully executed, as the dappling on the bird's belly, the texture of its feathers and the blending of shades was like nothing I'd ever seen. Well ... that wasn't true. I had recently seen something very much like it.

"Cop?" he asked, confident of my answer.

"Used to be. In the city. Nice ink work. Where'd you get it done?"

"Thanks." He pointed to his forearm, then his bicep. "These here I got in A.C."

"How about the bird? You get that done in Atlantic City too?"

"What are you, some kinda queer or something?"

"Or something," I said. "I knew your dad a little."

That wiped the arrogant smirk off his face and put a dent in his smart guy attitude. A city cop my age would know about what a corrupt piece of shit his father had been. In 1972, Raymond Sr., along with Larry McDonald and another thuggish cop I knew named Kenny Burton, had tortured and murdered drug kingpin Dexter "D Rex" Mayweather. Mayweather was king of the Soul Patch, the African-American section of Coney Island. But his execution wasn't some noble act of misguided vigilantism done to rid the Coney Island streets of drugs. Rather it was done at the behest of Anello Family capo Frankie Motta in order to cover up an ill-conceived partnership between his crew and D Rex.

"Yeah, so you knew my pops, so what?"

"I was in Frankie Motta's house the night he got shot."

Martello Jr. blanched, then burned hot. His face did somersaults. It was as if a colony of beetles were under his skin, pulling his face this way and that. He knew who I was without asking.

"You got some set of balls showing up here, Prager."

"You think?"

"I do. In fact, I think if you don't get off my property pretty soon, I'm gonna have to shoot you for trespassing."

"Your father tried to shoot me once and look where that got him."

Mayweather's murder remained unsolved until, seventeen years later, a low level dealer named Malik Jabbar was arrested by a very young and very ambitious detective named Carmella Melendez. During his interrogation, Jabbar claimed to know who had killed D Rex. That was all it took for things to unravel. Within weeks, Larry McDonald committed suicide, Malik Jabbar and his girlfriend were executed, and Carmella's partner and another 60th Precinct cop, a Detective Bento, were gunned down in a Brooklyn bar.

When I figured it out, I went to confront the terminally ill Frankie Motta. While I was there, Ray Martello and Kenny Burton showed up intending to do to Motta and me what they had done to D Rex. Things didn't work out quite the way they hoped. When the gunsmoke cleared, there were two men dead, one wounded, and one, me, still upright. Martello survived his wounds, but his heart crapped out on him on the operating table. He remained in a coma for a long time before they pulled the plug on him. The family might have better dealt with the tragedy and disgrace if, in the aftermath, the Brooklyn and Queens DAs hadn't held a televised press conference during which they made Martello the heavy in their little dog and pony show.

"Yeah, but I won't miss from this range," he said. "You'd look good bleeding from the eyes."

"Your dad thought the same thing."

"Smart man, my pops."

"That's not the words that come to mind when I think about your dad. Corrupt assassin is more like it."

The red of his face deepened and he coiled as if getting ready to strike. He didn't. Instead he shook his head at me.

"You want me to smack you," he said. "Well, fuck you, Prager. You'll get yours soon enough and you won't see it coming."

"You willing to risk everything on that?" I goaded him.

"To get rid of you, it'd be worth it. Any price to make you feel what we went through would be worth paying."

"Glad to hear you say it." I smiled.

"You're a sick fuck, Prager. Now I'm not going to warn you again. Hit the road, asshole."

"Don't worry, I'm going."

I left. There was nothing more to be gained by my further antagonizing him. I had a good feeling about Martello. He was the best-looking suspect I'd stumbled across. Ray Jr. knew good tattoo work. One look at that falcon on his back told me as much and I wasn't discouraged just because Martello didn't fit the description of the older man who had arranged for the kid's ink work. Whoever was doing this thing wasn't doing it alone. Maybe Cyclops was a relative or an old cop friend of the family's. Suffolk cops are the best paid in the country, so he had the means. Martello had just made it crystal clear he had the motive. And, as I was about to discover, Ray Jr. had something else that got my attention. I drove up the block a little ways to find a spot to turn around. Coming back past the Martello house, I looked down his driveway and saw that one of his garage doors was open. Parked in the garage was a new pewter Yukon.

CHAPTER SIXTEEN

I AGED A few years on the ride into Brooklyn, but no one sang "Happy Birthday" to me when I called into the office. At least everyone was now up to speed and, for the first time since this whole affair began, we were working the case like a case should be worked. Carmella gave Brian Doyle the shit end of the stick. His job was, for the time being, to be Martello's round the clock shadow. We'd get him some help as soon as we could. Not because we felt sorry for his ass, but because twenty-four hour surveillance is hard enough to do with a full team. It's nearly impossible for one person to maintain. The need for food and bathroom breaks gives the mark too many opportunities to slip away. And doing surveillance in the 'burbs is more difficult than in the city. Blending in isn't easy. Neighbors notice strange cars and unfamiliar faces.

Carmella said she would make calls to some friends in the Suffolk PD and the Suffolk County DA's office to check on Martello. Devo was getting credit reports and any other financial documents he could lay his hands on. When I walked into the office, both of them had promising news for me.

"I like him for it," Carmella said. "A captain I know out there says Martello's a prick."

"Brian Doyle's a prick too, but we hired him and he's not haunting my wife."

"There's more. This captain says—"

"This captain, how do you guys know each other?"

Silence.

"The mystery captain got a name?"

"Kirsten Rafferty. Why, you want her number?"

"I don't date women who outrank me."

"I'm not even going there," she said. "So you wanna hear this or what?"

"Go ahead."

"Seems Martello got divorced ten years back and the ex started dating a guy assigned to Highway Patrol named Cruz."

"Yeah, so …"

"A year later, Cruz was off the job and the ex was out of state."

"There's a punch line here, right?" I asked.

"The story goes that Ray Martello was like out of his mind over his ex dating another cop … Men and their macho bullshit. Anyways, he didn't confront either Cruz or the ex-wife. Instead, he hooks up with Cruz's barely legal little sister. Martello asks the sister to keep their romance quiet because he doesn't want to cause trouble with her big brother and she's only too happy to oblige. Problem is, she's also happy to oblige when Martello suggests they start videotaping themselves … You know what I'm saying? Do I have to draw fucking pictures for you, Moe?"

"So Martello lets Cruz know not only that he's been boning his sister, but that he's got the tapes to prove it. Cruz goes ballistic and assaults Martello, in front of several witnesses, no doubt."

"No doubt."

"Cruz gets kicked to the curb, the wife figures she needs to get far away from her crazy ex if she's ever going to date again, and Martello has his revenge."

"Gets better," Carmella said. "Because the story of why Cruz assaulted Martello gets leaked, the brass don't really want to bring criminal or disciplinary charges against Cruz. Cop vs. cop shit doesn't look good in the press, especially with what those guys get paid. Problem is, they need Martello's cooperation to keep it quiet."

"Nice way to make sergeant, huh? He gets everything he wanted and more, the vengeful dick."

"Vengeful is right. You gotta be a twisted fuck to go after a man's family like that. Sound familiar?"

"Unfortunately, it does," I said.

"Listen to this. Martello's movements over the past year fit the time frame we've established. He went out with a bad hip about eleven months ago and didn't return to active duty till June. That gave him all the time he needed to set this thing up. Devo's got more coincidences for you."

"Listen, Carmella, after I talk to Devo, let's get outta here for an hour, okay?"

"Sure. I could use a break."

I rapped my knuckles on Devo's door and walked in without waiting.

"What's that?" Devo asked, pointing at my left hand.

"Huh? Oh, this. Another videotape."

"I can see that, Moe."

"Right. It's from the gas station. It's got the kid and the guy who was driving him around on it, but you can't make much out. I figured it wouldn't hurt to let you have a try at it. Now I guess it's sort of beside the point."

"Maybe."

"Carmella tells me you—"

"Yes. Here, look at these." He slid some papers across the desk to me. "As you can see, Sergeant Martello was twice in cities—Los Angeles and Las Vegas—during the same time as the auditions were held in those cities. If we count New York, that is three cities. Of course, he may have been in many more of the cities, but Los Angeles and Las Vegas are the only two for which I have been so far able to obtain proof."

"Good work, Devo." I patted his shoulder. "Thanks."

"Moe ..."

"Yeah."

"It had nearly slipped my mind, but I did some analysis of the tapes you left with me previously. There is nothing much to be done, I am afraid, with the first security videotape. As you saw for yourself, it was terribly degraded and recorded over many many times. However, the phone machine tape did reveal something of interest. While I cannot say whether the voice is authentic or not, I can say it displays no obvious splices or edits, no abrupt clicks on or off. On the other hand, there is some very faint background noise."

"You mean like scratches and pops from a vinyl record, that kinda thing?"

"Nothing so obvious as that, no. I believe what I hear is the rumble of a cassette motor."

"Are you sure it isn't from the phone machine?"

Devo smiled at me like a proud father with his Little Leaguer. "A very astute question. I cannot be certain, but if that is in fact Patrick's voice, I would venture to say it was dubbed off a cassette tape and then filtered to suppress the other noise you would expect to find on an old tape. Find the person in possession of the original tape and you will be very close to having your answer."

THE SIDEBAR GRILLE was near empty when Carmella and I walked in. During ten months of the year, the bar would be four deep with ADAs, defense lawyers, judges, cops, court officers, and even the occasional investigator, but July and August were quieter times around the courts as judges and lawyers heeded the call of the Hamptons. Only cops and skells don't do summer hours. The Sidebar Grille was famous for its food and convivial atmosphere. More plea bargains and monetary settlements had been sealed in here with steaks and handshakes than in any number of courthouses.

Maybe it was the emptiness of the place or the humidity. Whatever the cause, it didn't seem that the Sidebar's renowned aura was having much of an effect on Carmella. While she may not have been exhibiting any obvious physical signs of the pregnancy, my partner was showing nonetheless. She sat across from me, squirming in her chair, unable to look me in the eye. Carmella was uncomfortable in her own skin and that just wasn't her. She was learning the hard lesson, that children change your life whether you carry them to term or not. Soon she would learn that it was a change from which there is no retreat.

Marco the maitre d' was about a hundred years old, but never forgot a face or a name or how to put one to the other. He took Carmella's hand in his, placing his other hand atop hers.

"*La bella* Carmella, what may I get for you this evening?"

"A Virgin Mary."

Marco screwed up his face like he'd been stabbed in the heart.

"She's been under the weather," I said, hoping to head off Marco's interrogation.

"So sorry, *bella*. You get better, soon, you understand?"

"And for you, Moses … Dewar's rocks?"

"How'd you guess?"

Marco winked, disappeared.

"You're still not drinking," I said. "Good."

"Good! Why good?"

"Because you're thinking of keeping the baby."

"I'm also thinking of not keeping it." She placed her right hand on her lower abdomen. She tilted her head down. "You hear me, you inconvenient little brat?"

"They're all inconvenient, Carmella. Every single one, always."

"I guess."

Marco brought our drinks over and chatted with me a bit, but I couldn't help but peer at Carmella out of the corner of my eye. She was in love and, inconvenient or not, that baby was to be born. Now the trick was getting her to know it.

CHAPTER SEVENTEEN

BRIAN DOYLE GOT relief, all right ... me.

I was certain Martello had taken notice of my car after our confrontation in front of his house the previous day. With the man's attention to detail and lust for revenge, he no doubt already knew my car and tag numbers. He probably knew my total mileage and how much longer I had before my next oil change. To guard against being easily spotted, I switched cars with Carmella Melendez. While she may have been a great detective and meticulous about her looks, the woman's car was a disaster area. There were enough old newspapers, gas receipts, and food wrappers in there to start a toasty bonfire and enough half full coffee cups to put the fire out. Still, the car smelled of her grassy perfume and that more than compensated for the mess.

I parked across Great River Road from the turn onto Martello's block. I nestled the car into a dark, cozy corner on the lot of a half-completed neo-Victorian just down the street from the theme park house, Night had long since settled in and the construction crews were well gone. My position afforded me a clear view of Martello's house, but it would be impossible for him to spot me without night vision equipment. I could also see the nose of Brian Doyle's Sentra. He was parked on Martello's block in amongst several cars that lined both sides of the street. Apparently, one of the neighborhood kids was having a pool party. I punched up Brian's number.

"Yeah."

"Okay, Brian, I'm in position. You can get going."

"You sure you don't wanna wait till my fuckin' bladder explodes?"

"Piss in a coffee cup, shithead. That's like on page one of your guide to surviving surveillance."

"Whaddayu, nuts? I got like ten people on the porch over here. I'm not gonna provide entertainment for the evening."

"Anything happening?"

"Nah. He got home from his shift around four forty-five and he's been in there jerkin' off ever since."

"Okay, go home and get some rest. I got him now."

It didn't take Brian long to split. He must not have been kidding about his bladder.

About three hours later, the pool party was breaking up. As the departing cars took turns passing me by, the blast and thump of hip hop fractured the silence of the suburban night before fading away in the distance. I was sort of glad for the action. My wrists were aching from holding up the binoculars. And when I checked the sun visor mirror, I noticed funky circles on my face from the binocular eyepieces. I looked like the oculist's billboard in *The Great Gatsby*. T. J. Eckleburg, I think that was the guy's name. It's weird what you remember sometimes, but stakeouts'll do that to you. The boredom fucks with your head.

Just when the last car headed past me, my cell buzzed. It was Sarah.

"Hey, kiddo. What's up?"

"The doctor says Mom can go home in a day or two. She's doing much better."

"No unexpected sightings? The sheriff's still got someone watching?"

"Twenty-four hours a day, Dad. And no, no ghosts or anything."

"And you've been keeping busy?"

"I go to the hospital twice a day and then I just hang, but I am kinda anxious to get back to school."

"Good. I'm pretty sure we know who's been behind this whole thing. I'm staking out his house right now."

"Really?"

"Really. He's the son of a dirty cop. I guess he blames me for his father's death."

"Were you, Dad … to blame, I mean?"

"No, but that doesn't matter if he thinks I am."

"Be careful."

"You too, Sarah. We'll talk in the morning, okay."

I occupied myself with the concept of blame for a little while, a very little while. Then I hopped off that slippery slope, picked up the binoculars, and tried getting back to work. The deathly quiet of the place gave me the creeps. How did Aaron ever adjust to living out here? Brooklyn at its most quiet is noisy and that noise had been my lullaby nearly every day of my life.

Things were changing in the Martello house. The strobe and colored flicker of his TV stopped, the front window going pitch black. A lamp snapped on and there was a brief show of Ray Martello's dancing shadow. About five minutes later, the porch and outside garage lights popped on. The electric garage opener whined, the door crawling up and out of sight. An engine rumbled. Puffs of exhaust fumes showed themselves like reluctant specters in the cooling night air. First brake, then backup lights flashed as the big SUV lumbered backwards down the driveway.

I supposed I was far enough away that he wouldn't hear Carmella's ignition catch, but I didn't trust the way sound traveled out here and decided instead to wait until he either passed me moving north or drove in the opposite direction along the border of the golf course. The Yukon's headlights rushed at me, sweeping from my left to right as the truck turned north toward Montauk Highway. I twisted Carmella's key; the engine perked right up. Still, I waited a beat or two to let Ray Martello get a block ahead.

Then, just as I put the car in drive, a cold chill made me twitch. I noticed movement in the shadows across the way: a slender figure emerging through the country club gates and turning onto Martello's street. I can't say why exactly, but I couldn't force myself to look away. I shouldn't have cared at all. It was probably some kid who'd met his girlfriend for late night putting practice on the ninth green.

"Keep your eye on the ball," I whispered to myself. "Keep your eye on the ball."

But as I rolled off the lot, my headlamps caught the slender figure, briefly bathing him in a harsh circle of light. Turning back, he squinted, shielding his eyes with raised hands. And in that brief second, all that I knew to be solid and real flew away, because standing there in that circle of light was Patrick Michael Maloney's ghost. Yes, this was the second time I'd seen him, but seeing him in the light that way ... Christ, it scared the shit out of me. My heart thumped so that I felt it pushing my chest against my sweat-soaked shirt. Suddenly, all the tattoos and videotapes were rendered irrelevant. What you think you know doesn't stand a chance against what you think you see.

I couldn't afford to scare him off, not this time. *Scaring off a ghost! Go figure.* Although only twenty yards ahead of me, I'd never catch him if he took off toward the golf course. So I forced myself to move, to not hesitate, pulling quickly off the lot and driving up the block in the opposite direction. I had the steering wheel in a death grip to insure that my hands wouldn't shake. Of course I knew how I should play it, but I wasn't at all sure I could pull it off. Having made a U-turn at the first intersection and doubled back, I eased the car alongside him and let the servo suck the window fully down into the door before I spoke.

"Hey, buddy," I said in as steady a voice as I could manage, "I'm kinda lost here. Could you tell me how to get to Brightwaters?"

The ghost kept walking, neither turning toward me nor away from me. All I could do was stare at his profile, at that too-familiar tattoo on his bare forearm, and the Shinjo Olympians on his feet.

"Listen, man, I—"

He stopped in his tracks. I stopped the car, clicked it into park. Slowly, I slid my right arm across my lap to the door handle and began tugging on it ever so gently. There was a frozen second there when it felt as if I could've watched an entire baseball game between breaths or counted the beats of a hummingbird's wings. Then ...

Bang!

He took off back the way he came, toward the golf course. The car was useless to me now, so I was out the door after him. He was agile and pretty damned swift, making it through the country club gates in only a few seconds. While I had some moves on the basketball court, speed—even before my knee went snap, crackle, pop—was never my forte. An additional twenty years, three knee surgeries, and fifteen extra pounds weren't exactly helping the cause, but with my heart rate already up and adrenaline flowing, I actually gained some early ground on him.

It was an anomaly, not a trend. Once we both hit the grass and open ground of the golf course, I fell back. My deck shoes were no match for his track shoes. Although darker out here away from the street and porch lights, there was enough natural light to keep him from being completely swallowed up by the night. He kept looking over his shoulder to see how far he'd extended his lead over me or if I'd given up. If he thought I was going to quit, he really didn't know me. I'd have to cough out my lungs and liver before my legs would stop moving.

Bulldog or not, the reality was that my persistence would only count for so much. Eventually, he would get far enough ahead to duck out of sight, while I chased my own dick around out there in the dark. I didn't have long to wait. Since we'd hit the grass—which couldn't have been more than a minute earlier, but felt like an eternity—the ghost had been heading due south toward the ocean holes, but now he decided to cut sharply east toward where the sun would be coming up in only a very few hours.

Shit! I lost sight of him for a second behind a raised green, but caught a glimpse when I made it around the other side. He was gaining confidence as he went, getting a better sense of my physical limitations.

Hugging the first cut of rough as he went, he would dart in and out of the small outcroppings of trees that dotted this part of the course. Then, he darted in, but didn't come out. I was about to go in after him when something four-legged and low to the ground shot out of the woods and skittered directly across my path. Two luminescent eyes stared back at me while I got my heart out of my throat. Free of the tree shadows and in the middle of the fairway, I could see it was a red fox. I hadn't run across many red foxes in Coney Island. Stray dogs, water rats, and horseshoe crabs, yes. Red foxes, no.

Before I could reorient myself, the woods coughed up the ghost fifty yards ahead of me and, like the fox before him, he ran directly across the fairway into a much larger stand of trees on the opposite side. Running as hard as I could, I took a diagonal line right to where he entered the far trees. I kept my eyes focused on that point, trying desperately to ignore my aching knee and the stitch in my side that felt more like a gash. As I approached the woods, an uneasy feeling came over me. I didn't sense danger necessarily. It was a feeling that there were more than foxes, owls, and fireflies in here. But whatever my concerns, it was too late to start worrying about them now.

In the woods, I knelt down behind a clump of thin-trunked trees. I could hear the ghost's footfalls—ghosts didn't have footfalls, did they?—on the dried undergrowth and fallen leaves that had accumulated over the years. Then I spotted him, but the irregular spacing of the trees made it difficult for me to follow his course. His silhouette flashed in and out of view. There it was again, that weird feeling. I tried to ignore it, to keep my eyes on the next clearing between the trees where I thought he would come back into view.

There he is! I'd gotten lucky. By keeping my place, I had confused him and he was now heading back my way. In a few seconds he would be passing about as close to me as he had been when he was caught in my headlamps. I eased myself up from the kneeling position and braced my back against the trees. Then I thought I was hearing things. The ghost's footsteps were now lost in an avalanche of crunching leaves. The woods were suddenly alive with a low thumping that had nothing to do with my heart. It didn't matter. I was committed.

I sprang. My timing was perfect. The sudden activity confused him too and it took him a second to realize I was almost on him. I was ten yards away, five, two, one … I was just stretching out my arms when something brushed my leg, knocking me off balance, but not down, Then, at the last second before I grabbed the ghost, I saw a blur hurtling at me. *Bang!* The wind went out of me even before my kidneys connected with the big tree behind me. When I got to my hands and knees, I got kicked in the head, hard. Unconsciousness took a while to take hold. In the meantime, I let the thumping rock me to sleep.

It wasn't quite light out when I opened my eyes, but there was light enough to see Patrick's ghost was gone. The thumping was now exclusively in my head. I felt the knot above my left temple. It was tender and the hair over it was stiff from dried blood. The bleeding seemed to have stopped. I stood up slowly, in pieces, making sure I didn't revisit any of my most recent meals. I had a pretty good headache, but was walking okay. I knew what day it was, where I was, and had a notion of what time it was. I took a leisurely pace as I headed back to Carmella's car.

Stepping out of the woods with the first rays of sun over my back, I tripped over something in the deep rough. It was the half-eaten carcass of a fawn: no doubt the handiwork of the red fox. Across the fairway, in the smaller woods, a herd of about twenty deer tried to look inconspicuous, standing perfectly still, trying to blend in with the trees. One of them probably had my blood on its hoof. I wasn't interested in finding out which one.

As I walked through the golf course's front gate, an older gentleman out walking his chocolate lab stopped me.

"You don't look so good, son. What happened?"

"I got mugged," I said.

"Mugged! By who?"

"Bambi."

That ended the conversation right there.

Carmella's car was where I left it, about two feet away from the curb, parked facing the wrong way, and the driver's side door ajar. At least I hadn't left it running. I seriously considered finding another cozy spot and keeping up the stakeout. That notion lasted until I spied myself in the mirror. I was never going to look in a car mirror again. I looked like shit, smelled like shit, and felt like shit. I was nothing if not consistent.

I closed the car door, started her up, and limped back to Brooklyn. It was the smart thing to do. The way I saw it, I had no idea if Martello had returned home. If he was home, he was probably sleeping and I could get someone from the office out here by the time he headed in for his shift. If he was still out, not knowing where wasn't as big a deal as it would seem. I had time to get coverage on him either here or at his precinct. Either way, there was little doubt that his young accomplice or stooge or whatever Patrick's ghost was to him, had already told Martello about our running with the deer.

Although I was far worse for wear and had failed to get my hands on the kid, my concerns about Ray Martello were confirmed: the asshole was behind it. You'd have to be from Pluto to think the kid's appearance at Martello's house was a coincidence. Now I had some choices to make. I could go to Vandervoort or the local cops with what I had, but, truthfully, I had *bupkis*. I had suspicions, a series of unlikely coincidences, and Ray Martello's palpable hatred for me. Unfortunately, none of it would stand up in court. That's why my screwing up with the kid really hurt. If I just had him, he could make the case for me. On the other hand, I didn't have to go the legal route. Judge and jury Moe had all the evidence they needed. There were ways to get back at people without taking them to court. If anyone could understand that concept, it would be Ray Martello Jr.

Driving back up Great River Road to Montauk Highway, I passed by a roadkill mother possum and two babies. I squeezed my eyes shut as I went, but all I could see in my head were the skittering red fox and the wrecked body of the dead fawn. I had had quite enough of the suburbs, thank you very much. It was time to get back to a place where I better understood the relationship between predator and prey.

CHAPTER EIGHTEEN

THE RINGING IN my head woke me up.

First, I felt for the lump on my head, then I reached for the phone. The swelling had receded a bit and the blood-stiff hair was gone. Hot showers are mostly forgettable events, but there are times when they're just a notch or two below desperation sex. This morning's shower was the stuff of top ten lists. My long nap had reduced my headache from crashing cymbals to the tinkle of a lone triangle and I no longer smelled like Sunday at Augusta.

"Yeah, what?" My voice was thick with sleep.

Silence.

"Okay," I said, "I don't have time for this bullsh—"

"How is your head?"

The voice was unfamiliar and it took a few seconds for the question to register. I guess there were parts of me other than my voice still thick with sleep. *Who knew about my head?* No one. I hadn't wanted to bother explaining about my getting KO'ed by Bambi, so I'd left that part out of my call in to Carmella and she was the only person I'd spoken ... *Holy shit!*

"The head's better. What should I call you?" I asked.

"Patrick."

"Don't be an asshole, kid."

"No, really, that's my name. It's weird, right?"

"After all this, why are you calling me now? We could have saved ourselves a lot of trouble and me a headache if you'd have just talked to me this morning."

"I'm scared of Ray."

"Ray Martello?"

143

"Yeah. When I spoke to him he was crazy mad at me for letting you get that close."

I started noticing things about the kid's voice. His accent was mostly flat with a bit of a nasally twang. Half the kids that Sarah went to the University of Michigan with had that same accent. I thought about what approach to take with Patrick, if that was his name. Should I play the understanding, avuncular stranger or the outraged victim? Should I play softball or hardball? I went with hardball.

"Ray's a scary guy," I said. "What do you want from me and why the fuck should I care? Don't forget, kid, you've spent the last few weeks terrorizing my family and committing felonies."

"I didn't know. I swear to God I didn't know." His voice cracked.

"What did you think you were doing?"

"Making a movie."

"Don't bullshit me, kid. I'm from Brooklyn and you're not." I threw a high hard fastball under his chin. "You need cameras to shoot a movie. Seen any of those around lately? Maybe when you got the job you believed that movie crap, but not anymore."

"Okay, you're right. I'm really sorry about what I did to your wife and all, but I was in too deep to …"

I had him and it was time to start pressing my advantage.

"How did Martello get a recording of Patrick's—?"

"If I come in, can you protect me?" His voice took on a real urgency.

"Sure."

"You don't sound so sure," he said.

"You blame me for not trusting you? Why should I believe a fucking word you say?"

"I swear to God, Mr. Prager, I'll come in. I just want to get away from this guy. He's got a crazy temper. I thought he was going to kill me this morning."

"That's twice you've invoked God in this conversation, kid. Stop swearing to God and start giving me some proof I should trust you. Where did Martello get a tape of Patrick Maloney's voice?"

"I don't know. I swear to—Okay, forget that, but I really don't know. He hasn't let me in on any stuff that doesn't directly involve me. I don't even know why he hates you so much."

"That one I have the answer to. Who's the guy with the eye patch?" I asked.

"I don't know. I guess he's an old cop friend of Martello's dad. He drives me around some of the time. That's all I know about him. We don't talk much."

"All right, kid, come on in."

"No, you have to come get me." It was his turn to play hardball.

I thought about calling his bluff, but couldn't afford to let him get away again. Besides, if what he was saying about Martello's temper was accurate—I had every reason to believe it was—and he sensed the kid was ready to bolt, he would cut his losses and get rid of the hired help. Bottom line was, I needed the kid alive. Without him there was no case.

"You win. I'll come to you."

Silence. He was having second thoughts. He might be scared but he was also likely sacrificing the most money he'd ever made. I helped his thought process along.

"Listen, Patrick, I'll pay you to come in and I'll do my best to shield you from the cops."

"Twenty grand."

"That means he's paying you ten, some of which you've already received. Five," I said, "and I'll have it with me when I pick you up. If you help me put this cocksucker away, I'll take care of you."

"Okay. Two hours."

"Where?"

"I'm pretty close to you."

"That doesn't help me, kid." I wasn't going to call him Patrick again if I could avoid it.

"Manhattan Court, number sixty-nine, downstairs. It's a garden apartment that he rented for me."

"Manhattan Court over by Coney Island Hospital?"

"That's it."

"You *are* close. Two hours?"

"Bring the money," he said, all the big bad fear gone out of his voice.

I thought about calling Katy and Sarah, but I remembered what her shrink had said. I could serve this kid and Martello up on a silver tray and Katy would still resent me. She had to deal with her issues and I had to deal with mine. That worked for me, for the time being.

SQUEEZED IN BETWEEN Avenues Y and Z and perpendicular to Ocean Parkway, Manhattan Court was a small, forgettable block of post-Korean War garden apartments with a row of low-slung garages behind. The "gardens" out front were actually lawns of weeds cut low to give the illusion of grass. Each unit had a brick and concrete stoop just large enough to hold a few beach chairs and a portable charcoal grill. I suppose Manhattan Court and the surrounding blocks of garden apartments must once have seemed like a little bit of heaven in the concrete and asphalt world of Brooklyn. Now it seemed in need of repair or bulldozing.

I knew Manhattan Court because Crazy Charlie had lived there. Charlie and I went to Cunningham and Lincoln together. We called him Crazy Charlie because he would do shit no person with half a brain would do. You tell him you'd give him twenty bucks to climb the Parachute Jump and he'd say, "Fuck, yeah," and climb it. Most kids, me included, were afraid to climb the fence that surrounded the ride, but there was Crazy Charlie two hundred fifty feet in the air screaming for his twenty bucks.

He also tended to be loose with his fists. For him, one a day wasn't a vitamin, but a description of how many fights he averaged. Sometimes he took Sundays off. "I'm a good Catholic," he'd say. Crazy Charlie didn't care how big you were, who you were, or who you knew. If you pissed him off—and, trust me, it didn't take much to piss Crazy Charlie off—he was going to smack you. Of course, throwing the first punch didn't always equate to victory I'd seen Charlie get the shit kicked out of him on more than a few occasions. There's no future for guys like Crazy Charlie. Last few times I saw him was in the mid-'70s when I was still on the job. I'm walking by the holding pen at the Six-O and I hear someone calling my name.

"Moe fuckin' Prager, that you?"

"Crazy Charlie, what the fuck you doing in there?"

"I ain't Crazy Charlie no more, Moe. I mean, I'm still crazy, but it ain't dignified for a man, that name, you know what I'm saying?"

"What are you going by these days?"

"Charlie Rolex."

"Selling fake watches, huh?"

"Good fakes. But yeah, a man gotta make a livin' right?"

"Right."

"So you should come by one day and have a beer with me."

"You still on Manhattan Court?"

"Yeah. My dad bit the big one, but Mom's still kickin'."

"Okay, Charlie Rolex. I'll do that."

And I did.

When I went over to his house that last time, he was shirtless, wearing an army helmet, and drinking beer out of a mixing bowl. Oh, yeah, he also had a loaded police special on the table. He let me drink my beer out of the can and we talked about the nutty stuff he used to pull. After a few minutes of reminiscing, he leaned over to me conspiratorially and whispered, "You're a Jew, right?"

"You know I am, Charlie."

He looked around to make sure no one was listening. "You don't see any of your people in jail."

Well, actually I did, but Charlie wasn't up for a debate.

"No, Charlie, you don't."

"See, that's what I'm saying."

Frankly, I had no idea what he was saying and I got out of there a little while later with fake Rolexes for Aaron, Miriam, and me. They all broke the first time we put them on. A few years later I heard Charlie had taken to living on the streets. From there it was only a short drop off the edge of the earth into oblivion. Like I said, there's never any future for guys like Charlie Rolex.

I put Charlie right out of my head the minute I turned left onto Manhattan Court from East 6th Street. Carmella and Brian Doyle were probably already here. I told them to park blocks away and walk into their positions: Carmella across the way on the even side of the street and Brian Doyle atop the garages around back. There was good reason for the precautions. Martello hadn't shown up for his shift that day—neglecting to call in sick—nor, apparently, had he returned to his house in Great River. Missing a shift without calling in meant he was getting sloppy, and sloppiness from a guy like Martello was a sure sign of desperation. To me it felt like he was preparing to cover his ass and that meant trouble for the kid.

I scanned the cars parked on both sides of the street. I had already circled the surrounding blocks a few times checking for pewter Yukons. None in sight. It was a good sign, but didn't mean Martello hadn't taken the same precautions as Carmella and Doyle. He was, after all, a cop and knew what we knew. At this juncture, however, I was certain he would be more concerned with being expeditious than judicious. I parked my car directly in front of number sixty-nine, collected the kid's five grand, and got out. Traffic was streaming in both directions along Ocean Parkway as I stepped up onto the stoop. I found comfort in the din of the traffic. I felt for the bulge at the small of my back and found comfort in that too.

The heavier front door pushed right back, exposing the staircase that led up to the second floor apartment and, on my right, the door to the kid's apartment. Ignoring the bell, I rapped my knuckles hard on the kid's door and waited. I could hear the sound of the TV coming through the door, but no footsteps.

"Hey, kid! Patrick, it's me. Open up." I wasn't shouting exactly. I tried the bell and waited a minute. Still no footsteps. I called the kid's cell phone. I heard ringing through the door. The ringing stopped when I hung up. I dialed Carmella.

"What?" she whispered.

"Maybe trouble."

"You want me to come across the—"

"No, stay put and keep your eyes open. I think the kid may have bolted or is ready to bolt. Call Brian and give him the heads-up."

"Okay."

I knocked again. Nothing. I tried the doorknob. It turned easily and the door fell back, but stopped after only a few inches. A dim shaft of light filtered through into the dark hallway. I pushed harder without completely shouldering the door and it moved a bit more, but not much. There was definitely something propped against the other side. I peeked through the four inches of space I'd managed to clear and was relieved not to see arms and legs. While I still couldn't look around the door to see what was blocking it, I saw the kid's cell phone on a beat-up coffee table. The sound from inside had come from a boombox stereo sitting on the bare wood floor, not from a TV.

"Kid. Patrick. Come on, it's me, Moe," I called, a little more urgency in my voice this time. No response. I hit the door square with my right shoulder and it gave way. I patted the wall for a light switch and found one. An overhead fixture came on and I saw the red plastic milk crate full of dumbbells and weights that had held the door shut.

I was standing in the living room. The coffee table and the boombox were the only things in there. This apartment had the same layout I remembered from Crazy Charlie's. There was a dining room ahead and to my right, a galley kitchen off that, a hallway to the left of the dining room with a bathroom on the right, a large bedroom on the left, and a small bedroom at the end of the hall. I slid my arm around my back, under my jacket, and pulled the .38 from its holster. I knelt down and killed the music.

"Kid. Patrick. I've got your five grand in my pocket."

I took the slow, measured steps of a tightrope walker, letting my gun hand lead. The dining room and kitchen were clear. There was no furniture in the dining room and no food in the kitchen. The living room closet set beneath the stairs up to the second floor was empty. When I stepped into the hallway a little gust of wind hit me square in the face. There must have been a window open in one of the bedrooms. A thunderstorm had been brewing all day and I smelled its inevitability in the air. There was another scent in the breeze that I couldn't quite make out.

The bathroom was the size of a closet and nothing much larger than a water bug could have hidden in there. The small bedroom was even more empty than the other rooms. It was totally barren except for cobwebs and the window was shut tight. No one had set foot in the room for weeks. The uncorrupted layer of dust on the floor told me as much. Stepping back toward the last unexplored room in the house, I caught another rush of air. Now I knew what that other scent was hiding behind the humid musk of the storm: blood.

"I'm coming in there, motherfucker!" I screamed like a madman and kicked the door above the knob. The door flew away and I ran in blind, fueled by fear and weeks of frustration. Crazy Charlie would have been proud of me. Not five feet through the door I tripped over something and crashed to the floor. Looking back, I saw what had taken my feet out from under me. This time, it wasn't a fawn.

When I crawled over to the kid, my hand slid in a pool of what I supposed was his blood. It wasn't warm, exactly, but it was fresh. I held my bloody palm up near my face. In the dimness, the blood almost looked like chocolate syrup. I put my other hand over the kid's heart and got nothing. He was still warm, as warm as he would ever again be. I found his neck. There was no pulse to feel. As I stood up, lightning flashed and I caught a glimpse of the kid. I didn't have to see him clearly to know he was dead. I found the light switch.

The kid's shirtless body lay so that his open eyes seemed to be looking straight through the ceiling, through the roof, into infinity. *How's the view, kid?* There wasn't a lot of blood anywhere except around his body, but the only visible wound was a long, diagonal gash across his liver. The blood that had seeped out of it was thick and dark. Yet as grisly as the gash was, I couldn't believe it could account for all the blood puddled on the floor. My bet was the detectives would find some nasty wounds in his back when they rolled him over. I dialed 911 and listened to myself talk to the operator as if from another room.

I didn't quite know what to do with myself. I was frozen, as incapable of movement as the kid. He did indeed resemble Patrick, but from here, in the stark light, it was clear he was no twin. He even looked a little different from that morning. I suppose getting murdered will do that to you. I knew he wasn't Patrick, not my Patrick, but his death dredged it all up again and the past twenty-two years—the lies, the secrets, and deceptions—came crashing down around me. Only this time it came down all at once. I tried distracting myself, gazing around the room at anything but the body.

There was an unfurled sleeping bag, a few pairs of jeans, some rock t-shirts from bands I never heard of, and two pair of those stupid Shinjo Olympians. The window was wide open and I thought I could already hear sirens, an army of sirens, coming my way. The wail of the sirens unfroze me and I stepped into the living room to wait. *Living room.* The phrase took on new meaning. Outside rain fell in solid sheets.

I must have been hallucinating about the sirens, because it took ten minutes for the first unit to arrive. The two uniforms were named Kurtz and Fong. Kurtz was nearly as old as me, too old to still be in a uniform without stripes, and Fong was a fresh-faced Asian kid trying hard to act blasé. By the time they came in, I had sufficiently recovered my wits and had since called Carmella and Brian and filled them in. I told them to stay away as the situation was going to get complicated enough without involving them. I did ask Carmella to give one of our lawyer contacts a heads-up.

I had my old badge out to show the uniforms. Neither Kurtz nor Fong were much impressed. After they patted me down, removing my .38 from its holster, checking out my wallet and credentials, we got to know each other a little. I didn't bother going into great detail about the reasons for my being at 69 Manhattan Court. *I was a licensed PI working a case. Blah, blah, blah ...* They seemed satisfied I hadn't killed the kid. *Yeah, Prager, whatever ...* Besides, making the case wasn't their headache.

"Hey," I said, "what took you guys so long to get here? I thought I heard sirens almost immediately after I called."

Both uniforms turned to each other and laughed. I must have missed the joke.

"Aren't there any fucking chairs in this place for a man to sit down?" Kurtz whined, rubbing his lower back.

"Nope."

"You did hear sirens," he said, still unhappy about the lack of chairs.

"We were right around the corner. You notice how wet we are?" Fong asked.

"Now that you mention it."

The bottoms of their trousers were dark with rain and beads of water covered the bills of their caps.

Kurtz shook his head. "My partner's not exaggerating. We had a traffic fatality at Avenue Y and Ocean Parkway. A guy ran right out into the traffic and got launched. When he came down he skidded and then got pancaked by like four other vehicles. It was ugly."

"Sounds it."

"Yeah, ugly," Fong agreed with his partner's assessment. "And really too bad. The guy was a cop."

That got my attention. "A cop?"

Kurtz sneered. "Yeah, if you consider them glorified, overpaid motherfuckin' meter maids in Suffolk County cops."

My heart was doing that jumping into my throat thing again. "A Suffolk cop?"

"A sergeant," said Fong.

"Was his name Ray Martello?"

Both Fong and Kurtz looked at me like Jesus walking on water. Lightning flashed again. If thunder followed the lightning, I didn't hear it. I thought I heard the rain falling.

CHAPTER NINETEEN

I SAT WITH Paul Dukelsky in an interrogation room at the Six-One precinct on Coney Island Avenue. The Duke, as he was known around the city's courthouses, was one of the best criminal defense attorneys in New York. Dukelsky was a shark with a square jaw, green eyes, and a good heart. For every rich scumbag he defended, there were two or three wrongly convicted men now walking the streets. We had done some work for his firm, but not enough to warrant his driving in from the Hamptons to play my white knight. That was Carmella's doing. Like most straight men with a pulse and a libido, he had a thing for my partner. Good looks and confidence are magnetic qualities in any woman, but when she carries a gun and can probably kick your ass … well, then, that's something else.

"So, Moe, let's go over this again," the Duke instructed, looking down at his wrist. I wasn't sure if he was checking the time or his tan. I did know he hadn't gotten his watch from Charlie Rolex.

"No."

"No?"

"No. Between you and the cops, I've been over this twenty times. The details aren't going to change. Ray Martello killed the kid, not me. Call Sheriff Vandervoort in Janus. Call my wife's doctors, for chrissakes! They'll tell you what's been going on. I've had it. It's what, like seven in the morn—"

"Eight-ten," Dukelsky corrected me.

"I'm exhausted and hungry and I'm not doing this anymore."

"As your attorney, I must insist you—"

"Go take Carmella out for breakfast or something and leave me the fuck alone."

He flushed red. I'd hit a nerve. "I don't see what that has to do with anything, Moe. I'm not here to discuss Carmella and me."

"I didn't know there *was* a Carmella and you."

He bowed his head, clearly trying to regroup. It never failed. Beauty and desire cut through the bullshit. For all the trappings of success, the Duke was, on the inside, like every other man I knew: an insecure fifteen-year-old boy who wanted to sleep with the prettiest girl in school.

"Listen, Moe ... I wanted to talk to you about—"

There was a knock on the door. Whoever was on the other side didn't bother waiting for permission before stepping into the room. It was Detective Feeney with Carmella Melendez in tow. Feeney was old school right down to his brush-cut gray hair, white shirt, and squeaky black shoes. He smelled of cigarettes and coffee and wore an expression that bespoke a perpetual sour stomach. The detective had his face in a file even as he walked. Carmella's expression was hard to read.

"Looks like you were right about Martello," Feeney said, pitching the file on the desk. "We've tentatively matched a hunting knife we found on his body with the weapon used to kill the kid. And there's a bloody sole print by the bedroom window that's a match for the shoes he was wearing. And I just got off the phone with that Vandervoort guy upstate. He confirmed your story."

"Do you have an identity on the kid?"

"The vic? John James, born August 18, 1981, San Pedro, California. He's got a sheet. Arrested several times by the LAPD for everything from shoplifting to sword swallowing, if you catch my meaning."

"That was his name, John James? Did he have an alias?" I asked.

"If he did," Feeney said, scanning the file, "it's not on his sheet. Why?"

"Nothing. Forget it." It was stupid, I know, but I was pissed off that the kid had lied to me about his name. I think maybe I was madder at myself for believing him. No one likes being played for a fool.

"We found Martello's Yukon parked on Ave Y. The sick bastard had human remains in the vehicle, a bag of bones complete with skull."

"My brother-in-law?"

"Probably. That'll take a few days to confirm. We'll be a week going over the stuff he had inside that SUV. All I know is, this guy musta hated you something wicked to go through this rigmarole. It was me and I wanted revenge, I'da just shot you."

Dukelsky's eyes got big. "I'm certain my client takes great comfort in that knowledge, Detective Feeney."

"Hey, I knew Martello's old man, the captain. He was an asshole too, but this is some crazy shit the son was doing. He made a cottage industry outta revenge."

"Is Mr. Prager free to go now, Detective Feeney?"

Feeney winked at me. "Sure, but don't go to the South Seas until this is all buttoned down, okay?"

He shook my hand and Carmella's, wished us both luck. Dukelsky was smart enough not to offer up his hand. Feeney was the type of cop who had no use for lawyers and would have told Dukelsky to shove his hand up his ass.

Outside, the wind in the wake of the thunderstorms was crisp, almost autumnal, but the strength of the sun, even this early in the morning, put the lie to that. The three of us stood there in front of the precinct. I just wanted to get home, take a shower, and get some sleep. I didn't care who drove me back to my car. Dukelsky kept looking at his watch, but didn't seem that anxious to leave. Carmella still had that funky, unreadable expression on her face.

"Would you guys like to go to breakfast? My treat," said the lawyer.

"No, thanks. I just need somebody to drive me back to my car before I collapse."

Carmella sighed with relief. "I'll take you. Come on."

"Just as well," Dukelsky said, "I've got to get back to Sag Harbor." He was lying and rather unskillfully at that.

"Thanks, Paul," I said, shaking his hand. "I can't thank you enough for helping me out. Send me the bill. I'm sorry about getting cranky in there. It's been a rough couple of weeks for me."

"Tell me about it. Don't worry about the bill."

"Okay then."

"So long, Carmella," he said.

"Bye, Paul."

Carmella drove me toward my house and not to my car. She said she would just arrange to have my car driven to my house and that she didn't trust me to drive in my present state. I didn't argue. I fell asleep before we made it to Sheepshead Bay Road.

CHAPTER TWENTY

THE SUN WASN'T particularly bright nor the sky severely blue. The clouds that drifted overhead weren't shaped like angels' wings nor were they ominous and gray. The wind blew, but only enough to disappoint. It was a plain summer's day that no one would ever sing about or write a poem about or paint a picture of. In this way, it was like most days of most lives: a nearly blank page in a forgotten diary. I think if we could remember our individual days, life wouldn't seem so fleeting. But we aren't built to work that way, are we? We are built to forget.

The Maloney family plot was, as Father Blaney had pointed out on that dreary Sunday in the rain, a pretty place to be laid to rest. And the priest, in spite of himself, presided over the third burial of Patrick Michael Maloney. It was a small gathering: Katy, Sarah, Pete Vandervoort, and me. I had thought to invite Aaron and Miriam and their families, but Sarah confided in me that she had had to lobby her mother just to let me come. Katy was still pretty delicate, her feelings raw, nerves close to the surface. We all had new things to work through.

Wisely, Katy had waited for the press to lose interest before putting her little brother into the ground for a last time. It was a hot story, but only briefly. Most of the reporting focused on the sensational aspects of the kid's homicide and the Martellos'—senior and junior—history of misdeeds. There were only a few oblique references to my involvement and nothing about Katy. I'm sure the press would have made more of it if they could have, but no one was talking. A story is like a fire, rob it of oxygen and it dies. Y.W. Fenn taught me that.

No one claimed the kid's body and John James was buried out in a field somewhere with the rest of the unclaimed, unwanted, and anonymous human refuse New York City seemed so proficient at collecting. I think in my younger days I might have made some gesture, maybe to pay for a decent burial or to find the kid's people. Not this time, not anymore. My time for the useless grand gesture had come and gone. I just couldn't muster much sympathy for the kid, even if he had gotten in too deep and hadn't meant to hurt anyone. It was petty, I know, but I was still pissed at his lying to me about his name. I also couldn't ignore the fact that his antics had helped shatter whatever fragile bonds that remained between Katy and me after the divorce. Sure, things might someday have collapsed under their own weight, but I would never know that now. Ray Martello had his revenge.

The day after the murder, I put in a call to Mary White to let her know how things had turned out. The awkwardness between us that began during my visit to Dayton had a long shelf life. I heard the strain in her voice during our conversation. I guess she just wanted to move on after all these years. Who could blame her? I wanted the same thing. There was genuine surprise in her voice when I told her about Martello's revenge.

"Really?" she said. "The police are certain it was him?"

"One hundred percent. His car was full of evidence linking him not only to the murdered boy, but to the plot itself. There were cash receipts, fake IDs, just a ton of stuff."

"If you're sure then …"

"Well, yeah. Jack's grave will be left alone from now on. I'm sorry for your troubles. Be well, Mary."

Blaney kept it short and managed not to scowl during the graveside service. Maybe the priest did have a heart. Still, he used it sparingly. Fallon hung back, waiting for us to clear out before filling in the earth atop Patrick's newest coffin. The caretaker had already done a masterful job of repairing the damage to the plot. The grass bore none of the scars of the desecrations, the hedges were trim and perfect, but Fallon was no miracle worker. It would be another month before my father-in-law's new headstone arrived, so Fallon had fashioned a serviceable wooden cross to mark the grave. The simple cross suited him well. In the end, Mr. Roth was right; Kaddish and ashes was the way to go.

With the last *Amen* of the day, the Prager family of Sheepshead Bay, Brooklyn, New York, broke fully and finally apart. I found myself thinking of what Howard Bland nee Judas Wannsee had said a few days back about the soft tissue of dinosaurs and how it was lost to history. So it was for us, the bonds that had tied us together as one were gone. In the grand scheme of things, the dissolution of my family was no more significant than the death of a may fly. The earth kept turning. There was now only Katy and Sarah, Sarah and me. I pulled Sarah aside.

"Listen, hon, I'm going to get out of here."

"I think that's best, Dad. Mom will be okay. This is her shit she's dealing with. Someday she'll be okay and we can be—get together, the three of us. What are you smiling at?"

"You really are the best of us, kiddo. So what are you going to do?"

"I'm going to stay with Mom until mid-August, then I'll head back up to school."

"I don't suppose the cute deputy sheriff has anything to do with your staying up here."

She cat-grinned. "Robby? Maybe a little."

"Stay away from cops. They're nothing but trouble."

"Not all of them." Sarah slipped into my arms and kissed me on the cheek. "Not you, Dad."

"Me most of all."

"I love you."

"Me too. Come down and visit before you go."

I watched Sarah and Katy get into Katy's car and drive off. Sarah looked back at me. Katy never did.

CHAPTER TWENTY-ONE

I HAD HEARD that it was possible for a man to float on quicksand, but I didn't know if it was possible for a man to walk across it. I couldn't have anticipated that I was about to find out.

The page was turning on the first week of August when Sarah came down to Brooklyn on the day after her birthday. We went to dinner at a Thai place in Sheepshead Bay, had Carvel for dessert, then we drove into Coney Island to ride the Cyclone and the Wonder Wheel. The Cyclone was great. I must've ridden it a thousand times since I was a kid. On the other hand, I despised the Wonder Wheel. I never met a Ferris wheel I liked and the Wonder Wheel was my least favorite. For one thing, it was gigantic and it had big cars that rocked and slid along rails as the huge wheel turned. My daughter always took perverse pleasure in watching me go pale and squirm.

"You crack me up, Dad. You'll ride any rickety, crappy, old roller coaster, but this thing scares you."

"I just always feel like the bottom's going to drop out."

Sarah clucked at me like a chicken.

"How's your mom?"

"Nice segue," she said.

"Seriously."

"She was doing well for the first week or so after the burial, now ... I don't know. She's been really quiet and to herself for the last couple of days. Kinda nervous and jumpy. I guess she's just got stuff to work through."

"I suppose. You all set to get back to school?"

"Yeah." Sarah frowned.

"Robby can come visit, you know?"

"No fooling you, huh, Dad?"

"Nope."

We had Nathan's hot dogs for a nightcap and Sarah dropped me back at my condo. She made some noise about wanting to get back up to Janus to see Robby, which was probably true, but I could tell she was worried about Katy. I hugged her tight, then let her go. I was doing a lot of that lately, letting go.

When I got inside, my answering machine was winking at me. I gave serious consideration to not listening. Aaron was pissed at me because I extended the time I'd taken off to work the case into a vacation. When he started ranting, I reminded him about what he had said about the stores thriving without me for twenty years. He didn't much care for my throwing his own words back at him. It was a big brother vs. little brother thing. Still, I've never been good at avoidance or procrastination. Bad news was better than no news. I pressed PLAY.

First message:

"Hello, Moe, it's me, Connie Geary … Oh, this is terribly awkward, isn't it? I'll just say it then. Truthfully, I got tired of waiting for you to call me, so I decided to call you. I hope you weren't simply humoring me that day when you said we could have dinner together. It was great seeing you and it brought back the happiest times of my life. Let's say you pick me up on Friday at eight. If I don't hear from you between now and then, I'll assume we're on. Okay then, that's Friday the eleventh at eight."

It had been a long time since I had that nervous feeling in my belly. Suddenly, I was back in high school again, staring at the phone, trying to summon up the courage to ask a girl out. Oh, God, the terror of those days. I had the phone in my hand even before listening to the second message. I put it down.

I wasn't going to live out the rest of my life in monk's robes and if I was going to be dating again, Constance Geary was a hell of a start. We had shared history, people in common, things to talk about. There wouldn't be any of those endless, awful silences to be filled in with uncomfortable stares or panicky trips to the rest rooms. And Connie was certainly pleasant enough to look at.

Next message:

"Yo, Five-O, dis Marlon Rhodes, man … You remember me … from Cincinnati? We talked once 'bout dat crazy lady, Jack White's sista. I got all up in your face and shit. Dat was a bad day when y'all called me. You still interested, I can be put in a better mood, if y'all hear what I'm sayin'."

End of new messages.

I heard what he was saying, all right, but that ship had sailed. Poor

Marlon had missed his big payday. Yet, I couldn't help but wonder why he'd chosen today to call.

I OPENED MY eyes on the Irish Wolfhound of dog days. It was nearly a hundred degrees by noon and the humidity was beyond ridiculous. You could have baked French bread on the sidewalk and grown orchids in your car. Even the stop signs were wilting. When I was a kid, this weather never bothered me. Back then, summer weather divided up only two ways: it was either raining or it wasn't; you could play ball or you couldn't. It was simple. Life was simple. My biggest concern was how many innings of stickball I could pitch. Nothing was simple now, especially not sleep.

Sleep was heavy on my mind because I woke up in worse shape than when I went to bed. After sending Sarah on her way, I hadn't been able to get to sleep and then, when sleep finally came, it kicked my ass. I tried blaming it on the weather. That was total bullshit. My condo was as cold as a meat locker. No, something was up besides the heat and humidity. It wasn't the stress of the final breakup or Sarah's impending return to school. It wasn't even those damned phone calls, though they were part of it. Connie's call made me happy and nervous. Marlon Rhodes' made me curious. Curious had its dangers.

The truth was that had I never received either call, I still wouldn't have slept well. I hadn't slept well since the day John James was murdered. I knew it was ridiculous, but it still bugged me that the kid lied about his name. I made the mistake of sharing that information with Carmella.

"Are you out of your fucking mind?"

"I told you I knew it was dumb."

"Dumb! This isn't dumb. This is stupid. I would never have closed a case if I looked for every little thing to make me miserable. The stars don't ever align the way you think they should."

"But why would he lie to me? He had nothing to gain from it."

"C'mon, Moe. You're looking for logic where there is none. The kid was a piece of shit. He was in the game. You know what hustlers are like. He lied because that's what skells do. It's a reflex, they don't think it out."

The cop's blanket answer for everything. I had known all of that before she said it. I'd uttered versions of it several times myself. I even agreed with her, yet …

I WAS WISE enough not to share with Detective Feeney the reason I asked him to lunch. We met at a Chinese restaurant on Avenue U near

Ocean Avenue. His choice. He was already seated in a red vinyl booth when I arrived. He was dressed as he was the first time we met: white shirt, same polyester tie. His hair must've been made of real bristles the way that brush cut stood up to the humidity. We shook hands and stared at the menus. I don't understand why people stare at Chinese menus. They always know what they're going to order.

"Food good here?"

"Who cares? The air conditioning's great." Feeney grinned.

Feeney was old school down to what he ordered: egg drop soup, chicken chow mein, and pork fried rice. Christ, it was like eating with my parents. I ordered crispy duck that wasn't especially crispy and was barely duck.

"So," he said, shoveling a fork full of fried rice into his mouth, "does this mean we're goin' steady?"

"I just wanted to say thanks for not making it as hard on me as you could have."

"Don't bullshit me, Prager." Funny, I had said those same words to the kid. "You got a bug up your ass about something. Wait ..." He put down his fork, wiped his mouth with his linen napkin, and then reached under his chair. "You wanna take a look at the file, right?"

"I do."

"Last person who said those words to me had my children."

"From me, you'll have to settle for the chow mein," I said.

He plopped the file on the table, but kept his forearm across it. "Before I let you take a look-see, I just wanna give you a chance to forget it, to finish your meal and walk away."

"And why would I do that?"

He tapped the folder with stubby fingers. "Because you ain't gonna find what you're lookin' for in here. The only thing you're gonna find is unhappiness."

"How do you know what I'm looking for?"

"I know. Believe me, Prager, I know. You think you're the first ex-cop I ever dealt with?" Feeney didn't wait for an answer. "Ask your partner, Melendez, she'll tell you."

"She already did."

"See, this here file contains the answers to questions of what and when, but that ain't what you want. You don't wanna know a what or a when. You wanna know a why. Am I right or am I right?"

"Right. But why agree to have lunch?"

"I was hungry."

"Very funny, but why do this for me?"

"I didn't do it for you. I did it for me, so I can get some peace. If I didn't let you see it, you'd be calling me with all sorts a stupid questions.

Eventually, you'd show up with a court order and I don't got time for that shit. I got cases on my desk from the year of the flood. This way, I figured to save me a lot of time and grief."

I didn't argue. Why argue with the truth? When I reached for the file, however, his arm didn't budge.

"Last chance, Prager. Take my advice. There's only more unhappiness waitin' for you in here."

"I'll take my chances."

"First, I wanna know what's eatin' you. Then you can see the file."

I guess I blushed a little bit.

"That stupid, huh?" he said. "Oh, this is gonna be good."

I explained about the kid lying to me about his name. Feeney had enough respect to let me finish before he started laughing. When he got done wiping the tears from his eyes, he slid the file across the table.

We didn't speak again for another quarter hour. During that time, Feeney finished his meal, had a dish of pistachio ice cream and a plate of pineapple chunks. When I was done, I slid the file back across the table to him.

"You satisfied?" he said, patting his full belly. "What'd I tell you? It's as solid a case as I ever made. We got every kinda evidence against Ray Martello that's ever been invented and then some."

"Yeah, it was like he wrapped himself up in a neat little package for you and then by getting himself squished, saved the mess of a trial. No loose ends. Nice and tidy. Pretty convenient all the way around."

"Perfect."

"Yeah, maybe a little too perfect," I said.

"What's that supposed to mean?"

"Let's take a ride."

Feeney agreed, a look of resignation on his face. My guess was he knew this was coming and he had already cleared a few hours to waste with me.

I PARKED MY car on Avenue Y in approximately the same spot Ray Martello had parked his Yukon on the night he killed the kid. As I slipped into the space, Feeney's resigned expression reshaped itself into a knowing smile. When I unlocked the doors, he didn't move.

He said, "Where're you goin'? We can do this in here in the air conditioning, you know?"

"Do what?"

"Weren't you gonna ask me to explain why Martello would park his SUV on the west side of Ocean Parkway while he committed the homicide on the east side? That's six busy lanes of traffic he had to cross at night to make his escape, right? Why would he do that? Then you were gonna point out to me that most of the witnesses, includin' the drivers that hit him, swear Ray Martello was runnin' not away from the crime scene but towards it when he got smacked. Am I right?"

"You know you are," I said.

"See, Prager, it's all those why questions, they're gonna make you miserable. I don't know why he parked his Yukon here. Maybe he couldn't get a spot on the other side of Ocean Parkway or maybe he didn't want anyone to notice his car. Why was he running the wrong way? Maybe he thought he forgot something at the crime scene. Maybe he got disoriented because he didn't know Brooklyn so good. Maybe because really killing someone ain't as easy as people think and it fucks 'em up a little. Maybe because he had twice the legal limit of alcohol in his bloodstream mixed with Xanax. You see, I don't have to know why he did those things. I only have to know that he did them."

"What about the alcohol and Xanax?"

"What about them?" Feeney asked. "You ever kill anybody?"

"No."

"You think if you were gonna have to kill someone you knew in cold blood, and a kid at that, that you might have to fortify yourself a little? I know I would."

"But he had enough alcohol and drugs in him to make an elephant loopy."

"He was a cop, not a pharmacist, Prager. Besides, maybe that's why he was disoriented and ran in the wrong direction."

What he said was making sense and it made me realize how silly and desperate I must have sounded, but I guess I'd already passed the point of caring just how silly.

"Did he have a prescription for the Xanax?" I asked.

"You're shittin' me, right? We can drive into your old precinct and within twenty minutes I could buy enough Xanax, Valium, methadone, and Oxycontin to put out a herd of fuckin' elephants. Trust me, Prager, as a brother cop and as a guy who's seen a lot of good men torture themselves over stupid details, leave it be. The answers you're lookin' for, you ain't gonna find here, not on these streets, not in that file. Ray Martello was a sick bastard who was willin' to go a long way to get his revenge. He killed the kid, panicked, and ran into traffic. End of story. You're never gonna know why the kid lied to you about his name. He just did."

I was almost ready to give in, but not yet. "What about this mysterious guy who drove the kid around, Martello's friend with the eye patch? You haven't been able to find him."

"Frankly, we haven't been lookin' real hard. Maybe he exists, maybe he doesn't. Bottom line, the people who matter in this case are dead," Feeney said, running out of patience.

"And the bloody shoe print … Why was there only one? Martello had to cross almost the entire length of the room to get out the back window, but he only left one print."

"'Cause Martello was part kangaroo and hopped to the window. Remember, I don't have to know why. There was only one print because there was only one print. Drive me back to the Six-One now, okay? You can keep a set of the autopsy photos as a memento of our date, but playtime is officially over."

When I dropped him back at the precinct, he thanked me again for lunch and warned me not to call him about the case. I promised I wouldn't, but I had my fingers crossed.

DURING MY RIDE into Brooklyn Heights, I went over everything Detective Feeney had said. The thing of it was, he was right. With Ray Martello and the kid dead, I could research the hell out of their histories, interview everyone who ever knew them, put their lives under the world's most powerful microscope, and I would still be asking why. It dawned on me, that the real question of why didn't have to do with the kid lying to me about his name, but about why I cared. I thought about what the late Israel Roth would have said vis-a-vis my state of mind.

"Mr. Moe," he'd say, "you are hanging onto the case because you don't want to let Katy go. Patrick bound the two of you together as powerfully, more powerfully maybe than wedding vows or gold rings. When in the hospital you told her about the fake Patrick and she got so angry, it was the same. It's like this number on my forearm, even if you could scrub it away, I would still be bound, for good or bad, to my past. If you said to me, come Izzy, I could get that thing removed, I'm not sure I would go."

It's funny, even when I imagined the words Mr. Roth might say, I heard his voice in my head. I put my hand to my mouth. I was smiling. By the time I got into the office, the weight of the whys had lifted. I walked directly into Devo's command center and released him from wasting any more time on my preoccupation.

"Devo, forget working on any of that stuff related to Katy's brother and tackle the backlog. We have to make some money around here with paying customers."

"Are you quite sure, Moe? I have sharpened some of the—"

"Forget it, I'm moving on. Just bag the stuff up and I'll return it."

"Okay."

Carmella was in her office and was standing by a file cabinet when she told me to come in. I couldn't help but stare. She followed my eyes.

"You're showing a little," I said.

"You're grinning like an idiot, Moe."

I didn't say anything, but walked up to her and reached out my hand to feel her little belly. I stopped myself. People often don't realize what an incredibly intimate and loaded gesture it is to place your hand on a pregnant woman's abdomen. It's reaffirming, connective, even sexual. I remembered complete strangers touching Katy without a thought of asking permission when she was pregnant with Sarah. It's almost instinctive, tribal, at least.

"It's okay for you to touch me."

And I did. She placed her hand on top of mine. "You're keeping it," I said.

"I am. It's a pretty amazing thing to have someone growing inside you."

"Now *you're* grinning like an idiot."

"Am I?" She blushed.

"We are going to have to rearrange things around here, if this little girl's go—"

"—boy. Little boy. I know it."

"If this little boy's going to get a healthy start."

She removed her hand from mine. "We'll talk about it when the time comes."

"Fair enough," I said.

Her grin faded as suddenly as it had appeared and her mood darkened. "Moe, I guess I should tell you that the baby is—"

"—Dukelsky's. I know. I knew the minute he showed up at the Six-One. It was a guilty favor he was doing. It all fit together. I think he tried to talk to me about you two, but I stopped him."

"Some of the things I said about him, they were … not fair. He just doesn't want a baby now or to get married. He's been married and divorced and has two kids. I don't want to marry him anyway. This was my fault. I chased him, Moe. I have for years."

"Why?" There was that question again. "You could have any man you want."

She brushed the back of her hand against my cheek. "No, I can't."

"Come on, Carmella, let's not do this again."

"That's right." Her eyes burned. "We can't be together because it makes too much sense. We can't be together because of your rules. Because some man raped me as a little girl, because it was you who saved my life, because my parents changed my name, because I lied to you about who

168

I was, because I got my shield and you didn't, because your wife tossed you to the curb, be—"

"Stop it!"

"Get out of my office!" she hissed. "Get out of here. At least Paul was honest with himself and me. Get out!"

Down on Court Street, the air was thick enough to swim through. Truck fumes coagulated around bits of dust, falling to the asphalt like volcanic ash. People on the sidewalk were defeated. A city bus stopped in front of me. A pair of brown eyes much like Carmella's stared out at me from an ad on the side of the bus. The eyes were set in the face of a watch. The copy read: *Timing isn't everything. It's the only thing. Harmony Watches.*

"Kiss my ass," I heard myself mutter. So too, apparently, did the woman standing next to me. She just shook her head no.

CHAPTER TWENTY-TWO

THE HEAT BROKE while I slept, massive thunderstorms washing away the haze and defeat. I bought a cup of coffee, walked across the street, and watched the fishing boats set out for blues or porgies or whatever else was foolish enough to bite at the thousands of tangled lines dropped into the Atlantic off the coast of New Jersey or Montauk. The decks were packed with beer-for-breakfast buddies full of good cheer and anticipation. A little chop on the water would wipe away those smiles in an instant, but for now the world was perfect. The boats' throaty motors revved up and one by one they headed directly into the rising sun. One hour down, the rest of my life to go.

As tired of the wine business as I was, I didn't do well with spare time. I'd made sure to never really have a lot of it. Between the wine stores and the agency and Katy and Sarah, I managed to keep myself pretty much occupied. But now with Sarah staying in Ann Arbor most of the year and with my more recent exile from Katy-ville, spare time seemed like it was going to be a bigger part of my life. I had at least the next two weeks off and I was bored silly an hour into my day. In the short term, my date with Connie couldn't get here soon enough. In the long term, Carmella getting fat with child would mean more work for me at the agency. *Hallelujah! Praise the Lord!*

I bought every newspaper I could find, another cup of coffee, and headed back upstairs to read myself blind. The phone machine came to my rescue. I was halfway hoping it was Aaron or Klaus needing me to fill in at one of the stores, but it was a confused and impatient Marlon Rhodes wondering why I hadn't taken him up on his offer. This time I called him back. I got his machine.

"Mr. Rhodes, this is Moe Prager returning your—"

"Yo, yo, yo! Marlon here, man." He referred to himself in the third person.

"Sorry I didn't get back to you sooner."

"So, y'all still interested in Mr. White's crazy-ass sista?"

"Depends."

"Man, don't play me like dat."

"How should I play you?"

"I play for pay, man."

"Yeah, I figured that out already. I got no problem with paying if I get a taste of what it is I'm paying for. But I have to warn you, Marlon, I'm not nearly as interested as I was that first time we spoke."

He thought about that a second. "Fair 'nough."

"I'm listening."

"Mr. White, he was a good man. He really gave a shit 'bout his students and all. Helped me out with money sometimes too. Got me into treatment and everything, f'all the good dat did. When he died, his sista tried to make us into like some fucked up little family, havin' us over for dinners and shit, but she wasn't like Mr. White. She was all spooky Jesus and shit. She be playin' us like old cassette tapes of Mr. White wishing her Happy Birthday or Merry Christmas. It was weird, man, hearin' his voice and all. Then she get judgmental and shit, tryin' to tell us all how to act. Mr. White, he wasn't never dat way."

"These cassette tapes, were they only Jack's voice?"

"Mostly, but sometimes there was this other man on there."

"Patrick?"

"If you say so. He was young. I *can* say dat. Been a long time, man."

My heart was racing and my mind was a blur.

"Yo, Five-O, y'all still there?"

"Sorry, Marlon. I got distracted there a second. What happened with these dinners?"

"Without Mr. White, most of us, we went our own ways. Some of us went farther then others, if y'all hear what I'm sayin'."

I read between the lines. "How long a stretch did you do?"

"Ten year bid in Kentucky for movin' a little rock."

"That's a long time inside."

"Man, when y'all doin' nigga time in Kentucky, ten minutes a long time inside."

"I can imagine."

"No, you can't."

Touché. "So what happened?

"I don't hear from his sista again until like eight weeks ago. I guess she heard I sometimes still went out to the cemetery. Dat's how she got my number, from one of the others."

"What did she say?"

"She all nice and shit now, sayin' how she appreciates me still visitin' her brother and all."

"But …"

"But dat she askin' everybody not to go out to the cemetery for a few weeks. She say some shit about them doin' some ground work."

"That's weird."

"I told you, man. She crazy."

"Marlon, I gotta ask. Why didn't you talk to me when I first called you and why'd you wait until now to call back?"

He didn't answer. It was price-setting time, but I didn't feel like haggling.

"How much?" I said.

"Five hundred."

"Sold. Now let's hear it."

"Y'ail think I'm some kinda fool nigga? Dat was way too easy. My price goin' up."

"Don't mistake my impatience with stupidity, Marlon. I'll throw you another hundred, but then the bank's closing forever. There's a limit to how much I'm willing to spend to satisfy my curiosity."

"Okay, cool. Six hundred."

"Six hundred," I repeated. "So what took you so long to call me back?"

"She call me last Friday, all apologetic and religious and shit. Kept sayin' she was sorry and dat the Lord will be with me. Hell, man, the next time the Lord is with me, dat'll be the first time. But I didn't disrespect her or nothin'. I guess she jus' a crazy old lady after all."

"Maybe," I said. "Maybe. Did she say what she was sorry for?"

"I didn't ask. Jus' wanted to get off the phone."

"Hey, Marlon, how'd you like me to hand deliver that money tomorrow?"

"Tonight would be better, but I s'pose I can wait."

"I suppose you'll have to."

CHAPTER TWENTY-THREE

I KNEW SOMETHING wasn't right the minute I turned the corner onto Mary White's street. There was a local agent's For Sale sign up at the edge of the meticulous little yard in front of her house. Hung beneath the larger sign was a smaller one. "Priced to Sell," it read. Both signs swung gently in the early afternoon breeze. A blue jay perched on the mailbox, cocked its head at the signs and flew away. He wasn't buying.

Marlon Rhodes had wanted to tag along and though I could've used the company, I decided to part ways with him and my money back in Cincinnati. Showing up on Mary White's doorstep with Marlon in tow would have been tough to explain away. Never mind Marlon, I couldn't think of what the hell I was going to tell her about *my* being there. I guess I needn't have worried.

There was no answer when I knocked or pressed the front doorbell. I called her number on my cell. The phone rang and rang and … That was funny. I knew she had an answering machine. I'd left messages on it. I could hear her old fashioned phone ringing out in the street. My belly tied itself in knots. I remembered what happened the last time I listened to an unanswered telephone. I walked around the house, cupping my hands against side and back windows. I knocked on the rear door. Mary White was gone. Coming back around the front of the house, a young, chubby-faced woman with dull brown hair and a lazy eye called to me from the adjoining yard.

"She ain't around," Lazy Eye said, a little boy crying from inside her house.

"I can see that."

"You interested in the house?"

175

"Might be," I lied. "Do you know where the owner is?"

"Traveling."

"Traveling?"

"Yup, that's—" She was interrupted by the boy's crying. "Shut up! I'll be right in. Eat your cereal."

"Do you know where she went?"

"Nah. My neighbor and me, we don't get along so well. But you can try the real estate agent. He's nice. Name's Stan Herbstreet. Sold me and Larry our house. Stan's office number's on the sign. You a family man?" she asked, with a suspicious twist of her mouth.

"Sure am. Got a grown daughter and a little boy about three from my second marriage," I lied some more. "Gonna do some work at the Air Force base."

She stepped toward me and whispered conspiratorially, "Please take the house. The old lady's a nasty bitch who hates my kid." On cue, the kid wailed. She turned over her shoulder. "Shut up! Mommy's talking to the nice man who's going to buy Mary's house."

"Well," I said, "I guess I'll make that call to the real estate agent. Thanks for—"

"Listen, if you are *really* interested ..." Lazy Eye stepped even closer, looking this way and that. "I know how you can have a peek around inside without bothering Stan. The old biddy keeps a key in the wood planter on the patio. This way when you call Stan, you'll have a better idea of what you should offer."

"Gee, thanks a ton ..." I offered her my hand.

She took it. "Roweena. Roweena with a double-e."

"Thanks, Roweena double-e. I hope I like the house."

"For our sake, I hope so too."

The key was right where she said it would be. I smiled and waved that I had found it. I walked very slowly to the back door, praying Roweena would go attend to her screaming kid. She did, finally. The key slid into the cranky old lock and turned with a little help. Stepping in, I held my breath. Finding the kid dead affected me more than I was willing to let on ... even to myself. When, at last, I inhaled, there was a bit of mustiness in the air, but nothing more.

The museum piece house was as neat and clean as I remembered it. All of it except for Mary's bedroom. Understandably, this room hadn't been part of the original tour. It smelled of camphor, cloves and orange peel; of lilacs and roses; of dried flowers from a dried-up life tied in a sack and tucked away in a corner somewhere amongst her unrealized dreams. Mary had packed in a hurry. Her ancient dresser drawers were all open and askew, the closet door ajar. Empty hangers were strewn about the room: on the bed, on the floor, at the foot of the full-length mirror. Her jewelry box was empty too, dumped upside down on the bed on a pile of hangers.

I searched the dresser drawers, remembering how my dad had grown odd at the end, obsessed with making lists of the inconsequential aspects of his life. He wrote reams and reams of lists on foolscap. When he died, we knew where his hankies and t-shirts, his pens and broken watches, his rings and school yearbooks could be found, but we could never find where his happiness had got to. We wondered if he had ever truly been happy at all. There are some things it's better for kids not to wonder about their parents.

There wasn't anything to be found in the dresser drawers or in the closet or beneath the bed, but in the nightstand drawer were old letters from Jack, all with New York postmarks. Behind the family Bible and photo albums on the nightstand shelf were twenty neatly stacked cassette boxes. Each box was labeled with Jack's name, an event, and or a corresponding date. *Jack, Christmas 1976.* There were tapes in nineteen of the twenty boxes. It did not take me long to figure out where that missing tape had gone. Questions filled my head. How had Ray Martello gotten to Mary White? What could he have told her? How much could he have paid her? What had Katy or I ever done to her except treat her with respect?

I shook my head, thinking Mary mustn't have understood what was going on. But in my bones I knew that was wrong. Not only had Mary White known, she was an active participant. Now I understood Mary's discomfort around me, her strange affect on the phone, the weirdness in the cemetery. There were never any roses on her brother's grave or, if there had been, Mary White placed them there herself. No one painted on Jack's headstone. Mary simply scrubbed the stone for my benefit: the missing dirt from where she'd washed it had been enough to convince me of the vandalism.

I slid a few of the cassettes into my pocket and headed toward the back door, but decided to take a second, more careful look around. In the kitchen, I found some flight information, two phone numbers, and an address in Kentucky scribbled onto a pad. Next to the address was the notation, #12. I ripped off the sheet and tucked it into my pocket with the cassettes. There was nothing else to see. I tiptoed out the back, replacing the key in the planter. Unfortunately, Roweena—double e, one lazy eye—had been keeping watch.

"Well?"

"Nice," I said, "but a bit claustrophobic."

She didn't look pleased. I fairly ran to my rental car. Her kid was still crying.

LOCATING THE CEMETERY proved more challenging than expected. With some help from a trucker, I found my way. Once through the gates, I was confident I'd be able to find Jack's resting place. Wrong. I thought I retraced the route Mary had taken—around the huge stone crucifix, two lefts, straight ahead twelve rows, a right and a left—but I just couldn't find the small chunk of stone adorning Jack's grave. I tried it three more times with some minor variations before admitting defeat and heading into the administrative offices.

The woman at the desk checked the book.

"You weren't wrong, sir. Mr. White is indeed interred there, but your confusion is understandable." She made a sour face. "The headstone has been recently replaced."

Had it ever. No wonder I hadn't recognized the site. In place of the tasteful block of beveled granite which had stood vigil at the head of Jack White's grave was a massive black tombstone vaguely reminiscent of the monolith in *2001*. I couldn't quite believe the scale of it: a sequoia among the shrubbery. Carved into the rich black stone were prayerful hands, crosses, scrolls, angels, and a rendering of Jack's face. There was a bible quotation, lines from a favorite poem. With all that, there was still enough empty space on the stone to have added the entire text of *War and Peace* or to list the names of America's war dead. All of them, ever. A mourners' bench had been added as well. It was constructed of the same black stone, tasteful only by comparison to the monolith. I suppose Mary could have tried to buy Cleopatra's Needle or Stonehenge, but she'd done okay on her own. Looking past the hideousness of the new monuments, I realized just how much they must have set Mary back. Ray Martello had paid her a pretty penny for her betrayal.

Without his sister around to scowl at me, I considered placing a rock atop Jack's new headstone. Unfortunately, Mary hadn't thought to include an elevator or build steps into the side of the headstone. I placed a pebble at the base of the black giant and walked away. Poor Jack. If anything ever cried out for a sledgehammer, it was that thing in my rearview mirror.

NOT UNEXPECTEDLY, THE address in Kentucky was a cheap motel near the airport. One of the phone numbers Mary had scribbled down was traceable back to room twelve at that same motel. The desk clerk, a

Pakistani kid, was happy to help. The fifty bucks I slipped him was more of an incentive than the bullshit story I laid on. I described Mary, gave him the date of her flight, and asked him to check on who had been registered in room twelve that day.

"No, I am very very sorry," he said in an Urdu-inflected lilt. "We did not have a woman like you describe in the room that day." He read me a list of three names, all men, none of them familiar. I asked if he remembered what any of the men looked like. "One was a nasty older fellow. Big, with an eye patch."

The desk clerk might have said something else, but I didn't hear him. I think I might have thanked him. So, there was a mystery man, but his existence raised some questions not even Feeney could ignore. Suddenly, I didn't feel quite so stupid or desperate.

Back in my rental, I called the other phone number Mary White had written down. Someone picked up. I could hear breathing on the other end.

"Hello," I said, feeling cocky, overplaying my hand.

He snickered at me and hung up. I got a chill, but not because I knew who had been on the phone. I didn't. I didn't need to know. I could recognize a ghost when I heard one.

CHAPTER TWENTY-FOUR

US AIR TO New York. Aer Lingus to Dublin. Those were Mary White's flight details. I had checked the numbers out at the airport before getting on my plane back to LaGuardia. Problem was, both of her flights were one passenger short. At least that's what Feeney told me. Mary White was somewhere, but it wasn't Dublin, Ireland. Dublin, Ohio, was more likely.

Detective Feeney was a stubborn bastard, not a fool, so when I returned from Cincinnati armed with a little bit more than desperate questions, he was, at least, willing to listen. I had to give the man credit. Most detectives with such a neatly closed case would have told me to go fuck myself. On the other hand, he wasn't exactly reopening the investigation. He agreed, if grudgingly so, to keep an eye out for Mary White. He'd also alerted both the Dayton PD and the Ohio State Police that Mary White was a "person of interest" for the NYPD—although she was only of interest to me—and that she might be on the run. But that was as far as it went. Feeney had no intention of looking for the mystery man.

"But why would this guy be meeting with Mary White after Martello was dead?"

"Don't push it, Prager. This mystery man's not my problem. Maybe he was a real loyal friend to Ray Martello and was fulfilling a promise or somethin'. You know, like makin' a last payment. Frankly, I don't know and I don't give a shit. I'll do you the one favor and keep tabs on what the Ohio cops come up with about the old broad, but this mystery guy's your headache."

So it was official, Cyclops was my headache. Now he was Brian Doyle's headache as well. I got Brian to take the few personal days we owed him. He was glad to do it seeing as I was matching his per diem—in cash—plus expenses. Double time and expenses: nice gig if you can get it. I just couldn't bring myself to march back into the office and reinvolve the staff, not officially. I'd already used the agency for my private business for too long. It was bad for business and bad for morale. Until I had something more substantial than a missing cassette tape from Mary White's bedroom and a meeting in an airport motel between an old lady and a one-eyed man, I would play it close to the vest.

The worst part was I hadn't told Carmella about this little arrangement between Doyle and me. I had no intention of telling her, not yet, anyway. She would murder me, and rightfully so, for going behind her back. But so far I wasn't getting much return on my investment. Brian was batting zero for two days. He hadn't found any of Martello's friends or family or fellow cops who either matched the mystery man's description or knew of someone who did. I thought it was kind of strange that Doyle had gotten nowhere. The one-eyed man, from everything Mira Mira and the desk clerk in Kentucky had said, was a hard man to forget. Let's face it, the eye patch alone would be pretty memorable.

"Anything?" I asked, squeezing the cell phone between my neck and ear.

"Nada, boss. No one knows this guy and believe me, Moe, I talked to a lotta people. I mean, I was going to hell anyways before you had me do this little job for you, but I've lied so much to so many people in the last coupla days ... I couldn't say enough Our Fathers or Hail Marys or light enough candles to atone for the bullshit I've been spreading. I'm telling the cops I'm Martello's brother. I'm telling his family I'm a Suffolk cop. I'm telling some of his friends that I'm a cop and some that I'm family. I'm lying so much, I can't even keep track. I wouldn't mind so much if it was getting me somewheres."

"Okay, listen, get into Brooklyn and canvass Manhattan Court."

"Where Martello killed the kid?"

"Right. Describe both Martello and our mystery man to the neighbors. Ask if they remember either man being around that day or ever."

"What's the point, boss? I mean, we know Martello murdered the kid."

"Maybe it's time to pretend we don't know anything for sure. Just do it, Doyle. For what I'm paying your lazy ass, you shouldn't be asking why."

"I'll leave in a few minutes. I'll be happy to get outta here. Long Island is creepy. Too quiet for me."

"I know exactly what you mean."

"Where you headed, boss?"

"Long Island." I hung up before he could ask any other questions. The last thing I needed was to try and explain my dating Connie Geary to him. I'd have to explain it to myself first.

AT EIGHT IN late June or July, the sun would have still been pretty well up. That's how I had seen the Geary manse the first time I came calling. Back then, I'd also gotten to meet Senator Steven Brightman. He was full of promise and full of shit: the perfect con man and consummate politician. I should've known I was being played by how hard everyone was working me. Thomas Geary threatened and bribed. Brightman charmed. In my own defense, I had been bullied into taking the case in the wake of Katy's miscarriage. I was still reeling from the turmoil that followed in its wake. On the heels of losing a baby of my own, how could I not take the case of a missing daughter of an ex-NYPD cop? How could I not save the politician who was going to save us all?

Brightman was the serpent to my Eve and I bit the apple hard. Not unlike Judas Wannsee, Brightman had that magical ability to make you feel like you were the most important person in the room, the only person in the room. He could talk to a crowd, but you felt—no, you knew—he was talking directly to you. And when we met that evening in 1983, he worked his stuff. The myth is that great politicians know when to lie. The opposite is the reality. It's how they parse the truth. The night we met, Brightman answered my questions directly, even admitting that he and Moira Heaton had slept together. He had inoculated himself by telling me a negative truth. It was brilliant, just not brilliant enough.

I'm not necessarily a big believer in the truth. Katy will tell you that about me, but that's not how I mean it. What I mean is that the truth doesn't conform to the rules of Sunday school or sermons, to clichés or adages. The truth doesn't always come out in the wash or in the end and it's frequently not for the best. The truth often makes things worse, much worse. The truth can be as much poison as elixir, cancer as cure. And I knew some ugly truths about Steven Brightman that had put an end to his political career, but that gave no comfort to the dead and grieving.

I put Steven Brightman out of my head. It was an August sun falling down over the brim of the earth. The sky was a heavy shade of dusk, the stars more than vague hints of light. The darkening air was rich with the sweet scent of nicotina and lavender from the gardens—their sweetness playing nicely against the predominant smell of fresh-cut grass drifting over from the golf course next door. I pulled up to the house, my shirt slightly damp from nervous sweat. But I was enjoying the delicate buzz of excitement and anticipation I had going. It had been a very long time.

Connie met me at the door, her blond hair swept back, her white smile and clear blue eyes sparkling. We sort of stared awkwardly across the threshold at each other, not knowing quite what to do. She reached out, taking my hand, and pulled me into the house. When I was inside, she kissed me shyly on the lips. I kissed her back as shyly. No one ran screaming. We had gotten by the first hurdle. Both of us took deep breaths.

"Hi, Moe. God, I've been so nervous all week. I was worried you'd cancel. A scotch?"

"Sure."

"Come on into the den."

I followed. She was dressed in a clingy floral print and open-toed shoes with a low heel. Her muscular calves flexed as she walked to the bar. I noticed not only what she was wearing and how she looked, but the pleasant effect it was having on me.

"I've been looking forward to this as well, I think even more than I knew," I said.

"Really?" She handed me my scotch and we clinked glasses. "What's been going on in your life?"

I thought about not answering or deflecting the question with the usual nonsense, but thought it would be a bad precedent. I told her.

"My lord," she said, refilling my glass. "What madness. Can revenge really be such an obsession?"

"Apparently. It was so important to my father-in—to my late father-in-law, that he wanted it from his grave. Good scotch."

"You sold it to me. Your store did, at least."

"Listen, Connie, can we stay off the subject of graves and revenge for now? I've spent a little too much time in cemeteries lately."

"Absolutely."

Connie put her drink down, pressed herself against me, and kissed me in a way I would not describe as shyly. I returned her kiss and then some. Connie had other talents besides playing the piano. Kissing Connie didn't come with the baggage of kissing Katy nor with the depth of feeling and darkness of kissing Carmella. It was, in any case, an amazing sensation. Other than those two weak moments I shared with Carmella and the spontaneous moment with Tina Martell, Connie was the only woman beside Katy I had kissed in the last twenty years.

"How's your dad doing?" I changed subjects.

"I'm afraid he's taken a bit of a bad turn. He's in the hospital, but should be home next week some time."

"Sorry to hear it."

"What can one do? It's the nature of the disease. Mom will be back by then. At least my son doesn't have to deal with it. He's up at football camp for the next two weeks. Come, let's get out of here and leave these depressing things behind us. In fact," she said, reaching into her clutch and pulling out her cell phone, "can we make a deal? How about we shut out the rest of the world for the evening and focus only on the two of us?"

"Deal," I said, making a show of shutting off my cell phone.

She put hers down on the bar.

"I'll drive," I said.

"Oh, no you won't. The car will be here in a few minutes. We're focusing on each other, no distractions."

My first impulse was to argue. I didn't. It felt good to give in, to turn control of things over to someone else for a change.

"Would you like me to play for you until the driver gets here?"

"Maybe later," I said, pulling her close. "Maybe later."

I HADN'T BEEN on a date in about a quarter century, so nearly every inch of the night was a revelation. Around our second bottle of old vine Zinfandel, when it became clear that bed had gone from our possible to our inevitable destination, the rate of revelation picked up speed. The odd thing about marriage is that it lulls you into a comfortable forgetfulness. You forget that the dance you do can be nearly the same and yet be almost completely different. You forget what it's like to discover excitement instead of relying on it. You forget that even awkwardness has its potent charms and that first times do still exist in the universe. You can know in your head that every woman has a different taste, a different scent, a different feel, but to be reawakened to the sense of it was an indescribable and unexpected shock.

Connie Geary was everything I would have wanted for my debut in the world of the recently single. She was good company, familiar enough, but not too familiar. She was comfortable with herself, at ease with me, smart, skeptical, not cynical. She was unembarrassed by her family's wealth, but not blind or unsympathetic to the plight of the rest of the world. In bed, Connie was eager, sharing, unafraid. She was all of those things and yet I knew I would never visit her bed again.

The night had been both wonderful and hollow somehow. For all the laughs and kisses, wanting looks, flirtatious touches, and orgasms, there didn't seem to have been an ounce of spontaneity in the entire evening. I don't want to say it all felt staged—no man wants to think the moans and clenches, the screams and spasms, are the result of careful rehearsal and not passion—but I couldn't escape the sense of things having been storyboarded, that each step had been premeditated. Even when I got up at five to shower, I knew Connie Geary would follow me in a few minutes later and take me in her mouth. Knowing didn't stop me from enjoying.

Perhaps the strangest aspect of the whole experience was the parting. We had, it seemed, used up all our awkwardness in our twelve hours together. Our farewell was almost business-like: pleasant, courteous, distant. There were no hard feelings, no angry words, no accusations. Pulling down the driveway, I could see Connie in my sideview mirror. She stood at the edge of the portico, giving me a goodbye wave so slight it was barely noticeable. The look on her face was unvarnished and predatory.

Is this, I wondered, what being alone did to you? Had Connie played out this scene over and over again with any number of men? Had they all disappointed her? Was she disappointed even before they showed up? Is that why it was, in spite of all the heat, so empty an experience? Christ, it was all so very odd. Heading back to Brooklyn, I didn't find myself missing Katy so much as the marriage itself.

CHAPTER TWENTY-FIVE

I KNEW THE second I walked through the condo door that the world had changed when I wasn't looking. My phone machine was flashing without pause. I'd never seen anything like it. Reflexively, I reached for my cell and remembered the deal I'd made with Connie Geary about leaving distractions behind. The second I turned it back on, it buzzed. It was an easy choice for me between answering machine and cell. I preferred hitting one button to cell message retrieval.

First message:

"Dad, it's Sarah, listen … We've gotta talk. Something's up with Mommy. I … I think she's losing it. I think she's seeing Uncle Patrick again. Please call me back. I'm supposed to leave for Ann Arbor tomorrow, but I don't really want to leave with Mommy like this. Call me back as soon as you get this."

The second and third messages were much the same only more frantic. Sarah was increasingly worried not only about Katy, but by her inability to reach me. The fourth and fifth messages were from Aaron and Carmella, respectively. Both had gotten calls from Sarah concerning my whereabouts and why I wasn't picking up my cell phone.

Next message:

"Yeah, Prager, this is Detective Feeney. We got a location on Mary White. She never made it outta the Ohio-Kentucky area. The airport cops found her in the trunk of her car in the short-term lot. The tags had been switched. Preliminary report is the old lady was strangled. Give me a call."

There was another round of calls from Sarah and Aaron, alternating between panic and anger.

187

Next message:

"Hey, boss, it's Doyle. It's weird, but no one on Manhattan Court can ever remember seeing Martello. I even showed his picture around. Nothing. But the minute I mentioned the guy with the eye patch, like ten people knew who I was talking about. And here's the really weird thing, two or three of the neighbors remember the guy with the eye patch being there the night the kid bought it. Gimme a call. Whadaya want me to do from here?"

I picked up the phone and dialed Sarah's cell, half listening as the messages continued playing. *One ring.* The next message was from Sheriff Vandervoort. *Second ring.* Sarah had called the sheriff's station and was panicked. *Third ring.* When Sarah got up and went to check on Katy, she was gone: her bed unslept in. Her car still in the garage. *Fourth ring.*

"Dad, where the hell have you been? Mommy is—"

"I know, kiddo, I'm listening to my messages."

"Where have—"

"It's a long story, Sarah. Tell me what's going on."

She pretty much repeated what Pete Vandervoort had described and then started losing it.

"Shhhh, Sarah, calm down, calm down. It won't help anyone if you lose control. You said you thought Mom was seeing Uncle Patrick again. What makes you say that?"

"She was acting weird, like … like she was before she tried to—"

"Weird how?"

"She was all nervous, always looking over my shoulder when we were together. She started staying in her bedroom all the time, smoking cigarettes. I could smell them through the door. She tried to get me to stay at Robby's or to come back to your place. Dad, I'm really scared."

"We'll take care of it. Your mom'll be fine," I said, in spite of all the evidence to the contrary. "I'll be up there in a few hours. In the meantime, put in a call to her shrink, okay? I'm on my way."

I stayed and listened to the remainder of the messages. They were from Aaron and Carmella, another one from Pete Vandervoort. All wondered where I was and why I still hadn't picked up my cell. Walking to my bedroom to change, I half-listened to another message, the last message. It was mostly silence, a vague, familiar silence, a chilling silence. Then a snicker.

End of new messages.

I HAVE SELDOM in my life been thankful for traffic. Being thankful for traffic is akin to joy over an exit wound, but I was thankful for it that day.

With the Belt Parkway jammed in both directions, I hadn't even gotten out of Brooklyn. And given all that was going on, I'd've thought my mind would be cluttered by fear over Katy's disappearance, worry for Sarah, the news of Mary White's murder. Then there was the peculiar nature of what Brian Doyle had said about no one having seen Martello on the night of the kid's murder. Never mind the call from the snickering ghost.

Yet, there in the traffic, the radio blasting "Black Coffee in Bed," my progress measured by inches, not in miles per hour, all I could think about was Connie Geary and the expression on her face as I drove away that morning. I looked at my sideview mirror as I had earlier, trying to recreate her face with the paint of memory. Her expression was predatory, almost feral. Again, I wondered where it had come from. I wondered if she meant for me to see it. It was always the small details: Connie's expression, the kid lying to me about his name, Katy seeing … Suddenly, I was short of breath and then the world went away.

Things became so clear to me that I hurt, I ached. I wanted to peel my skin away from my muscle, tear my muscle away from my bone, wrench all feelings away from my heart. Horns filled the air, but I could not move, could not blink, could not … All senses deserted me. I was numb and deaf, dumb and blind. The only thing I tasted was my own bile. I heard the horns again. They were angrier now, even vengeful. Beneath the blare was a distant tapping. Still, I could not move. The tapping grew more insistent.

"Hey, buddy … pal …" The tapping had a voice. "Buddy, you okay?"

The world rushed back in as I turned to see a man's face pressed against my window. I looked ahead and the traffic had broken up.

"Yeah, I'm fine. Sorry."

He shrugged his shoulders, hitched up his eyebrows, the corner of his mouth. He tapped the window one more time and said, "Okay, then let's go."

I stepped on the gas and drove blind.

ALTHOUGH IN MY heart I now knew who had been pulling the strings all along, I wanted some confirmation, something tangible I could show Feeney and Pete Vandervoort. Too many times in my life I had operated on whims and hunches. Not this time, because if what I suspected was true, *was* true, then Katy's life, Sarah's, and mine were in real danger. Everything, even the murders of Mary White, the kid, Martello—yes, Martello—had been the preliminaries, the overture and first two acts. Before I went rushing upstate, I needed to know for sure.

I called ahead to Vandervoort and Sarah and warned them I might be delayed in getting to Janus. Car trouble, I'd said. The sheriff knew

I was full of shit and Sarah believed me out of desperation and habit. I considered telling Vandervoort the truth, but changed my mind. There was too much to explain and if I was wrong, I didn't want to risk the sheriff shifting the focus off the search for Katy. If I was right about who had her, she'd be safe for now. The last act required me as audience.

Devo was already in the office waiting for me.

"I have it queued up for you, Moe."

The lights in his office were dimmed and he had me sit in front of one of his computer monitors. He stood behind me to my right.

"The view, I am afraid, is far from sharp, but you can make out a face," Devo said, then began explaining the mechanics of how he had coaxed the image from the gas station's security video.

"Just show it to me."

"What you will see is a continually sharpening image. When the image is at its highest resolution, the frame will freeze." He touched the mouse.

There on the monitor was the image of a slightly tinted driver's side window of a 2000 GMC Yukon. *Click.* I could barely make out the ghostly silhouette of someone in the driver's seat. *Click. Click. Click.* In tiny increments the window tinting seemed to brighten and, as it did, the silhouette became less and less ghostly. *Click.* A human face began to emerge out of the darkness. *Click.* A few seconds later I could make out a black bulge over the left eye of the emerging face. *Click.* Then, just before the frame froze, I recognized the face of the mystery man. In that brief second before the fear and resignation set in, I smiled. For now I knew where a bullet I fired in Miami Beach in 1983 had landed. I'd shot out Ralphy Barto's left eye.

Mira Mira had almost been right. While Ralph Barto wasn't a cop, he had been a U.S. marshal and a PI. Bullet wound or not, this wasn't about revenge for his missing left eye. After all, the prick was trying to kill me when I returned fire. No, Ralph Barto was a professional lackey, not a master of the universe. Dead roses, ghosts, and graves were not his franchise. If Barto had wanted revenge, he'd have sought me out long ago, stuck a gun in my mouth, and made like Jackson Pollock. This wasn't about Ralph Barto, at least not directly, but about his boss, a man who had murdered a little boy and a political intern in coldest blood.

In 1983, Ralph Barto had two bosses: Joe Spivack and Steven Brightman. Spivack, another ex-U.S. marshal, had owned a security firm in the same building where Carmella and I now kept our offices. His firm had done the initial investigation attempting to clear Steven Brightman from any taint in connection to his intern's disappearance. After I got involved and we cleared Brightman, Spivack went to his cabin upstate and blew his brains out. Spivack's suicide, along with some other nagging doubts, led me to question my own conclusions about Brightman's innocence. At Spivack's funeral, Ralph Barto offered his services to me. I had no way of knowing that he was Brightman's boy, a mole meant to keep tabs on me. When I got too close to the truth, he tried to kill me.

I could understand Brightman wanting revenge as much or more as Martello, but why now? Why seventeen years later? Something had had to set him off and I wanted to know what that was before we crossed paths.

"Devo," I said, "do me a favor and get on the internet."

"Sure, Moe, but why?"

"Steven Brightman."

"What about him?

"Everything, but especially about his ex-wife."

CHAPTER TWENTY-SIX

CONNIE GEARY HAD made it happen. I knew that without Devo having to look it up. She was in this. I just didn't know how deeply. She had planted the idea of our date weeks ago. She made the call. She set the time. She made sure we were alone and I was unreachable. She arranged for the car. She picked the restaurant. She gave me the first kiss. Christ, even fucking was her idea. At least she let me choose the wine. Had she known what Brightman really had in mind? I'd like to think not. She had probably financed him. Financing Brightman's campaigns seemed to be a Geary family habit.

For a little while there, I thought about heading to Crocus Valley and grabbing her ass for trade bait. It was a good thing her son wasn't around, because I was in the kind of mood to have used him too. That's how fucked up I was. But even if I had been far gone enough to have used them both, it wouldn't have mattered. Bargaining requires that the parties value what the other party possesses, but Brightman wouldn't care about Connie or her kid. Too bad Connie was blind to that. She wouldn't be for much longer. If she had understood the end game and not involved herself, then maybe Brightman would've been forced to come directly at me instead of my family. That wasn't his way.

I was pretty sure I had some time and that Katy was in no immediate danger. My guess, my *hope* was that Brightman needed my presence to bring down the final curtain. Was I certain? No. I'd been wrong about almost everything else, but I knew Brightman, the way his twisted mind worked. So before heading into town, I stopped at the cemetery to talk with Fallon. I don't know why it had taken me so long to realize what was right in front of me from the first: that a man with a backhoe, a shed full of pickaxes, shovels, and sledges, a man with unfettered access to the Maloney family gravesite, was a more obvious suspect than neighborhood kids, vandalous ghosts or avenging angels. That the sheriff had also neglected this point was of no comfort.

The crunch of the gravel beneath my tires brought it full circle. I once again thought of that long-ago winter's day in the cemetery with Mr. Roth. God, how I missed that man, but the love I felt for him was always tainted with guilt over my father. We're funny creatures, us humans. We live in hope that even the dead will change. I know I did. My dad loved us. We loved him, but he had cut himself off from us. He could never bring himself to meet us halfway. *So far, no further.* He was a failure at business. Even his failures were unspectacular. I don't think Aaron, Miriam, or I cared about that, but he did. We saw him as a failure because he saw himself that way, because he failed us that way. Israel Roth came with none of that baggage. That baggage was reserved for his son. He was the father I chose. I was the son he wished he had. It was a cruel bargain for everyone but the both of us.

I parked in front of Fallon's neat little bungalow, but I didn't make it up the front steps. The shed door was open, creaking as it swung lazily in the early evening breeze. I reached around for my .38. Something was wrong. I could feel it in my bones. Besides, cemeteries just tend to throw me off my game. No one likes confronting the inevitable. When your life spreads out before you, there are countless possibilities. Not in the end. In the end, it's all the same. Death is the most egalitarian of things. Cemeteries, like a constant whisper in the ear, had a nasty way of reminding you of that fact.

"Fallon!" I called out. "Mr. Fallon. It's Moe Prager, Katy Maloney's ex."

The only answer was the whine of mosquito wings. They'd come out for a light supper. In the distance I heard a faint *clink, clink, clink*-ing. When I grabbed hold of the door and peeked around, I saw why it refused to close. Mr. Fallon's work boots were doorstops. The caretaker lay face down, one end of a pickaxe stuck so completely through his left shoulder blade that the handle nearly rested on his back. There wasn't much blood, not on his back anyway. His head was pretty well smashed up. The little blood that had pooled around the wound was thick with mosquitos.

I looked up at the door header and ceiling of the shed as I backed out. Fallon hadn't been killed in the shed. No way an assailant could have swung the pickaxe high enough to gather the momentum it would have taken to gouge through the body that way. I took a look around. On the far side of the equipment barn, I found the source of that faint *clink, clink, clink*-ing. Fallon's abandoned backhoe was still running, the exhaust cap popping up and down in rhythm to the puffing of diesel fumes. The blood missing from the shed was all here, but not pooled all in one place. The caretaker had received quite a beating before dying.

My cell phone buzzed even as I grabbed it to call the sheriff. It was Brian Doyle.

"You were right, boss," he said. "The tattoo babe confirmed it."

"Thanks."

I clicked off and called the sheriff.

"Pete."

"Yeah, what's up?"

"Have you seen my daughter?"

"Sarah? She was just in here with Robby, why?"

I let out a big sigh of relief. "Keep an eye on her."

"Why? What's up?"

I didn't bother explaining. "Listen, Fallon's dead."

"Fallon, the guy from the cemetery?"

"Yeah. I'm at the cemetery now. Fallon's in the tool shed, a pickaxe sticking halfway out his back. My guess is—"

I never finished the sentence because a baseball bat had, at that instant, introduced itself to my right kidney. *It's way back. The leftfielder's on the warning track ... at the fence ... looking up. That ball is ... outta here!* I'll be pissing blood for a month, I thought, crumpling to the ground, if I live that long. My cell phone seemed free of the bonds of gravity and flew off somewhere, far far away. The involuntary tears and choking mucus that filled my eyes, throat, and sinuses was the least of it. The nausea, the puking, that was the bad part. It made everything else that much worse, especially the pain. When I was done puking, someone slipped a pillowcase over my head, taped it closed around my neck, and cuffed my hands behind me. Two men—I guessed there were two and that they were men—dragged me by my elbows along the dirt and gravel. I was shoved into the back of a car—my car, by the sound of it—and driven away. Someone spoke. The voice was familiar, but it wasn't Brightman's or Barto's.

"You didn't think you was gonna blow up our kitchen and get away with it, did ya?"

It was Crank.

THE RIDE WAS a fairly short one. That much I could say, but I was still disoriented from the whack in the kidney and the growing pain in my head. The tape, tight around my neck, wasn't helping my respiration any, and the buildup of my own vomit-sour fumes in the pillowcase was hard to take. When we stopped, I was yanked out of the car and dragged along some new dirt and stone. A door opened. I was bent into a sitting position with my legs and ass on a cool, damp floor and my back against a rough wooden wall. Something tore open the linen cocoon around my head. The rush of fresh air made me swoon. If there had been anything left in my guts, I would have puked again. As it was, I dry-retched until my head nearly exploded. Someone kicked me in the ribs and the dry heaves stopped. I wish I had known that trick in college.

"Okay, Prager," Crank said, straddling my legs, twisting my shirt in his hands. "Who are you working with?"

"The KGB."

"Funny man." He backslapped my face, but not as hard as I supposed he could have. There was also something in his eyes that belied his angry demeanor. "We know there's someone working for the Feds inside this organization and you're the outside contact."

I didn't answer right away. Instead, I looked around the room. We were in a cabin not unlike the one Crank and I had been in the last time. For all I knew, it might have been the same cabin. Standing behind Crank were four bikers from central casting. Behind them was a suit. The bikers wore black leather and greasy cut denim, beards, big boots, belt buckles, and bandannas. The suit had cop written all over him, but he wasn't local. No, Suit's brown eyes had the requisite sheen of condescension found primarily in Feds.

"ATF or DEA?" I asked the suit.

He smiled. I didn't. Suit opened his mouth to speak.

"Come on, Prager," Crank interrupted, "talk to me now and we'll skip the blowtorch and pliers bullshit. Gimme a name."

"Make some suggestions and I'll give you a name. I'm not joking here. I just don't know what the fuck you're talking about."

"Get the barbed wire," said Suit to the bikers. "We'll rearrange his face a little and when he sees how much blood pours out, then maybe he'll—"

"Wait a second!" Crank barked. "This is my thing. The lab blew on my watch. I'll handle this shit."

"Yeah," Suit said, "like how you let him slip away the same night you let a few million dollars of potential income go up like a Roman candle? I don't think so."

Crank jumped up, pulled a hunting knife out of the sheath on his belt, and stuck it right under Suit's chin. For a barrel-bellied guy, Crank moved more like a ballerina.

"Listen, Swanson, you dickless motherfucker, don't start giving me fucking orders. You get your cut from us, not the other way around. Remember that."

"And I fucking protect you guys," said Agent Swanson.

"And we're paying for your retirement, asshole."

"Gee, and I thought cops were the only ones who hated Feds."

Crank back-kicked his leg and hit me square in the belly with his heavy boot. "Who the fuck asked you? Unless you got a name for me, shut the fuck up."

That one hurt, but the damage could have been much worse had he got me in the jaw. Probably would've broken it. As it was, I couldn't catch my breath.

Crank refocused on Swanson. "Back the fuck off, you suited prick. I don't take orders from nobody. Just ask my Desert Storm commander. I broke his arm in three places, one place at a time."

Swanson tried to look cool, but there was real fear in his eyes. "Okay, okay, but we need that name."

Crank pulled the knife away from the agent's neck and put the blade back in its sheath. He turned his attention back my way, lifted me off the ground and shoved me into a chair. He spoke softly to me, almost cooing, trying to cajole an answer out of me.

Wouldn't I feel better getting it off my chest? Wouldn't I rather avoid the torture, which would surely come? Wouldn't I like a chance to live until morning? Wouldn't I …

I would have been happy to give him an answer had I any notion of what he was going on about. I felt like a character from one novel who had fallen through the looking glass into another book: *Alice in Fatherland*, maybe. My mind drifted, I wondered if this was all part of Brightman's grand scheme. But when I retraced my steps to my original contact with Crank, I rejected the idea. This was wrong place, wrong time at its worst. Yet in spite of the threat and bluster, not much was happening. Crank even got me a drink and cloth to clean me up some. More than an hour must have passed since I was first brought into the cabin. I got the sense that he was playing for time.

"This is bullshit!" one of the gang of four bikers growled. "Are we gonna kiss this guy's ass until he gives us a name or what? Deuce and Deadman are gonna be here any minute and they're gonna wanna know what the fuck is what."

Swanson raised his hands like a traffic cop. "Hey, don't look at me. That's one of your boys talking, Crank, not me."

"All right, Max, get the wire," Crank said matter-of-factly. "Prager, gimme a name now, or you're gonna bleed."

Only I could see Crank's face. His back was to the bikers and Swanson. There was something both imploring and reassuring in his expression. It was if he was telling me that things would be okay if I could only give him something to work with. I scoured my memory, trying to recall how things had played out the night the lab exploded. If I wasn't already motivated enough, seeing the razor wire kicked it up a couple of notches.

"Cutter," I said. "It's Cutter."

Crank winked at me in a brief second of calm. Then one of the bikers, a rough looking dude with a long beard, sunglasses, and prison tats lunged at me.

"You lyin' motherfuckin' snake."

Well, now I knew who Cutter was. Instinctively, I pushed back and my chair went down and I tried to roll away. Crank threw out his left fist, catching Cutter in the Adam's apple. Cutter, gasping for air, went down on top of me.

"Get ZZ Top off me!"

Agent Swanson actually laughed at that. The other bikers were on Cutter, punching him and kicking him even as they pulled him off. A few minutes of that and he'd look like Fallon sans pickaxe.

"Gag the rat and cuff him!" Crank ordered. "We'll let Deuce and Deadman deal with him."

Then, as if on cue, the quiet of the woods was ripped wide open by the distinctive throaty rumble of twin Harleys. The two bikes pulled up almost to the front door. The woods again went silent. The door opened. Two more bikers joined us. They didn't look any more fierce or rough than Crank and the four that were already here, but it was evident from the look in everyone's eyes that these two were players: princes among the common scum. There was a round of ritualized hugs and handshakes between the boys. It had the feel of a meet and greet at a Masonic temple. The bikers kept their distance from Swanson. They seemed to regard him as an infectious disease.

"You got my cut?" Swanson said. "I can't be here for the pleasantries."

"Shut the fuck up, man," said the shorter of the two princes. "Ya'll get your money when I'm ready to give it to ya."

Crank pointed at me. "That's the ex-cop. He fingered Cutter as the rat."

Cutter struggled against his restraints and tried to say something. One of the bikers kicked him in the ribs and told him to shut the fuck up. Apparently, I'd chosen the right fall guy. Neither the original gang nor the two princes acted at all surprised by the news of Cutter's disloyalty. Swanson was fidgeting, clearly worried about witnessing what would surely happen to Cutter and me.

"Deuce, pay the cunt and get him outta here," said Deadman, the short prince.

Deuce reached around his back and pulled out a duct-taped brown paper bag. Swanson's eyes got big, but he didn't reach for the stack. Deuce threw it on the cabin floor like scraps for the dog and Swanson couldn't pick it up fast enough. The second the Fed grabbed the package, the world hit a speed bump. There was a flurry of activity outside: gunshots, shotgun blasts, tires skidding, running feet on gravel, motorcycles rumbling. The cabin flooded with blinding light from all sides.

"Inside the cabin, this is Special Agent William B. Stroby of the Federal Bureau of Investigation and Combined Meth Task Force. The cabin is completely surrounded. You are all under arrest. Any attempt at escape will be futile and will result in additional charges. Please follow my instructions promptly and to the letter and no one will be injured. A failure to do so will force me to use all necessary means to effect your arrest. Open the cabin door and throw out all weapons. Then, when I give the word, I want you to knee-walk out of the cabin in single file with your hands clasped behind your heads. Any variation in this procedure or attempt at escape will result in your being fired upon. Starting now I want …"

As Stroby droned on, Deuce looked my way.

"We got us a bargaining chip," he said, reaching for the butt of a handgun tucked into his pants.

"I don't think so," said Crank, pressing the muzzle of a Glock to Deuce's head. "Prager, stand up." With his free hand, Crank reached into his pants pocket and removed a cuff key. He handed it to Deuce.

"Uncuff him."

"You fuckin' mother—"

Crank slammed his boot into the side of Deuce's knee. Something snapped and the prince crumbled, yelping in pain. I almost felt sorry for him. Almost. Crank then ordered one of the original bikers to undo my cuffs. He did so.

"Prager, get that hogleg from Deuce and come over here with me."

I followed Crank's instructions. Deuce's gun was a Colt revolver. The barrel on the damned thing was the size of a deer femur.

"Jesus Christ! Will you look at this thing," I said, pulling back the hammer. "Please, somebody move. I'd love to see what a bullet from this thing would do to you."

Crank got a kick out of that, but then his face went all business. "All right, boys, all weapons out on the floor now."

Stroby was still at it when Crank yelled out the door. Some of Shakespeare's plays had less acts than this guy's speech. Until that point

I had been successful at focusing on saving my own neck and not letting my mind drift to Katy's plight. If I got myself killed, Katy had no chance. But now that my freedom was at hand, it all came rushing back in.

"Stroby, will you please shut the fuck up!" I thought I heard some of the assault team laughing. "This is Agent Markowitz," Crank yelled. "The code word is pelican and the color is green. I repeat, this is Markowitz. The code word is pelican and the color is green."

Stroby shut up.

No one was stupid enough to make a run for it and within fifteen minutes, the weapons had been collected, the bikers and Swanson arrested, the tension gone. Crank—Markowitz—had an EMT look me over. He gave me something for the pain, but that ache in my kidney was going to require weeks of healing and something stronger than glorified aspirin to take the sting out. The EMT had some stuff with him to help me wash up. He even had some mouthwash. Still, I looked and smelled like last week's garbage.

"You okay?" Markowitz asked, handing me back my cell phone and .38.

"Define okay." I checked my phone for messages. None. "Listen—"

"Yeah, pretty dumb question, huh?"

"I've heard dumber, but not many. Listen, I've gotta get outta here."

"In a minute," he said. "I've got to get clearance for you to leave from my C.O."

"So, you want to tell me what the fuck this was all about? I mean, I can figure out that you're a Fed and that you've been undercover in this meth ring, but why drag me into it?"

"I'm ATF and I didn't drag you into it. You put yourself in it. Who told you to come looking for me? Who told you to show up the night I blew the lab?"

"*You* blew the lab!"

"Sshhhhh! Keep it down, Prager. Technically, I'm not supposed to destroy evidence like that, but the case wasn't ready yet and we were going to ship out a huge volume of product. I couldn't let it hit the streets, not even for the case. This shit's like a plague, a fucking cancer. If you thought crack was bad ... You ever see what a tweaker looks like after a few months on this shit?"

"Okay, I get it, but why reinvolve me?" I asked, looking impatiently at my watch, wondering when his C.O. would clear me to leave.

"I didn't reinvolve you. They've been keeping eyes out for you. They knew someone was leaking info to the cops and Feds. I told you that night the lab blew that your timing sucked. These kinda guys don't believe in coincidence. You show up and their lab goes boom ... When you got away, they started looking at me. I couldn't afford that, so ..."

"So you told them there was someone inside and a contact outside. I was the obvious candidate for the outside contact."

"These guys are cutthroats, not geniuses, and they sample a little too much of the product. Too much and it makes you paranoid as all hell. I just fed their paranoia a bit. Yeah, so someone spotted you on the road leading to the cemetery earlier. Good thing I was around."

"Tell that to my kidney."

"Sorry about that."

"Listen, Markowitz, I'm not joking. I gotta get outta—" My cell phone buzzed. "Excuse me," I said and stepped a few feet away.

"Remember my voice, Moe?" It was Brightman.

"I remember."

"You were pretty smug the last time we spoke. You feeling smug now?"

"Not at all."

"Good, but you're late," he said.

"Late for what?"

He ignored that. "You were doing so well and then you seemed to disappear on us. Where have you been?"

"Before or after I found Fallon?"

"That, oh, well … how about after the cemetery?"

"You wouldn't believe me if I told you."

"Try me."

"No."

Brightman moved his mouth away from the phone, but not so far that I couldn't hear him. "Hurt her," he said. There was a second delay and then a woman screamed. He got back on the phone. "Don't do that again, Moe. I want to kill her in front of you, but if you put me in a bad frame of mind, I'll do it and they'll never find her body."

"Okay. What do you want?"

"I can't have what I want, but short of that I want you to go for a ride, alone, and keep your cell phone available. I'll call you when it suits me."

"Where should I—"

"Head toward the County of Kings. Yes, that suits me fine. Take the thruway and remember, Moe, old stick, alone."

"I'll remember."

I clicked the phone shut.

"You don't look so good," Markowitz said. "Who was that?"

"The man who is going to murder my wife."

CHAPTER TWENTY-SEVEN

I HAD JUST pulled onto the New York State Thruway, heading south toward the city, when Brightman called. He had changed his mind, he said. It seemed I wasn't destined for Brooklyn after all. He had me circle back north and head into the Catskills. Then as he continued reciting the directions, it hit me. I knew where he wanted me to go. I shaped my lips to form the words Old Rotterdam. I wasn't even certain I had spoken them aloud until Brightman answered.

"Yes, Moe, Old Rotterdam, very good. Do you remember the grounds of the Fir Grove Hotel?"

"I do."

"Then I'll see you in an hour or so. Now, without hanging up, toss your cell phone out your car window. I want to hear it hit the pavement. Toss the phone."

"No," I said. "First, I want to talk to Katy. And don't give me that 'hurt her stuff' again. Put her on the phone and then I'll toss it."

Again, he moved his mouth away from the phone, but not far away. "Bring her over here."

I heard some background noise, the shuffling of feet, then, "Moe. Moe, what's going—" It *was* Katy.

Brightman got back on the phone, his voice edgier, the threat closer to the surface. "Don't try anything cute. You're being watched. Now, toss the fucking phone!"

I tossed it. The phone bounced once before being crushed under the wheels of a semi coming up fast on my left. I used the opportunity to check my mirrors to see if Brightman was bluffing about my being followed. It was impossible to tell in the dark in the midst of hundreds of cars. Even when I turned off and circled around, too many other vehicles exited and entered for me to have spotted a tail. It was moot. Destiny lay ahead, not behind me.

THE FIR GROVE Hotel was gone. It had been gone that first time I drove up its huge semi-circular driveway in 1981. All the bulldozers and dump trucks that had leveled the compound and carted away the debris were mere formalities in the aftermath of the workers' quarters fire, the broom and dust pan sweeping away the refuse of shattered crystal. No, not crystal. Glass, cheap glass. The Fir Grove, The Concord, all the Catskill hotels that had pretentions were never really anything more than baloney sandwiches. Once people saw what the rest of the world had to offer, the Catskill Mountains became the lunch meat option, a vacation spot for poor schmucks and sentimental fools. In spite of what the locals thought, the Fir Grove fire was nothing more than an exclamation point on the Catskills' death certificate. My eyes adjusting to the darkness, I noticed that now even the grand driveway was gone. I couldn't tell if anything more than memories remained.

I parked down at the bottom of the hill and popped my trunk to get my flashlight. People say the crisp mountain air is good for you, that it smells fresh without the taint of the city. They say a lot of things. All I could smell was smoke from the distant fire that killed Andrea Cotter, the first girl I ever loved. A cop becomes intimately familiar with what fire does to the human body. The image of Andrea's charred body flashed into my head and I shuddered. Although it felt like a million years since I'd last done crowd control at a fire scene, I could taste the acrid stink of burnt hair on my tongue and in my nostrils.

Bang! I stopped in my tracks, trying to remember the date. August … Christ, it was the anniversary of the Fir Grove fire. *Was it the thirty-fourth anniversary? The thirty-fifth?* I couldn't recall. It had been so many lies, so many secrets, so many lifetimes ago. Brightman had done his research. He was going to kill the last woman I loved where the first had been murdered. It was all so symmetrical in a twisted kind of way.

I had to put Andrea Cotter out of my head. Three and a half decades had passed and she was as dead as she was ever going to be. She had met the end of time, the clock had stopped ticking on her nevers and forevers. Katy's clock was still running. She was who I had to think about. I couldn't let Brightman play with my head. He already had too much of an advantage. I slammed my trunk shut.

"Stop!" a voice came out of the darkness.

"Ralphy Barto."

"You remember?"

"I remember. Hitting you in the eye like that, it was a lucky shot."

"Not for me."

"As I recall, you were trying to kill me at the time."

"There was that," he said, a smile in his voice. "You carrying?"

"I got my .38 tucked into the small of my back. You want me to—"

"No, thanks," he said, stepping out of the darkness. "I'll handle it."

He was carrying a submachine gun of some kind, a long, thick sound suppressor on the end of its barrel. In spite of the eye patch and years, Barto actually looked better than he had in 1983 and I told him as much.

"Yeah, I take care of myself these days. Anyone in the car?"

"Brightman told me to come alone."

"That's not what I asked."

Before I could say anything else, Barto sprayed my car with bullets. The rate of fire was amazing, the suppressor—silencer is a misnomer—keeping each shot down to a loud snap and hiss. He paid careful attention to the trunk and backseat.

"No," I said too late. "I'm alone."

"That you are, my friend." He replaced the clip, took my .38, and patted me down. He knew I wouldn't risk Katy's life by trying anything. "Christ, you smell like puke. You're scared, huh? Somehow, I didn't figure you as a puker."

"Bad shrimp."

"Cute," he said. "Listen, he's gonna kill her one way or the other. There's nothing I can do about that, but if you wanna run, I won't shoot you. I'll lay this thing down and you can split."

"I can't do that."

"I know, but I figured I'd ask. Come on. Up the hill. You try anything now, I'll wound you and it won't change anything."

"Is she okay?" I asked.

"She's a little freaked, I guess."

"Has he hurt her?"

"Not really."

It was a tough climb up the hill. We stopped at the top to rest a minute before heading toward where the guest parking lot had been. The parking field was gone as were the wildly overgrown hedges that had once marked the rear boundary of the lot, but the concrete steps that led down to where the pool area and ball courts used to be still remained. The same could not be said for the pool and courts themselves. Now nothing but a great flat field with hills in the distance appeared in the beam of my flashlight. We started across the field.

About fifty yards on was where the late Anton Harder had established his angry white boys town: a collection of ratty trailers, abandoned cars, and abandoned souls. The people who lived there were a ragtag collection of losers, misfits, and bigots. Harder had his own reasons for choosing the Fir Grove property as base camp. His mother, Missy, a hotel chambermaid, had died in the fire. As the flames had consumed his mother, the hate had consumed him. He had even built a shrine to her not very far away from the foundation of the workers' quarters.

"Come on, let's go." Barto nudged me along with his gun.

We kept on ahead, insects hurtling themselves into my hand as they flew toward the source of the light.

"Did you kill the kid?"

"Yeah," he said, as if he were telling me the time.

I was glad I hadn't run when he gave me the chance. He would have shot me. I could see where this was headed. Brightman would kill Katy and Barto would kill me. It was to be a neat and tidy little package of revenge.

"The other kid, the one really named Patrick, are you going to kill him too?"

"You know, Prager, that's pretty good. How did you know there was two of them?"

"I wasn't sure until earlier today. The tattoo artist confirmed that wasn't her work on the autopsy photos of John James that my man showed her. But I think I had doubts the night I found the kid's body. He just didn't look quite right and I could never figure out why the kid would've lied to me about his name when there was nothing to gain by it. I guess Patrick is the one that looks more like Katy's brother."

"I don't know. They looked the same to me. Maybe it's the one eye thing. You ask me, it was a lot of trouble to go through because of a grudge, but I'm not paying the freight."

"You think Connie Geary knows what she's been paying for?" I asked.

"Moe, you figured a lot of this shit out. I'm impressed. I gotta hand it to you, you're pretty fucking smart."

"Yeah, just not smart enough. I'm the one walking with the gun stuck in his back. So, Ralph, you didn't answer me. Are you going to kill the other kid?"

"Nah."

"No!"

"No. He's already dead. Brightman killed him in front of your wife. Wanted to give her some closure after all we put her through. It was the least we could do." Barto snickered as he had on the phone, his true nature showing itself.

That did it. I lost control and spun around swinging. I caught Barto off guard, but I wasn't quite quick enough. I got in one good punch, but it glanced off his jaw. He simply stepped back, letting my momentum and gravity pull me down.

"Nice try," he said. "I'm gonna enjoy killing you. Let's go!"

I ignored the threat and tried to regain my equilibrium. I couldn't let him get to me anymore. I started talking.

"What about Martello?"

"That asshole, what about him? Truth is, it took you a lot longer to get to him than we figured. We thought you'd interview him right away, but you never was very conventional in the way you did things. I suppose if you were, I'd still have my left eye, you'd have your gold shield, and Brightman'd be president. You shoulda just left things alone back then, Moe. What did finding the truth get you anyway?" Barto coughed and spit. "Fucking bugs keep getting in my throat."

"That's why you picked a pewter Yukon, because Martello drove one!"

"Right. Good thing he liked a roomy ride. It would've been hell for me if he drove a Miata. I'd look pretty stupid driving them kids around behind the wheel of one of those little things. Woulda looked like the clown car at the circus. Let me tell you something about that guy Martello, Moe, he mighta come after you one day on his own. He fucking hated you."

"When you told Ray what you had in mind for him, did he feel any better about you sacrificing his life in a just cause? I mean, you did drug him up, stick the murder weapon in his pocket, and force him to run into the traffic on Ocean Parkway."

Barto snickered again. "You shoulda seen him bounce and skid, man. It was pretty cool."

We had nearly reached the crest of the hill. Just a hundred feet ahead and down the hill, in a small glen was where the workers' quarters had been. I had no doubt that was where Brightman and Katy were waiting. Only a few yards before the crest, Barto ordered me to stop.

"Turn around!"

When I turned, I saw Barto raising his weapon at me. *What the fuck are you doing? This isn't the way it's supposed to happen, asshole.* I opened my mouth to say something, but found I was so angry I couldn't speak. He ordered me to back up to the crest. When I stopped, he put twenty or thirty shots at my feet and above my head. I didn't have time to react. He shook his head at me.

"Nah, you ain't a puker," he said, regarding me with a sick kind of admiration. "You look more pissed off than scared."

"Can I ask you one thing before we go?"

"Sure."

"Do you really think you're going to get away with this?"

"Me, I *am* gonna get away with it. As for Brightman … I don't think he gives a shit whether he will or not. I think he's sorta beyond that. Now, let's go."

When we came over the crest, I saw the little campsite set up where I remembered the foundation had been. There was a sizeable fire going, a pretty big tent, and not another thing in sight. This was no place for a Brooklyn boy to die. Still, any place was better than a hospital, I thought. As we approached, the tent flap opened and Brightman emerged. Katy was nowhere to be seen. That wasn't good for a lot of reasons. While I was still confident he hadn't killed her, I had no hope of saving her if I didn't know where she was to be saved.

"Hello, Moe. Still not feeling very smug, are you?"

"Where's Katy?"

"She's close enough."

"Where's Katy?"

"Ralph, please teach our guest some manners."

I clenched in anticipation of the blow, but it didn't come.

"Cut the shit, Brightman," Barto said, "and let's get this over with."

"Where's Katy?"

"Goodness, Moe, you sound like a broken record."

"CD."

"What?"

"There are no records anymore, Brightman. It's CDs and soon there won't be any of those. That's your problem, you're living too much in the past."

"Oh, yeah, do you think so? I'll show you what *your* problem is."

He went back into the tent and came out dragging Katy by her hair. She didn't struggle. That scared me. She was trussed up, hands to ankles behind her, a strip of duct tape across her mouth. He pulled her up onto her knees. She wasn't bleeding and there were no obvious cuts or bruises on her, but her eyes were impassive. I hoped it was just shock, but I knew it was more, much more. The last month had plunged her into a deep well with slick and very steep walls. Brightman had an automatic in his waistband, but asked Barto for my .38.

"*This* is your problem, Moe," he said, pulling back the hammer of my .38 and pressing the short barrel to Katy's temple. He didn't pull the trigger. It wasn't time. He hadn't gone through all of this to shoot her within two minutes of my arrival. That was good. The longer he took, the better our chances of getting out of this, if not unscathed, then alive.

"I'm not playing, Brightman."

"Yeah," Barto seconded, "shoot the bitch so I can kill this asshole. Let's get outta here."

"Quiet! I want to savor this. Once she's dead, I don't care what you do to him. That's the deal."

"Whatever," Barto said.

Brightman got on his knees next to Katy and wrapped his free arm around her shoulder. "I just want you to know that this is all your ex-husband's doing. Did he ever tell you about what really happened between us? Shake your head yes or no."

Katy, her eyes still impassive, shook no.

"I didn't think so. Moe does like his secrets, doesn't he?"

Silent tears began rolling down Katy's cheeks and I nearly collapsed. Secrets, the gifts that keep on giving. The pain my silence had caused seemed endless. In a voice barely above a whisper, Brightman explained to Katy how instead of accepting my gold detective's shield and living happily ever after, I had reopened the investigation into Moira Heaton's murder. He told her how I had backtracked and discovered that he, Brightman, not Ivan Alfonseca, had murdered Moira.

"Moira knew too much," he said. "She knew that I had killed a neighborhood boy when I was a kid. I hadn't meant to kill him, not really, but what do intentions ever have to do with anything, especially in the face of murder?"

The flow of tears was much heavier now and Katy's body shook, the tape muffling her sobs.

"But did your husband go to the police with the truth? No, he didn't. Moe, tell Katy what you did."

"I told you, Brightman, I'm not playing."

Barto shoved me in the back. "Do it!"

"No."

"Okay, then *I'll* do it," Barto said. Brightman's eyes got angry, but Barto had the bigger gun. "Moe set Brightman up and goaded him into a confession. Even made him piss his pants. What Brightman didn't know was that his wife and Thomas Geary had watched and listened to the whole thing. There. Now, can we get this over with?"

I could see in his eyes that Brightman was getting ready for the finale.

"How could I go to the police?" I said. "I had no proof and all the witnesses were dead."

"I thought you weren't playing," he said.

"I waited until you started lying."

He shoved the .38 into Katy's ribs so hard she crumpled in pain. He pulled her back up. The passivity was gone from her eyes.

"That's right, instead of being satisfied with ruining my career, he had to hurt my wife. Ruining me professionally didn't really cut it for Moe Prager. No, he wanted to punish me in a personal way, so he used my wife."

"I always regretted doing that. I realized I'd punished her more than you."

"Katerina divorced me in about thirty seconds. She couldn't understand how she could have shared her bed with a murderer and not have known. That question haunted her for the rest of her life. Did you know she—"

"—died last summer. Yeah, I know. I'm sorry. Katerina was really sweet and one of the most stunningly beautiful women I've ever met," I said. "Cancer, right?"

"No, it wasn't cancer, it was the haunting and the guilt."

"Guilt?"

"Oh, so there are things you don't know?" Brightman taunted.

He whispered something into Katy's ear that I couldn't hear. There was immediate and crushing ache in Katy's eyes. I hadn't seen anything like it since the miscarriage, since Connie Geary's wedding day, when Katy sat sobbing in a stall of the women's bathroom at the Lonesome Piper County Club. She sobbed now so that even the tape couldn't contain the sound of it. She cried so hard that her body seemed to convulse.

"Do you want to know what I told her, Moe?"

No. "Yes."

"I told her that a week after you confronted me on the street and got me to confess my sins, Katerina had an abortion. She was empty after that, empty ever after. That's what killed her, not cancer."

More than anything, I wanted to call him a lying motherfucker. I wanted to accuse him of fabricating that story so he could torture the both of us with it, but I knew he was telling the truth even before the words were fully out of his mouth. And now, finally, I understood why he had gone to such elaborate means.

"Kill me," I said, spreading my arms out. "Just leave her alone. Don't repeat my mistake."

Brightman aimed my .38 as his mouth formed the word no, but I couldn't hear him. I couldn't hear anything above the *thwap thwap*

thwap of the helicopter blades. The downwash kicked up a storm of dirt and rocks. An intense and blinding spotlight encircled us. I shielded my eyes. There was the bark of gunfire. I spun. Barto's head rocked back. Crimson spray danced in the light. A flash. Several flashes. Something bit hard into my ankle and burned its way into the bone. I went down. More shots. I pushed my face out of the dirt. Brightman was no longer standing. He was on his back, arms thrown out, one leg bent completely beneath him. I crawled over to Katy.

The pain in her eyes was gone, with it had gone the light. I pulled the tape off her mouth and put my lips to hers. They were still warm, but the pressure of my weight on her body forced blood out of her mouth and onto my lips. I smeared her blood across my face. I hoped my tears would never wash it away. I was wrong about my destiny. It didn't lay in front, but behind me.

There was a hand on my shoulder. I turned to see Agent Markowitz standing at my back, a mournful, pleading look on his face. He was speaking but it was all just twisted lips and a jumble of noise. He pointed at my wrecked ankle, the blood gushing out of it, mixing with the dirt, mixing with the blood of the dead. Markowitz pulled off his shirt and pressed it hard against my leg, his mouth moving the whole time. I was starting to catch words now, a few at a time. He was shouting the same thing at me over and over again. Finally, I understood.

"How do you feel?"

I didn't answer. Brightman's words were so loud in my head, I didn't think I would ever hear anything else again. *How does it feel? How did I feel? How would I feel?*

Empty.

Empty ever after.

EPILOGUE
SPREADING THE ASHES

SARAH RECEIVED THE videotape about a week after we buried Katy. The tape was from Brightman, mailed by proxy—maybe his lawyer, but probably Connie Geary—shortly after his death. On the tape, he confessed to the murders of Carl Stipe, the little boy from his home town, Moira Heaton, and Patrick Farner, the other Patrick Michael Maloney impersonator. Ralph Barto, he said, had murdered John James, Fallon, Martello, and Mary White. He explained to my daughter why he had murdered her mother. It was, he said, my fault for having slowly killed his ex-wife. He took great pains to discuss the details of my involvement.

When Sarah came to me, there was little I could refute. I hadn't left things well enough alone all those years ago. I had indeed rejected the offer of the gold shield I had so desperately wanted in order to dig and dig and dig until I found the truth out about Steven Brightman. When I found the truth, I set Brightman up to confess in front of his wife. I had wanted to punish him by using her. And in the end, I shared the truth with almost no one who was directly involved. Carl Stipe's mother and Moira Heaton's father went to their graves without knowing what had actually happened to their children.

Sarah hasn't spoken to me in nearly a year. She took a leave of absence from the University of Michigan and moved into Francis Maloney's old house on Hanover Street in Janus. To think that I lost Sarah to him not because of anything he did, but because of my own blindness is irony beyond even my ability to comprehend. Sometimes on rainy nights when I can't sleep, I imagine I can hear him laughing at me. On those nights I pour myself a Dewar's, look out my window at the black waters of Sheepshead Bay, and raise my glass to him. "Yes, Francis," I say, "I do believe in ghosts."

Pete Vandervoort keeps me updated about Sarah. She's still dating Robby, the deputy sheriff. Pete tells me they're pretty happy together and that Robby's a good cop. I've got nothing against the kid, but I hope like hell he finds another job or Sarah finds another man. Mostly I hope that Sarah can someday forgive me and try to understand that I meant for none of this to happen and that if I could bargain with God, if there was a god to bargain with, I would gladly sacrifice myself to take back even the least of the damage. But as Brightman remarked that night, "What do intentions ever have to do with anything, especially in the face of murder?"

Brightman gave a lot of other information on the tape, stuff only of interest to me and Feeney and the Ohio and Kentucky cops. He explained how he and Barto had picked Martello as the fall guy—*He hated your father maybe more than I did and he tended to act out*—how they arranged for fake credit cards in Martello's name—*Ralph Barto was well acquainted with a Nigerian gang that specialized in identity theft*—how they induced Mr. Fallon to do the grave desecrations—*Money, and the phony deed to a nonexistent house on Galway Bay*—how they got Mary White to conspire—*We falsified some New York City Department of Public Health forms indicating that Patrick Maloney had been the one to infect her brother with HIV. Of course, Patrick had died years before anyone had ever heard of HIV or AIDS, but our money helped cloud Mary's memory.*

Steven Brightman didn't deem either John James or Patrick Farner worthy of explanation. Why would he? Chess players don't bother explaining the sacrifice of their pawns. There was also one other glaring omission in his taped confession. He hadn't discussed how he managed to finance his revenge. I chose not to discuss it either, at least not on the record.

In October, I was thumbing through the *Daily News* when I saw the obituary for Thomas Geary. He had been buried in a private family ceremony days before the story was released to the press. I waited out the week before driving to Crocus Valley. When Connie saw my face on the security monitor, she said nothing, buzzing me through the front gate even before I pressed the intercom. Riding up to the house, I passed some teenagers tossing a football around on the lawn. I watched for a little while. It was easy to pick out Connie's son, Craig Jr. He had the Geary genes. He was tall and handsome and had perfect form when throwing the football.

"Hello, Moe," she said, relief in her voice and resignation on her face. "I've been expecting you for months."

"I know you have."

"You're limping."

"I'll be limping for a long time," I said. "The cast just recently came off."

"Well, you better come in."

We did what we did. Connie played and I drank scotch. No show tunes today. I didn't question her, but just let her speak when she was ready.

"The first time I slept with Steven, I was sixteen years old. It was magical. He was nothing like the boys I'd been with at camp or at school. He took his time with me, treated me like a woman, always pleasing me first. Of course he would treat me that way. He was a man, not a boy. He taught me how to enjoy my own body. Even now, knowing all that I know about what a horrible man he was, I'm wet thinking about him. I disgust you, Moe, don't I?"

"This is your story to tell, Connie," I said, pouring myself more scotch.

"Of course I think my father knew almost immediately. Sixteen-year-old girls think they are very good at keeping secrets, but they're almost transparent. You would know that. You have a girl."

I knew more about secrets than sixteen-year-old girls. Having a child doesn't make you an expert on children; it doesn't even make you an expert on your own child. I didn't say a word. Connie took that as a cue to continue.

"My father gave his tacit, if not spoken, approval to our relationship. It was a useful tool that helped him control us both. Controlling people, that was very important to my dad."

"I know."

"Yes, you would know. My father's approval came to an end when he saw that Steven had an unlimited future as a politician. He made us break it off, but not by confronting me. He went to Steven."

"I bet your dad didn't have to threaten Brightman, did he?"

"I don't actually know, but my father could be incredibly persuasive without ever having to resort to direct threat."

That was another aspect of Thomas Geary's personality I was well familiar with. Connie went on to explain that they hadn't fully broken it off until Brightman got engaged to Katerina.

"Of course he loved Katerina. She was wonderful and god-awfully beautiful. I know women who had crushes on her." Connie Geary blushed. "After their divorce and the resignation, my dad kept Steven afloat. I suppose he felt responsible for him, like Dr. Frankenstein for his monster. It wasn't a week before we were sleeping together again."

She went on explaining about how her own marriage fell apart—*I never really loved Craig. I didn't even love the idea of him*—and how, after her father's illness, she managed the family's funds. Brightman's stipend grew ever larger. But they had never managed to recapture the early magic. *Even when he was fucking me, he was fucking her.*

"You see, Moe, it was easy for me to act the whore for you. I had been acting as a whore for years. And," she said, reaching across the piano placing her hand on mine, "you made it easy on me. You were good and you were present."

I pulled my hand away.

"I didn't know about the murders, I give you my word. I did know about the scheme to frighten and confuse your wife with the actors. I helped him. I financed him, but I was desperate to exorcise Katerina's ghost. After she died, her ghost took up more and more room in our bed."

There was a knock on the front door. I stood up. "That'll be the police," I said, pulling the wire out from under my shirt. "I'm through keeping secrets, Connie. The secrets stop here. Don't worry. I doubt you'll do time."

If I was expecting anger or defiance, I didn't get it. Constance Geary, I think, wanted this over as much as anyone. The wealthy understand the cost of doing business and paying a fair price.

ISRAEL K. PRAGER was born on March 29, 2001. He weighed exactly what Sarah had weighed at birth. It was to laugh, no? Who can explain these things? Klaus thinks the K is for him. Kosta thinks it's for him. Carmella and I let people think what they want. When he's old enough to understand, I will explain it to him. The three of us live pretty well and happily in my condo. Although I'm not sure my single neighbors are too thrilled with the arrangement. I guess we'll eventually buy a house somewhere, but not yet.

Before Carmella and I got married, I asked if she wanted to change her name back to Marina. It was, after all, her real name, the name she had when we first met. For me, there never was and never will be any shame associated with it. She said no, that as long as we knew the truth about who and what we were, that was the only important thing. I suppose it was. To say I love my son as if he was my own is cliché. It is nonetheless true. He is magic. Sometimes at night, I hold him in my arms and tell him about his big sister. I tell him that if we could make a family out of broken parts and discards, there's always room for one more.

NOT LONG AFTER Katy's funeral and the fallout from Brightman's tape, I was called to testify in front of a federal grand jury. The government was preparing its case against the bikers and I was a peripheral witness. My testimony, as the U.S. Attorney explained, was the cherry on the whipped cream on top of the cake. Even without me, all of these guys were going away for a very long time. I had been a part of and around law enforcement long enough to know that the Feds believed in piling on. Why charge someone with a hundred counts when you can charge them with a hundred and one? If the government wants you, you're in trouble. Once they've got you, you're fucked.

Outside the grand jury room I walked past a man in a neat blue suit and silk tie.

"Moe!" he called after me. It was Agent Markowitz.

"Crank in a suit. You clean up pretty good," I said. "You've lost weight. I didn't recognize you."

"Crank," he repeated shaking his head. "Great name, huh? I just wanted to apologize again about—"

"Don't apologize. You guys nearly pulled it off. It was my fault, not yours."

"It's just that using the tracking device on your car, we couldn't get men in place in time. We had to use the chopper." He pointed at the cast on my leg. "How's the ankle?"

"Hurts like a sonovabitch."

"The funeral, how did that go?"

"Divorce fucks everything up, including death. It's a long painful story, so let's forget it."

"Okay."

We shook hands and I hobbled out of the courthouse. I didn't look back. It hurt too much to look back.

IN DECEMBER, STEVEN Roth and I flew to Warsaw, Poland, carrying a very special piece of cargo, the urn containing the ashes of Israel Roth. I had held onto his ashes for nearly ten years. For in spite of what Mr. Roth had said to me in my car on that long-ago day when I'd taken him to say Kaddish at his wife's grave, I hadn't known where to spread his ashes. I hadn't known until fate and a false ghost interceded.

We took a train from Warsaw to Krakow and hired a car. At six the next morning we met our guide and an official of the Polish government at the hotel. Both the official and tour guide checked our papers and we set off for Oswiecim or, as most of the world knows it, Auschwitz-Birkenau. The ride took a little over an hour, but seemed to have taken much much longer. It might have helped if someone had uttered a single word.

The weather was just as Mr. Roth had described it to me. It was cold and dreary. A mixture of rain and snow fell on us as we walked from the car. The camp, a museum since 1947, opened at 8:00 a.m. The government official was keen that we finish our business before the gates opened. He wasn't mean-spirited about it, just nervous. I got the sense that what Steven and I were doing wasn't standard operating procedure. Our guide was crestfallen, but he needn't have worried. No matter how many newsreels, movies, or documentaries you've seen, no matter how many books you've read, no matter what you know or what you think you know about the Holocaust, being at Auschwitz, even for a few minutes, changes you. But as hard as it was for me to be there, it was much worse for Steven. For the sins visited upon his father had lived on to be visited upon him. There were victims of the Holocaust yet to be born.

We explained to our guide what we were looking for and he said he knew just such a place. He walked us over to the spot. It's hard to say that one frozen patch of snow-covered earth is better than another, but for our purposes this patch of earth seemed well chosen. We asked the guide and the government man to excuse us. After they left us, Steven and I spread handfuls of Israel Roth's ashes onto the slippery ground. When there was nothing left in the urn, I took a card out of my coat pocket and began to recite Kaddish, the mourner's prayer. "*Yis-ga-dal v'yis-ka-dash sh'may ra-bo, B'ol-mo dee-v'ro* ..."

As I read off the card, Steven Roth joined in. He didn't need the card. After finishing the prayer and saying our amens, I held Steven's hands in mine.

"Kaddish and ashes, it's what he wanted," I said. "I guess part of him never left this place."

"Part of us will never leave here either."

Who was I to argue?

AFTERWORD

Many years ago, I asked Lee Child when he would know the time had come to pull down the curtain on his Jack Reacher series. He was incredulous. His answer was something like, "Why would I ever do that?" It was only after reading several more of his series books that I completely understood his response. Reacher is untethered to a specific place. He travels light, very light. His past is shadowy and malleable. And, if there's an overriding series arc, Lee has masterfully disguised it. Though I am surely not the first person to point this out, Reacher is the *High Plains Drifter*. It was only through understanding the very clever way Lee had constructed the Reacher series that I came to understand why I had asked him the question in the first place. I asked because I knew that someday I would have to close the door, or, more aptly, turn the page on Moe Prager.

You need only look at my sales figures to know Moe Prager is no Jack Reacher. In many ways, Moe is, in conception, at least, the antithesis of the *High Plains Drifter*. Moe is utterly tethered to a specific place—Coney Island, Brooklyn—to his family, to a business he despises, to secrets, but, most of all, to his past. Moe's history is his history. He knows only what he knows. There can be no fudging or blurring of lines. Moe ages during the course of the series. He is in his thirties in *Walking the Perfect Square* and his fifties in *Empty Ever After*. When I wrote *Walking* … I included sort of an artificial timeline for the series—1978 to 1998. This was the one thing I knew I could, if necessary, dispense with. As long as Moe didn't die in 1998, I could continue the series. One problem: you can't continue a series without a publisher. If only readers understood the profound effect the business end of publishing has on the books that are written. Alas.

I had a two-book contract with Bleak House Books. *Soul Patch*, the fourth book in the series, was done and I had one more Moe book to write. It was an interesting challenge because I didn't know if there would be another contract. *Empty Ever After*—a title taken from a song by the Brooklyn rock band The Shirts—would have been a different book had I known for sure it would be the last book in the series. As I didn't know that to be the case at the time, I had to write a book that would on the one hand give loyal Moe readers a sense of series closure and, on the other, leave the door open for the series to continue. No easy task, that. Yet, even had I known there would be more Moe books to follow, I realized that things had to change. The books had become too heavily burdened with backstory. Moe's past was essential to the success of the books, but it also became an albatross. I found I was spending too much time explaining details from the earlier books. I also realized that the story arc concerning Moe's keeping of Patrick Maloney's secret was played out. I had done all I could do with that conceit and, frankly, I wasn't interested in trying to breathe new life into it.

So the challenge became an opportunity. *Empty Ever After* would allow me to wrap up all the loose ends left over from the previous four books in the series and to introduce some new characters and situations that might extend the life of the series. What better way to move on emotionally and practically, I thought, than by ritually burying the past. It is no accident that the prologue takes place in a cemetery. The cemetery motif recurs throughout the novel and is meant to symbolize the death of the story arc surrounding Patrick Maloney's disappearance and murder. In the novel, Moe revisits all of his old cases and interacts with many of the most memorable characters from the earlier books. This was done so the loyal Moe readers could pay their respects and say their farewells. Me too. I was always curious about what had happened to Nancy Lustig and Judas Wannsee and Connie Geary. Ultimately, I wanted to bury Mr. Roth—the moral center of the series—as well. Along with death comes rebirth and this was why I brought back Carmella Melendez. The birth of her son Israel is symbolic on two levels. His arrival marks a new turn for Moe and the series, but by naming him Israel—after Israel Roth—I would tie any future Moe books to the older books in the series.

Reed Farrel Coleman
June 2010

Dear Readers,

When my great friend Israel Roth died many years ago, he bequeathed me some money, many of his old photographs, and the contents of the house he owned and rented out in the Midwood section of Brooklyn. He had long since made Florida his permanent home, but Israel Roth was a man who, in spite of his best efforts, could never let go of the past. That's why he could never bear to sell that old house. The house was part of him as sure as his own arms and legs. He was a man who understood history, not as a stream of facts or dates and places or as a list of names of generals and despots to be remembered and recited on cue, but as a living breathing thing. As a concentration camp survivor, he was a small piece in the puzzle of man's ugliest moment in time.

Unlike many survivors, Mr. Roth was not shy about discussing his years in the camps, but I was completely stunned by what I found in a trunk in the attic of his old Midwood house. In a large white envelope that had yellowed and was more a memory than an envelope—it disintegrated in my hands—were a collection of several legal pads covered in faded handwriting I recognized immediately as Israel Roth's. On the pads were several short stories Mr. Roth had written based upon his brief time in Treblinka and his torments in Auschwitz. I recognized some of the incidents described in these stories as being directly inspired by Mr. Roth's own experiences, but not all the incidents described were about him nor was the camp he described in the stories identifiable as either Treblinka or Auschwitz. I don't think that was the point nor was Mr. Roth the point. He wanted to leave behind the essence of the overwhelming inhumanity to which he had borne witness and to try and explain how one could survive in such places and still be a human being. I now share one of those stories with you. Learn from him as I learned.

With Sincerest Love and Respect for Israel Roth,

Moe Prager

FEEDING THE CROCODILE
BY
ISRAEL ROTH

THE BAKER SANG as he always sang while kneading the dough. It was a sad song, a song that once made his late wife spill her tears into the mother yeast, the yeast he still used to make his loaves rise. Although his son thought he was a superstitious old fool, the baker swore that his Anya's soul lived in the yeast and no one could convince him otherwise. It was why his bread was so prized by all the people of this small Polish town.

Everyone, Jew and gentile alike, Bolsheviks and National Socialists from the German side of the border, came to Baruch's tiny shop in the ghetto. And it was a fight over the last loaf in the shop that had led to the blood feud between the two families.

Exhausted and hungry, Isaac Becker closed his tattered notebook.

"More!" barked Kleinmann. "What happens to the old baker's daughter? Does she escape Poland with the documents? Does Pavel, the dirty Bolshevik scum, help her or turn her over to the Gestapo to save his own worthless hide? More!"

"Not tonight, I'm afraid, Herr Lieutenant Kleinmann. I am feeling weak. There was much much work on the ash heap today. Have you ever shoveled wet ashes?"

"You Jews! Always complaining. Always ungrateful. Remember, Becker, if not for me, you would be in the heap and not on it."

"I remember. Every day, I remember. I thank the God of Israel for your kindness."

"Good, then write well tonight, Becker. Pray to that God of yours to inspire you, for I will dream again of the old baker's daughter and what will become of her."

"But my rations ... what about—"

"You will have your crusts and soup," Kleinmann said, cutting Becker off mid-question as he always did.

It was as ritualized as the dance of bees, these nightly exchanges between Werner Kleinmann, the SS lieutenant, and Isaac Becker, the Jew. With the exception of Becker's tales, even the words they spoke had become formalized, as if they were the names of words instead of the words themselves. Any implied irony or threat that may have been a part of the ritual when the dance partners took their first awkward steps together had long since been forgotten.

"Thank you, Herr Lieutenant Kleinmann." Becker bowed as he always did, as was expected.

Becker waited for the words. *You're welcome, Isaac.* These words never came. The lieutenant dismissed the prisoner with a curt, backhanded slap of the air as a finger of flame might snap at an impudent moth. Lately it dawned on Becker that things omitted from a ritual are part of the ritual too, but this revelation did not quench his thirst or fill his belly.

Closing the door behind him and plodding through the mud back to his barracks, Becker cursed Kleinmann in several tongues. In hell, one is educated in many things. He loved Hungarian curses best of all. He delighted at the sound and rhythm of the language, and the creativity of the curses was unparalleled. He had never been to Hungary and once had dreamed of some day visiting. But he had months ago stopped dreaming of walking the streets of Budapest and just listening to the people chatter about the magnificent and the mundane. His current hell was as close to Budapest as he would ever get.

So caught up was he in his cursing, Becker hadn't noticed the approach of Jacob Weisen. Weisen and Becker were from the same small village on the German side of the Polish border. They had met for the first time when they were five, their hate for one another immediate and mutual. The depth of their loathing was beyond social, beyond merely molecular. It was metaphysical. At home, they had managed, for the most part, to avoid contact. That proved impossible in the camp, their having been assigned to the same barracks. Worse for Becker was Weisen's position as head of the retribution squad.

A death camp is a special kind of prison, but a prison nonetheless. In all prisons, there are rules and there are lines and there are lines not to be crossed, ever. Given the cheapness of life and the ever-hungry machinery of death behind the barbed wire and electrical fences, no one seemed keen on appeals or second chances. This was especially true of the prisoner enforcers. Yes, at its basest level, life inside this place was all about survival: a few more minutes, an extra day, two weeks, perhaps a month. But at what price? How close to the line should one step?

"So, Isaac Becker, you have again been feeding the crocodile," prodded Weisen.

"The crocodile? What nonsense are you talking now, Weisen?"

"Have you never heard it said that the frightened man feeds the crocodile in the hope that he will be eaten last?"

"I am a teller of tales, not a chef. I work on the heap just like you and the rest of the men in our barracks."

"But you eat better than us, don't you?"

This stunned Becker. Lieutenant Kleinmann had assured Isaac that none of the other prisoners would ever learn of their special arrangement. The change in Becker's expression was not lost on Weisen.

"How typical of you to assume you are the only lost soul in hell to have made a deal with the devil. Fool! Do you ever wonder where your rewards come from? For every one of your extra rations, there is a little more smoke, the heap gets a little taller."

Becker felt as if Weisen had just whacked him across the ribs with a plank. He was short of breath, suddenly nauseous, and might've vomited right there in the mud had there been enough food in his system to bring back up. He had never wanted to consider from where his extra rations had come. He hadn't wanted to think about it because he knew. He had known from that first day the lieutenant pulled him off the pile.

"You are the storyteller," said the SS man. "In such a place as this, your talent is a commodity as precious as gold fillings and hidden diamonds, Becker." The SS man had pointed at the crematoria. "If a man's soul is gray when he is stationed here, the smoke will blacken it. If a man's soul is already black …"

"And yours, Herr Lieutenant Kleinmann, what is its hue?"

"Never mind my soul, storyteller. Your job is to make sure that a little sun shines through the smoke."

And so the deal had been struck. Becker would provide the sun, Kleinmann the bread and soup.

"What's the matter? You've gone gray, Becker," Weisen asked, snapping the storyteller back into the moment. "You walk a very thin tightrope between us and the crocodile. His protection extends only so far. One day soon, you will be part of the pile and your rations will go to some other scum who has traded in your soul for one more day in paradise. Sooner or later, Becker, we are all eaten by one crocodile or another."

Becker opened up his mouth to explain, but the words would not come. He knew he could not risk telling another inmate of his plan. Weisen's threats had only reinforced Becker's belief that there were no secrets in Hades.

o   o   o

WHEN HE WAS certain that the baker's daughter was well into the tunnel beneath the shul, Pavel twisted the hand grenade fuse and pulled Herr Ernst, the Gestapo man, close by his black leather lapels. First, confusion washed across the crystalline azure sea of the Nazi's eyes, then fear like a raging storm roiled the waters. Herr Ernst pounded his fists against the Russian's chest, but to no avail. Pavel simply smiled.

In that brief second, he was as at peace as any man who had ever lived. He could see his mother's weathered face set against the swaying field of golden wheat, her red and blue babushka snapping in the wind. He smelled the sweet aroma of onions frying in chicken fat and the fragrant steam rising from the boiling buckwheat. When he was certain there was no turning back, Pavel released Ernst's lapels. He pressed his fingers softly to his mouth, remembering the feel of Esther's lips against his. Then nothing.

When the old baker heard the explosion from the street outside the shul, he smiled and pressed the stolen Luger to his temple, his tears pouring into the mother yeast. He would not survive to knead the next batch of dough. That would be for new hands, but he and his wife would live on, their souls bubbling up together as long as the new baker fed the yeast. Perhaps they would live forever.

Becker closed the tattered notebook.

It was time for the dance of bees to begin, but it did not. When Becker looked up, he noticed tears streaming down Kleinmann's cheeks. In that moment Becker felt a level of revulsion and hate for Kleinmann, for his own writing, for himself that he never imagined possible. How, in this place where the worst atrocities were perpetrated by one human against another on an hourly basis, could his story make Kleinmann weep? He had witnessed Kleinmann execute prisoners for the mildest perceived slight, even for slipping on the heap, sometimes simply for sport. Nor was Becker blind to the teenage girls Kleinmann had brought into his office. The crocodile was hungry for more than stories.

226

"Bravo, Becker. Bravo!" The lieutenant raved, wiping away tears between claps. "Thank you. Thank you."

At last, Kleinmann uttered the words Becker had longed to hear.

"There will be meat for you tonight, Isaac Becker. Triple rations."

In his head, Becker heard Weisen's voice. *Triple rations. The smoke grows more dense. The heap grows taller still.*

The SS man smiled. "Or maybe you would prefer some companionship instead? Man does not live by bread alone, eh, Becker?"

Now Becker wanted to rip his own eyes out of their sockets. "That is most kind, Herr Lieutenant Kleinmann, but the rations will be fine." On the verge of tears himself, Isaac Becker stood to go.

"I have not dismissed you, Becker. Here, bring me your book, that magic book of yours."

Becker's body clenched in fear. "The magic is in me, not the book."

"The book, Becker! Now!"

What choice did he have really? He slid the book across the desk to the SS man. The Nazi stroked the book, patted it, picked it up and caressed it. Then, when he opened the book, Becker had to prop himself against the desk for fear of fainting. The scowl on Kleinmann's face did nothing to improve Becker's equilibrium.

"What is this, Becker? What language is this?" he growled at the storyteller.

Becker sighed silently, thankful for the lieutenant's lack of language skills. He got some string back in his legs and said, "Hungarian, sir, Magyar."

"Hungarian! The Magyars were once Aryans, but are now inbred pigs. Why don't you write in German or even Yiddish? Is this some kind of trick, Jew?"

"I don't dispute you about the Hungarians, Herr Lieutenant Kleinmann, but their language sings to me. Learning the language has occupied my mind here and it helps me with my writing. Even you, sir, have said that one's mind must be occupied in such a place as this."

The scowl evaporated. "Yes, I have said this. Whatever helps you with your magic. I suppose the language in which you write is irrelevant, so long as when you read to me . . ." Kleinmann again became emotional. "You are dismissed. Go to the rear of Building Five. Your rations will be waiting." Becker stood his ground. "What is it now? I said you can go."

"But my book, Herr—"

"You have no possessions here, Becker, only the illusion of possession. That illusion is solely dependent upon me. Savor your meat. Take the night off from your writing. Tomorrow, I will keep you off the ash heap and I will have a new notebook for you and pens, the best pens."

Becker dared not show his anger. He bowed, turned, hurried through the door, and, for the first time in his life, sought out the company of Jacob Weisen.

"DO YOU KNOW what they will do to you if you are caught, Becker? For this, it won't be anything as gentle as the gas and that's no treat," Weisen warned. "It would be better if they shot you."

"No. You must see it happens as we discussed it."

Weisen shook his head. "All this for a book of tales. If I had known you were such a fool, I wouldn't have despised you quite so much."

"Then it is a fool's errand and I will pay for the folly, not you."

"Very well."

Becker grabbed Weisen's forearm. "You will give the book to the Gypsy and he will get it out of the camp."

"You have my word."

JACOB WEISEN HAD explained how it was possible to get back to Kleinmann's office without drawing unwanted attention. This part of the camp was dark and not well patrolled. No need, really. On those rare occasions when prisoners got loose, they did not run to the ash heap. They knew they would get there soon enough without helping their murderers. Now Isaac Becker, the teller of tales, lay face down in the mud, waiting. For nearly an hour he had listened to Kleinmann forcing himself on one of the blank-faced girls. *Bitch!* the pig would call her, slapping her hard as he grunted. Then there was silence. A few minutes later, two guards showed up at his office door.

"She looks like she could use delousing," one of the guards joked.

"Yes, a shower would do her well," said the other.

"No, not this one, not tonight. I am in high spirits tonight. Clean her up and send her to the enlisted men's brothel," Kleinmann said, as if he were a genie granting the girl her first wish.

Shortly after the guards left, the lieutenant headed to his quarters.

HE HAD UNEXPECTED company.

"Becker, what are you doing here? Are you mad? You know this isn't permitted. You could be shot and there isn't a thing I could do about it. Come, walk in the shadows with me." He looped his arm through Becker's and pulled him into the dark.

"My book, please, Herr Lieutenant Kleinmann."

"What did you say, Becker? Did you again call it *your* book? You Jews are a stubborn race. I—"

Pushing the SS man against the side of an empty hut, Isaac Becker covered Kleinmann's mouth with his muddied hand and plunged a sharpened wedge of glass—the other end padded with a stolen sock—into the SS man's liver. When he was certain it was in very deep, Becker snapped the glass off so there would be no hope of removing the makeshift blade. Just like in his story, there was confusion in the blue eyes of the victim, then fear. Death came soon enough and more mercifully than it would come for Isaac Becker. The storyteller took back his precious book and retraced the path Weisen had laid out for him.

IT TOOK BECKER three days to die on the cross. They had tortured him first and then let him heal enough to make the crucifixion worth their trouble. The cross had been centrally placed so the prisoners would be forced to pass by the dying man while going to and from their barracks. Those prisoners who lacked ringside seats had been marched over to watch the long spikes driven into the storyteller's body.

"You got the book out?" Weisen asked the Gypsy, both staring out at the cross.

"This morning in a bag under the ashes for the local farmers. They use it for fertilizer, you know, the ashes. One of the farmers is a Polish Resistance man."

"Where is the book going?"

"An address in Budapest somewhere, I think."

Weisen turned to the Gypsy. "Did you look in the book?"

"I can't read. Did you?"

"No. Becker gave it to your man before the guards came for him. I wonder what was in it."

"Nothing worth that, I can tell you," the Gypsy said, pointing to the crows pecking at the storyteller's body.

"It was to him."

The Gypsy laughed. "No it wasn't. The first time they jolted him with electricity or burnt him with lit cigarettes, I can tell you, he stopped thinking it was worth it."

"Then it was a good thing there was no turning back. Still, I wonder what was in that book."

"Enough! Wondering won't feed us or keep us alive in this place," the Gypsy said. "I'm hungry."

So both men turned their backs on Becker and went behind the barracks to divide up the extra rations Weisen had received for turning in his old nemesis.

Somewhere a crocodile closed his eyes and fell into a deep asleep.

ABOUT THE AUTHOR

Called "a hard-boiled poet" by NPR's Maureen Corrigan, Reed Farrel Coleman has published twelve novels, including two under his pen name Tony Spinosa; *Tower*, co-authored with Ken Bruen; and his newest Moe Prager book, *Innocent Monster*. He has been twice nominated for the Edgar Award and is a three-time winner of the Shamus Award. Reed is the former executive vice president of Mystery Writers of America and was the editor of the anthology *Hard Boiled Brooklyn*. His poems, short stories, and essays have appeared in *Indian Country Noir, Damn Near Dead, Wall Street Noir, The Lineup, Crimespree Magazine,* and several other publications. Reed is an adjunct professor in creative writing at Hofstra University and lives with his family on New York's Long Island. Visit him online at www.reedcoleman.com.